HIS REASON TO BREATHE

CAUGHT UP IN A DECEPTION

A WITH ALL the HEART and SOUL NOVEL

B. E. STALTER

This is a work of fiction. Names, characters, places and events portrayed in this book are either the product of the author's imagination or are used fictitiously. Any similarity to real persons, living or dead, business establishments, events or locales is coincidental and not intended by the author.

Paperback ISBN: 978-1-7371340-3-9

Cover design by: DDDesigns

Dedication

To my brother Tim, who just happens to be the best brother ever, and my sister-in-law, Denise, who is passionate about love stories.

Love you both!

TABLE OF CONTENTS

INTRODUCTION

Welcome to the Circle R Cattle Company Ranch where the residents, though not all bound by blood, do share a wealth of admiration and friendship, as well as an abiding love for the land and animals in their care.

Former Ranch Owners:

William Roberts (Bill) and his wife Peggy Roberts (both deceased)

Current Ranch Owners:

Roger Michael Willis (Mike) and

Emilia Addison Willis (Emi)

Twin children:

Roger Michael Willis, Jr. (Roger) and

Addison Mackenzie Willis (Addie)

Mike's and Emi's oldest daughter:

Eloise Lianne Whrite-Thompson (Elli)

Elli's 1st husband:

Richard Blair Whrite (Rick / Blair) - (deceased)

Whrite-Thompson Children fathered by Richard Blair Whrite:

Jessica Blair (Jess)

Triplets:

Richard Blair (Blair),

Peggy Lynne (Peggy) and

Tyler Logan (Logan)

Elli's 2nd husband:

Tyler Logan Thompson

Children fathered by Tyler:

William Timothy (Billy)

Lianne Susanna (Lianne)

Twins:

Alastair Lachlan (Alex) and

Caelan Angus (Angus)

Twins:

Patricia Emilia (Patti) and

Anna Bella (Annie)

Tyler's father and step-mother:

Alastair Caelan Thompson (Alex) and

Annabelle Thompson (Anna)

Nephew of Peggy Roberts:

Timothy Lee Jones (Tim)

Wife:

Jeannie Jones

Jeannie's daughter by previous marriage:

Sophie Hannah Brown

Ranch Foreman:

Sean Fitzpatrick Hannity (Sean)

Ranch Hands:

John Andrew Marshall (John)

Jacob Campbell MacGowan (Jake)

Thomas Graham McKinney (Tom)

HIS REASON TO BREATHE

CAUGHT UP IN A DECEPTION

PROLOGUE

JUNE 14th, 11:39 p.m., Elli woke with a start. At first, she was disoriented, expecting to awaken in her bed at the *Circle R Cattle Company Ranch*. Then she remembered that the Whrite-Thompson brood had arrived earlier that day at the new home they'd built in Stillwater, New Jersey. In a few minutes, it would be June 15th. The family was here to celebrate the life of Richard Blair Whrite. It would have been Blair's 33rd birthday if he had lived. It was also her daughter Lianne's 2nd birthday.

The family always celebrated here on the Whrite farm, home to the Whrite clan for generations. Elli thought about the day she had returned to Stillwater, her daughter Jessica in tow. Blair's daughter, born of a single night of passion they'd shared after high school graduation. That lone night had given Elli the gift of that beautiful daughter. But time and circumstances, and bad choices had prevented Elli from sharing that gift with the father of her child.

Then, when Elli was twenty-four, circumstances brought her home to Stillwater, and Blair learned the truth that she had withheld from him. He was a father. Everything happened in a blur after that, and she, Blair, and Jessica became a family. A family with three more on the way. Triplets, Richard Blair, Peggy Lynne, and Tyler Logan. The marriage gave Blair the family he'd craved, but he died soon after in a farm accident.

A silent tear slid down Elli's cheek. Blair was Elli's heart, and she'd loved him so very much for such a long time. Elli thought she would never be whole again after his death.

But always there, just slightly out of reach, was the man who held Elli's soul. Tyler, Blair's best friend and Elli's protector, confidante, and business partner, shared a moment of passion. Then Tyler left her, too. But the connection that brought them together had given her another gift.

Thankfully, with the help of a stranger, Tyler finally realized that what he needed and loved was the person he'd left behind. That, someone, was Elli, and she was here in Stillwater waiting for Tyler to come home. They married soon after, and Tyler gifted Blair's children with his last name by adopting them. As a result, all of the children became Whrite-Thompsons.

Elli's heart and soul were whole again. Tyler loved her too, and he had given her a beautiful son whom they'd named William Timothy.

She and Tyler have been married for almost eight years now. That union has gifted them with five more children in addition to Billy. Lianne Susanna, Alastair Lachlan, Caelan Angus, Patricia Emilia, and Anna Bella. Elli freely admitted that she was blessed and would be forever thankful.

Elli glanced over at her slumbering husband, Tyler. He was lying on his back with his left arm thrown over his eyes. Elli studied his sleeping form and tried not to drool. She'd never get tired of looking at Tyler's body. Tyler liked to sleep in the nude, so there was plenty to ogle. At 6'2" tall, Tyler was all broad shoulders and firm muscles. He had the softest dark brown hair, both on his head and other appropriate regions of his body. His hair was so dark that it almost looked black. Elli loved to run her fingers through the down on his chest and trace the ridges of his eight-pack. For some reason, it always seemed to calm her when she was stressed. Thankfully, Tyler wasn't sporting an erection at the moment, or Elli might feel the need to do something about that huge problem.

Thoughts of making love to her husband weren't the cause of waking up before midnight. Instead, she was jarred awake by a pressing need to go to Blair's gravesite in the family plot. A need that wouldn't allow her to wait until morning.

Elli slipped from the bed and scanned the room for her white cotton nightie. Finally, she found it draped over the nightstand on Tyler's side of the bed where he'd thrown it after ripping it off her a few hours beforehand.

After placing a gentle kiss on Tyler's cheek, Elli tiptoed to the bedroom door and closed it softly behind her as she stepped out into the hall. The master bedroom was at the other end of the house from the rooms occupied by their ten children. So Elli wasn't worried that she might disturb their slumber as she made her way to the kitchen. Before Elli slipped outside, she grabbed a flashlight from a bench near the back door. Then, tiptoeing quietly down the stairs to the patio, she edged past the sliding glass doors leading to the suite occupied by her in-laws, Alex and Anna.

Stepping out onto the lawn, Elli switched the flashlight on. Then, keeping the light aimed toward the ground, she followed the path through the patch of woods behind the house that led towards the family cemetery and the original Whrite farmhouse beyond. The old house was currently the home of the farm's caretakers, the Davenports.

A light misty fog coated the trees, lacey ferns, and rocks in a raiment of dewy droplets that sparkled like diamonds. When Elli reached the gate to the family plot, she found it already open.

Elli trained the flashlight at the headstones while making her way to the southeast corner. She didn't really need that light to guide her. She had traversed the ground to her first husband times too numerous to count.

It was now, June 15th, 12:01 a.m.; Blair's birthday. When Elli reached his grave, she covered her mouth with her hand to hold in the moan that threatened to escape, startled by what the light revealed. Leaning casually against the headstone was the shimmering form of her deceased husband. Other than in her dreams, this was the first time Elli had actually seen Blair's ghost.

"Hi, darlin'!" the apparition greeted her.

"Blair?" Elli gasped. "How is this possible?"

"Oh, it's possible, darlin'. People can see if they truly want to. Most don't want to, so they can't. I've missed you, Elli, since you moved away. You don't come to see me all the time like you did when you still lived here on the farm. Being so far away makes it harder for me to watch over you and our children, but I try by coming to visit you in your dreams."

"Can Tyler see you too?" Elli wondered.

"No, darlin'. I try not to show myself to Tyler. I don't want to interfere with his love for you. I don't show myself to our children either because that would only confuse them. Tyler's their dad, now, and that's as it should be. So I won't interfere with their relationship. It wouldn't be fair to any of them."

"Thank you for that, Blair. You're such a good man, even if I'm probably just hallucinating right now," Elli smirked.

"That's alright, darlin'. I don't mind that you'll wake up thinking that I was just a dream. Just needed to let you know that the love is still there. So you get to take that with you if nothing else."

The ghost form wavered and moved towards her. When it reached Elli, it leaned down and placed a misty kiss on Elli's lips. Her lips were wet when the apparition backed away.

"Love you so much, darlin'. I have so many regrets where we're concerned. The only consolation is that we'll all be together someday."

"I also need to say thank you, Blair, for warning me that something was going to happen and that I should lean on Tyler. I don't think I would have survived the loss of my grandmother and grandfather otherwise. I think I would have lost my mind when I found out about my real parents on top of that loss," Elli admitted.

"My pleasure, darlin'. I'll always watch over you and try to keep you safe, but Tyler's the one who can do that best. That man loves you more than life itself."

"Now, there is something that you need to do," the ghost continued. "A woman will be applying for a position on the ranch.

Hire her. Her friend is going to need your help. Also, put Sean Hannity in charge of training the woman. That's important."

Confused, Elli said, "Okay. I don't understand why, but I can do that."

"Good. Other than that, you'll all be fine. All of the kids are going to thrive, Elli. At some point, you'll need to suggest that Tyler start bringing Blair, Jr. to the farm. He will take over running the place when he's older and be a farmer just like his old man. He'll meet a girl in college, and they'll fill that big house Tyler built for you with lots of grandbabies."

Elli started to cry. "Oh, Blair. I miss you so much it hurts."

"I know, darlin', but it's as it was meant to be. Go on back to Tyler, now. He woke up, and he's worried about you." With that, the apparition dissolved, and the shimmering droplets fell to the ground.

Elli placed a kiss on the headstone that marked her first husband. "Happy Birthday, my love."

Then she worked her way between the graves to the wrought iron gate. Closing it behind her, she made her way back through the woods to the house. There, she met Tyler on the back porch.

Elli could see that Tyler took in her damp appearance with a worried countenance. Then, throwing herself into his arms, she wrapped herself around him and hugged him tightly. The fierce kiss she gave him took Tyler by surprise.

When they broke apart, Tyler looked at Elli questioningly. Before he could ask her anything, however, Elli told him, "I'm just fine, Tyler. I'm sorry that I worried you. Now, take me to bed, husband-mine. I need you inside me, right now, and I want lots of orgasms."

Tyler smiled, kissed his wife just as fiercely, and said, "I think I can manage that." Then he lifted Elli in his strong arms and carried her back to their bed.

The Whrite-Thompsons spent July 15th enjoying a mild day. The sun was a fuzzy orb in a sky covered by an opaque layer of blue-gray altostratus clouds. A rainstorm was expected, but the weatherman said it would hold off until early the following morning.

Elli, Tyler, their children, Jessica, Blair, Jr., Peggy, Logan, Billy, Lianne, Alex, Angus, Patti, and Annie, plus Tyler's father Alex and stepmother, Anna, spent time in the cemetery. The babies rested in carriers on their parents' chests as the family tidied and placed fresh flowers on all of the graves. Jessica was in charge of Alex and Angus and kept them from eating the weeds as they were pulled and put in buckets. Then, as everyone stood around the grave of Richard Blair Whrite, Tyler told the kids stories about his best friend. He told them how that good man had fallen in love with the beautiful princess, their mother, when he was only twelve years old. Also, Tyler reminded them that he loved the princess and would take good care of her and Rick's legacy.

When they were finished, the family held their picnic on the back patio, where a gentle breeze stirred the leaves of the trees behind the house. It was a day of celebration of the man who had brought them all together and of the little girl born out of that love whose birthday it was, also.

Tyler went back to the cemetery later in the day to spend some alone time with his best friend. Tyler missed Rick and always would.

Later that night, as they lay in each other's arms, Elli told Tyler about the dream concerning Blair's predictions. They'd promised each other when they got married that they would never keep anything from each other, and this was something that Tyler needed to know.

Tyler didn't scoff at what Elli's dream revealed. She'd had other dreams about Rick and his warnings, and those dreams had come true. Also, if Blair, Jr. showed any interest in the farm, Tyler would support the boy in his goals.

Elli kissed Tyler for being the best husband any woman could hope to have, then rewarded him with a fantastic blowjob. Tyler fell asleep that night with a smile on his face.

The family spent two weeks in Stillwater, enjoying the unseasonably spring-like weather. While Elli and Tyler took the older children to play laser tag, mini-golf, to an arcade, a water park, and an aquarium, the little ones were watched by Alex and Anna. They all spent quality time playing with the younger children. One evening, everyone piled into the van Tyler had purchased. It was big enough to seat all of them. Tyler drove them to the Stillwater Elementary School, where they played baseball on its ball field. Of course, the little ones, watched over by Alex and Anna, just cheered from the sidelines. It was mainly just hitting and catching and chasing the ball, but the family had a lot of fun.

When their mini-vacation was over, the family paid one more visit to the grave of Richard Blair Whrite to remind him how much they all loved and missed him. Elli was the last one to leave the gravesite. Placing a kiss on the headstone, she told Blair. "I'll see you soon, if only in my dreams, and again, thank you. Love you so much!"

Then the family went home to the *Circle R Cattle Company Ranch* in Montana.

When Elli received an application from a woman seeking employment on the *Circle R*, she would remember what Blair had told her. The woman was applying for the new programs that Elli thought might pull more revenue for the ranch. After exchanging a few emails and phone calls, Elli told the woman that the job was hers if she wanted it.

CHAPTER 1

ONE month earlier, Makailyn Elsbeth Jamieson, known as Mak, watched as a flutter of butterflies took wing above the pinkish-purple florets of a patch of wavy-leaf thistles. She and her mount had startled the insects as she checked the fence line on the north pasture that afternoon. Mak gasped as one butterfly lit on the horn of her saddle, followed by another that touched down briefly on her gloved hand as she held the reins.

Butterflies had always brought Mak luck. The few times something genuinely wonderful had happened in her life, she had spotted a flutter of butterflies beforehand. Mak thought it was a little early in the season to view such a fantastic combination of butterflies and thistles in Chilton, Oklahoma. Still, it had been unusually warm of late. The weather must have caused plants to bloom sooner than expected.

The sighting made Mak think about the gift given to her by her best friend Jo for her eighteenth birthday. They had gone together to a tattoo parlor in Oklahoma City that was jointly owned by a brother and sister. The business was called *No Regrets, Ink.* Mak asked the female co-owner to design a tattoo consisting of a flutter of tiny butterflies poised above several long-stemmed thistles.

Jo asked Mak, "Why thistles? Daisies are your favorite flowers."

Mak responded that yes, daisies were her favorite flowers because they were unassuming and straightforward, just like Mak herself. But thistles tended to be tenacious, and Mak hoped that maybe she might be a little bit like that, too.

Mak wanted to carry her good luck with her wherever she went. So, that tattoo now graced the side of her ribcage and trailed up over her left breast. The tiniest butterfly rested on the tip of a thistle floret just above her heart. One lone butterfly, the largest, had flown away from the rest of the flutter to light on the top edge of her right nipple.

With too much work to do and no one to help, Mak didn't have time to think about what that sighting in the north pasture might mean.

So, she put it out of her mind. Then, turning away from the beauty, she headed back to the barn, where she promptly got lost in her thoughts.

Mak often daydreamed while mucking the stalls and tending to the horses. Sometimes those thoughts were about her childhood. Mak and Jaymiee Joanna Johnston, known as Jo, met in first grade and spent every day of their childhood together after that. When they were little girls, they enjoyed playing dress-up and tea parties on rainy days and helping to do chores and tend the livestock on good ones. By tenth grade, their friendship had progressed to where Mak would cover for Jo when she'd sneak out after dark on Friday and Saturday nights. It was a good thing Jo's bedroom was on the ground floor, and the window didn't stick. Then, Jo would meet up with her latest beau down by the swimming hole. Mak always marveled that Jo habitually forgot her swimsuit but still managed to go swimming and come home in dry clothes. Mak was grateful for everything Jo had ever done for her, so she was happy to help her best friend out.

Jo was the one who held Mak when she cried inconsolably over her mother's defection when the woman ran off with a traveling salesman. Mak was only eight at the time, and the image of her mother had slowly faded. However, Mak vaguely remembered that Mom had long blond hair and pouty lips painted a deep red. Mak also recalled her graceful hands and dainty feet with fingernails and toenails painted to match her lipstick.

Mak's father, Lyle Duncan Jamieson, was a rugged-looking cowboy with a rangy build and hair the same color as his only child's. Mak remembered the smell of his aftershave when he'd hoist her up for a hug and when they snuggled on the sofa while watching television.

Mak cringed at the few memories of how her parents always fought. After her mom's clandestine meetings with other men, she would try to sneak back into the house. Mom always smelled of booze, cigarettes, and the current man's cheap aftershave. Thank God Mak didn't know what a person smelled like after having sex when she was a kid. Her mom probably smelled of that, too. That thought brought a smirk to Mak's face. The only reason she knew now was because of Jo. During college, Mak had accidentally walked in on Jo and one of her many boyfriends going at it hot and heavy.

Mak learned the truth about her conception during the very last fight her parents had before her mom skipped out. Her mother confessed that she'd never loved her father. Mom had only married him because she was pregnant with Mak. She told Mak's father that he'd never amount to anything, so he would never be able to give her the life she desperately wanted and deserved. She believed she was meant for bigger and better things. So, she refused to be stuck on some rundown ranch in the middle of Nowhere, Oklahoma raising a kid. Mak hasn't heard from her mother in twenty years. Mak knew that the woman wasn't much of a mother anyway, so good riddance to bad rubbish, as the saying goes.

Jo consoled her again when Mak's father was killed in a hit-and-run accident when Mak was twelve. It was a stupid way to die. He'd parked the truck in the entrance to the long dirt road that led to their home and had gotten out to check for mail. Unfortunately, someone ran off the road and took out Mak's dad and the mailbox, plus part of the fence that lined the field. His body was discovered when the school bus stopped to drop her off. Thankfully, Mak was the last stop on the route, so it was just her and the bus driver. No lookie-loo kids peering out the windows of the bus so they'd have all the gory details to relay to their friends at school the next day. Mak remembered that her father's old pickup truck had been idling in the driveway but was almost out of gas. Whoever killed her father never came forward, and with no clues to follow, the culprit was never caught. Lyle Duncan Jamieson was an excellent father, and Mak still missed him every day.

Mak was not technically an orphan because her mother was admittedly out there somewhere in the world. The child welfare lady assigned to Mak's case tried to find Wilma Jamieson. However, she was unsuccessful in her endeavor, and Mak was relieved about that. Still, Mak was terrified that she would end up in foster care and be shuttled from one family to another. Therefore, Mak counted herself the luckiest girl in the world when the Johnstons added her to their large brood of children by taking her into their home.

Jo also shared her tampons with Mak and showed her what to do when Mak finally got her first period. Jo was a few months older and had gotten hers when she was thirteen. Mak was a late bloomer. Her monthly flow didn't rear its ugly head until she was almost fifteen. That missing mother should have been the one to help Mak navigate the signs of impending womanhood. If only she'd bothered to stick around long enough to raise her own daughter.

Toward the end of ninth grade, Jo saved Mak once again. Mak had forgotten a book that she needed to complete her homework. So, Jo asked her brother, Bill to drive them to the high school. Jo then diverted the janitor's attention so Mak could sneak off to her locker. After retrieving the book, Mak was on her way back to the school entrance when two junior boys from the swim team cornered her and shoved her into the empty locker room. While the one boy had Mak pinned, the other tried to divest her of her shorts and underwear. Mak tried to scream as she struggled to escape the boys' evil intentions but only partially succeeded before her own shorts were crammed into her mouth. Thankfully, Jo had gotten curious as to why Mak was taking so long to retrieve her book. So, she came looking for Mak. Hearing the commotion, Jo came busting into the room. Beating the boys about the head with her fists, Jo clobbered the boy holding Mak down so hard she broke his nose. Then she bit the other boy on the ear after she jumped on his back, of course.

After that terrifying incident, Mak and Jo made a pact. If either was ever in real trouble, the threatened one would send the other a one-word text. That would let the other know that she needed to come running. The girls puzzled over what that one word should be and finally settled on the word "*Savior*" because that was what Jo had been that day. Mak's savior.

Then there was the way Jo stood up for her when Mak's date left her sitting in the corner at the junior prom. The boy had abandoned her so he could make out with the girl he'd really wanted to escort to the dance. It was Mak's first and only experience dating during high school. She'd only agreed to go because Jo's boyfriend, Tony, coerced his best friend, Bruce, into asking Mak, so they could double-date.

Jo got right up in Bruce's face and gave him a dressing down. Then bitch-slapped the girl Bruce had been smooching with when she started badmouthing Mak. It only added fuel to the fire, however. Jo was very vocal when she got riled up, which meant the popular girls in school got to witness Mak's disgrace first hand. Word spread like wildfire, and it seemed like everyone was enjoying a good snicker at Mak's expense. They were laughing over the tale about the poor girl left crying in the corner. Mak's confidence took a broken-cabled elevator ride straight to the basement after that night of humiliation. She hid her feelings behind a wall of indifference as she navigated the halls of the high school. Mak kept herself pretty much invisible for the balance of her junior and senior years. She still felt inconspicuous to the rest of the world due to that experience and probably always would.

The number of times that Jo had taken care of Mak was too numerous to count. Except for when Jo pushed Mak out of her comfort zone, no one could ask for a better friend.

Having been raised on a ranch, it was only natural that Mak and Jo would go off to an agricultural college together. They both got Associate in Applied Science degrees in Equine and Ranch Management. Unfortunately, while they were getting their degree, Jo's father suffered a heart attack. As a result of Mr. Johnston's health issues, Jo's parents sold their ranch. They moved to California before the girls got their diplomas. With no family ranch to go home to, Mak and Jo were now on their own.

Shortly after graduating, Mak applied as a ranch hand on the *Rockin' R Ranch* in Chilton, Oklahoma. After being interviewed, the ranch owner, a wizened old codger named Willis Riordan, said, "Just call me "*Will.*" I don't stand on formalities. The job's yours if ya want it."

Mak asked Will if he had an opening for another ranch hand because her best friend needed a job, as well. Thus, Jo has worked beside Mak on the *Rockin' R* ever since. Even though it has been eight years, at times, it has felt like only yesterday.

Helping the ranch owner run the *Rockin' R Ranch* has kept Mak and Jo so busy over the years that Mak felt she hardly had any time at all to breathe. The women helped the *Rockin' R* institute new programs to pull in customers and additional revenue to keep the ranch viable. Besides raising quarter horses, Australian Shepherds, and registered Black Angus cattle, they performed equine massage therapy. In addition, Mak and Jo gave classes for young beginner clients in natural horsemanship and roping and reining. They also assisted with the ranch work and working the small herd of cattle.

Mak and Jo could definitely pass for one another if a person didn't look too closely. Both women had hour-glass figures, heart-shaped faces, high cheekbones, and small noses. Neither woman was a slouch in the measurement department, either. Having the same body type, they often shared clothing they wore to do their chores. However, Jo's style was more flamboyant, so Mak tried to avoid the outfits Jo liked to dress up in when Jo forced her to go out.

Mak was 5'8" tall, with a 38" bust, 29" waist, and 40" hips. Though she weighed 140 pounds, it was all lean muscle from her daily ranch work. Jo's brown hair had red highlights, while Mak's had natural golden streaks that most women spent a fortune at the beauty salon trying to replicate. Both of them wore their long hair in ponytails when they were working. They each had brown eyes, but Mak's were lighter to go along with the lighter skin tone and hair color.

Life on a ranch could be pretty dull at times, with no one around to talk to except the horses and cattle. Especially when her best friend was in California visiting her family relations. It was a good thing the horses were excellent listeners and didn't mind when Mak went off on a rant about her lack of eligible male suitors. Unfortunately, Mak's shy nature didn't help when it came to the possibility of dating. Whenever Mak met anyone new, she got all tongue-tied. Having an actual conversation with another adult, especially of the male persuasion, was torture. It was like having a dyslexic mouth. All of her sentences came out backward and jumbled. She found that it helped if she didn't actually look the person in the eyes while talking. She could better order her thoughts that way. Not looking at a person you were talking to was supposed to be a sign of deceit. Mak was anything but. She'd never told a lie and didn't plan to in the future.

It also didn't help that the only sober men Mak got to meet were fathers who brought their young children to the ranch to be signed up for the programs the *Rockin' R* was becoming well-known for. Even though the men were married with children, a few of them had hit on her. Mak respectfully declined any attempt at a dalliance by always asking after the wife. Then she'd immediately move on to the topic of their child's progress and what the parent could do to support and encourage said child to help that boy or girl succeed. That seemed to throw the philanderer off his game by reminding him of his obligations.

Jo had a vivacious personality and liked to go out bar hopping on Friday or Saturday night when she was hunting for a new boyfriend. On those occasions, she always made Mak dress in a pair of Jo's tight skinny jeans and a skimpy top or one of her short slinky dresses. Then Jo would drag Mak along.

Mak wasn't one for drinking because she didn't seem to have any tolerance or taste for the stuff. Nor did she enjoy having sweaty, drunken guys grope her or push their dicks against her backside while she was enjoying the music on the crowded dance floor. Swaying to the beat of the music was the only time Mak let her mind soar free of the confines of her inhibited body. She didn't understand why men seemed to think that was some sort of open invitation to get intimate. Mak didn't realize that she was really something to behold when she was lost in the rhythm of a good song. Those poor men were just drawn to the spell of seduction she was weaving.

"Mak, for heaven's sake. Where did your mind wander off to? I swear, your head is always lost in a fog. I've been tryin' to get your attention so I can introduce you to my new friend," Jo exclaimed as she reached out and grabbed her best friend's arm to give it a shake.

Mak was fantasizing about a handsome white knight on a jet-black stallion who would come riding into her life, rescue her, and then whisk her away. There would be a lot of passionate kissing involved and hot sex in a huge bed. The bed would have to be big. Her fantasy white knight was actually a hot studmuffin of a cowboy who would own a large ranch full of horses and cattle. A tall cowboy, at least 6’3”, lean with broad shoulders, well-defined muscles, narrow hips, and long muscular legs. He’d need to be very strong. Mak imagined him lifting her into his arms as if she weighed nothing, then gently depositing her in the middle of that big bed so he could have his way with her. He’d have to come complete with a ten-gallon hat and boots, of course. The cowboy would strip those off along with his shirt, jeans, and boxer briefs. Mak licked her lips at the thought of what would be revealed when he shed those unmentionables. Yeehaw!

While Mak was hankering after that ideal lover, she figured she might as well throw in big, callused hands. She’d want those hands all over her. The thought of those rough hands touching her in certain places made her rub her thighs together. Maybe the friction would relieve some of the sexual frustration she was experiencing at the moment. But, unfortunately, being so busy meant not having any spare moments to pursue finding that cowboy she dreamed about nightly. The dreams had become so vivid she could almost see the cowboy’s face.

Yanked back to reality by her best friend, Mak prayed that her face didn't show any signs of what she'd been thinking about. Mak had no control over her facial expressions whatsoever. Anyone could tell what she was feeling. It always showed on her stupid face. Good thing she didn't play strip poker. She'd lose her shirt and most or all of the rest of her clothing as well.

Stepping forward, Mak enveloped Jo in a hug and asked excitedly, "Jo, when did you get back? I wasn't expecting you home from your parents' place for another week. I've missed you so much."

Jo squished Mak to her and admonished, "You need to get your head out of the clouds, stop working so hard, and take time out to enjoy life, girl. God, I've missed you, too, sister-mine. It's so good to be home. I couldn't take any more of my youngest brother's and sister-in-law's kids. They are such spoiled brats. Mom and Dad watch them while their parents are at work and let them do whatever they want. My folks sure have mellowed. They would have beat us black and blue if we'd pulled half the stunts those little monsters get away with. It was time to get the heck out of there and come home so I can regain my sanity."

Turning to her companion, Jo grabbed his hand and saucily said, “Mak, I met this good-lookin’ fella’ at the airport in California. We were on the same flight and seated together. I bent his ear during the entire trip and then actually kidnapped him by offerin’ him a ride when we landed at *Will Rogers Airport* in Oklahoma City. This is Jack Hamilton.”

“Jack, this is the woman I’ve been tellin’ you about. This is my sister by another Ma and Pa. This is Makailyn Elsbeth Jamieson, but I’ve always just called her Mak.”

Jack reached out his hand and said, “Hello, Mak. It’s a privilege to meet you. The two of you really look like sisters. You could almost pass for twins. This is my lucky day, meeting two such attractive women.”

Mak rubbed her palm on the thigh of her jeans before accepting Jack’s handshake. She could feel the heat rise in her cheeks due to the comment about her looks, which meant she was blushing. Why couldn’t she be self-assured like Jo instead of acting like a silly tongue-tied schoolgirl?

Mak studied the man’s shoes as she ordered her words to form a reply, “It’s a pleasure to meet you, Mr. Hamilton. What brings you to Chilton, Oklahoma, or are you from the area?" Once the words were out, Mak looked up and studied Jack's face.

"Call me Jack. Mr. Hamilton's my dad," Jack said with a cheeky grin and a wink. "Actually, I'm here to help my friend move into his new home, plus I'm to be his houseguest for a few weeks. My friend just purchased a custom waterfront home on Lake Eufaula. Maybe you know him. His name is Brian Hillhouse. Brian and I were roommates in college, and we're both attorneys. I was in California visiting some dear friends. I'm godfather to their twin daughters. I plan to spend time with Brian before starting my new position at a law firm in Philadelphia, Pennsylvania. That's where I hail from, and I'll be headed there after my visit."

Mak glanced shyly at the handsome man standing beside her lifelong friend. He looked to be about 5'10" tall with a close-cropped head of black hair, aquiline nose, wide-spaced eyes, and square jaw. With a lean runner's build, Mak would bet good money that he ran several miles a day. It was no surprise that the man was so good-looking. Jo had a bubbly personality that drew handsome men to her like flies to honey. Her figure and beauty didn't hurt any, either.

Thinking about Jo's success with men caused Mak's mind to slip back into the past to when Jo lost her virginity. It happened in eleventh grade on the night of that junior prom, but not with Tony, the boyfriend who was her actual date. After the incident involving Bruce, Jo dumped Tony like a hot potato when he tried to stick up for Bruce's lousy behavior. But, of course, a good-looking guy was standing in line to take the spurned boy's place. That young man may have gotten lucky that night, but it would be his first and last time with Jo. Jo didn't think someone who would kiss and tell was worth her time.

Since they were so close, Jo shared all the juicy details with Mak about her sexual escapades from that night and the string of male friends Jo has run through since.

Mak felt a longing to be so carefree in sharing her body with a man, but she steered clear of dating. Mak's mother's dalliances had tainted Mak's life, and she didn't want to be considered the apple that didn't fall far from the tree. Mak had heard the whispered remarks concerning her mother by those popular girls who belonged to cliques in high school. They liked to gossip and give Mak sly looks behind their hands as Mak walked by. Plus, Mak knew firsthand after the prom fiasco what it was like to be spurned by a boy. So, she was guarding her heart as well as her body. Mak didn't want to give it to just anybody. She wanted her first and last experiences to be with the man who would hold her heart for the rest of her life. Since he hadn't made an appearance yet, Mak, at twenty-eight, was still a virgin. Hence, the sexual frustration.

Mak realized that she'd zoned out again when she heard, "Brian and I plan to do some celebrating. He was just offered a partnership in his father's law firm in Oklahoma City. The firm's letterhead will now read *Hillhouse, Bow, and Hillhouse, Attorneys at Law.* It is supposedly a top-notch firm catering to the elite of Oklahoma and the surrounding state."

Releasing Jack's hand, Mak replied, "I can't say as I've heard of the law firm or Mr. Hillhouse before, but I don't get away from the farm very often. I definitely don't require the services of a fancy law firm, either. Maybe you can offer your friend my congratulations on making partner." Wow, Mak thought. I actually managed a coherent response. Will wonders never cease?

"Well, not getting away from the ranch very often is going to change right this minute, Jo interjected. "I've volunteered us for manual labor, so you can offer the man your congratulations yourself when you meet him. Git a move on and wash up. And change your clothes. You smell like a horse."

"I don't think that's a good idea," Mak began, but Jo interrupted by saying, "No, you are not stayin' in your room again tonight watching reruns of old *John Wayne* westerns. Go on now. Git. I'm not leavin' here without you. I'll show Jack around while we wait on you to get ready."

Chagrined at Jo's outing of her unimpressive social life, Mak went off to do as she'd been told. Even if she didn't really want to spend the evening in the company of strangers, she'd missed her friend and wanted to please her.

After taking a quick shower, Mak slipped on a filmy, sleeveless wrap dress and ballet flats. Pulling her hair into a French twist, she applied some lip gloss and a spritz of her favorite perfume. Giving herself a once over in the full-length mirror, Mak deemed her appearance good enough. Grabbing her purse, she was ready to go.

CHAPTER 2

WHEN Mak exited the rear seat of Jo's car, she stood with her mouth hanging open in an "o." So, this was how the other half lived. The house was huge. She could tell that it was constructed of high-quality materials. It was a two-story home with a natural stone exterior and included a two-bay attached garage. A stunning, pearlescent red *Bentley* convertible sat proudly in front of one of the bay doors.

As Mak spun in a circle to take in the beautiful landscaping, the front door opened. The man that stepped out to greet them was even more handsome than Jack. He was tall with broad, well-defined shoulders that Mak knew didn't come from hefting hay bales. He had dirty-blond hair that was slicked back in a wave. As he got closer, Mak could see that he had piercing blue eyes, a patrician nose, and a gently rounded jawline. The only thing that marred the perfection of his face was his thin lips. They gave him an arrogant appearance. He wore a t-shirt and khaki-colored shorts that hugged his muscular chest and lean hips but left his muscular arms and legs exposed for a female's viewing pleasure. The man's legs were covered with fine blond hair a little lighter in color than the hair on his head. Mak wondered if the hair was coarse or soft like a downy chick. The attorney spent a substantial part of his life at the gym if this was Brian Hillhouse. Mak didn't believe bodies like his came naturally. Especially the bodies of attorneys who sat behind fancy desks all day and never did any manual labor.

Mak knew she was correct in assuming that this was Brian Hillhouse when Jack yelled, "Brian, I've brought you a present. Well, actually, two. These beautiful women are here to act as our slaves. They're going to assist in helping us unpack your stuff."

Brian greeted Jack warmly by gripping Jack's hand and pulling him into a man-hug. Then turning towards Mak and Jo, he eyed them speculatively and joked, "Which sex slave is mine?" At least, Mak hoped Brian was joking.

"No sex," Jack laughed and clapped Brian on the back. "Just slave labor. Brian, this lovely young lady is Jaymiee Joanna Johnston. You can call her Jo, and hands-off. She belongs to me."

"That's good," Brian responded, "because that means this scrumptious dish is all mine." Then he pulled Mak into his arms and tried to plant a kiss on her mouth. Fortunately, Mak turned her face just in time, and the kiss landed on her cheek. Unabashed, Brian winked at Mak and said, "What's your name, doll face?"

Mak, famous for her blushes, did precisely that as Jack answered for her, "Brian Alexander Hillhouse III, I'd like to introduce you to Makailyn Elsbeth Jamieson. I guess everyone calls her Mak."

Brian grabbed Mak by the hand and gave it a light squeeze. Then taking in the sight of both beautiful women, he said, "Welcome to my new home, Mak and Jo." After retrieving Jack's luggage from the trunk of Jo's car, Brian led his guests up the walk and into the house.

When they were all standing in the foyer, Brian turned to Jack and said, "When did your flight land, Man? You were supposed to text so I could come to pick you up at the airport."

Unabashed, Jack laughed and responded, "Well, that's the thing. I was kidnapped by this magnificent specimen of femininity." Then, indicating Jo, he clasped her face, leaned in, and locked lips. Mak could almost see steam rise from the intensity of that kiss. It seemed to go on and on and on.

Turning away, Mak felt a little bit envious at the ease with which her friend gave her affection to any man. To hide the blush on her cheeks, she studiously pretended to examine a small grouping of western-themed paintings that hung on the wall. It looked like Brian had already unpacked some of his belongings. Mak wasn't an expert by any stretch of the imagination, but she would bet the paintings were originals. Moreover, they were all signed by someone named *S M Long*.

Brian laughed at Jack. "Not fair." Then he turned Mak towards him. Before she knew what hit her, Brian was kissing her, and it wasn't on the cheek this time. When Brian slipped his tongue into her mouth, Mak pressed her hands to his chest and pushed a little to break the kiss. She needed to put some distance between them because she'd felt his erection pressed against her. Mak wasn't sure how she felt about such intimacy. Especially since they'd only just met. Mak thought she saw something in Brian's eyes before he stepped back. It almost looked like anger, but it was gone so quickly.

With a deprecating sniff and thinning of his already thin lips, Brian turned to the others and said, "Let me give you all a tour of the house. Then, after, we can eat and get acquainted before I put my slave laborers to work. How's that sound?"

When they all nodded their heads in agreement, Mak thought maybe she'd been mistaken after all. Brian grinned boyishly, then laughed, "Well, as you may have guessed, this is the foyer. The house has four bedrooms and five bathrooms."

As he walked them through the rooms, he guided Mak with a warm palm to the small of her back. Certainly, Brian wouldn't show her such respectful consideration if he was angry with her?

Mak marveled at the home's luxurious features. All of the rooms had highly polished hardwood floors and high ceilings adorned with beautiful mahogany crown moldings. The living room, dining room, and master bedroom had stone fireplaces with marble mantles, but her favorite room was the kitchen. It was a cook's wet dream come to life. There were granite countertops, a kitchen island, a huge subzero refrigerator, and separate freezer, glass-fronted upper cabinets, a huge range, and double wall ovens, plus two dishwashers. It was definitely designed for preparing meals for hosting parties and fancy sit-down dinners.

The five bathrooms were all Italian marble wonders to behold. The master bathroom even featured a clawfoot tub big enough for two.

When the tour of the inside of the house was complete, Mak's thoughts were, "What the heck was a single guy living all alone gonna do with a house designed for a large family? Unless, of course, he had plans to marry and fill the house with children." She kept those thoughts to herself.

Mak believed she was having a dream when they all stepped out onto the covered patio to view the backyard. A long sloping swathe of well-manicured green lawn led down to a broad expanse of placid water. The home was graced with a gorgeous view of Lake Eufaula. The sun casting crystal sparkles of light off the blue water of the lake actually hurt her eyes. It would be a shame to wear sunglasses to deaden the view, however. It was just so spectacular.

"We'll take a cruise around the lake when it gets dark," Brian promised. Then he pointed, "See the boat slip and the boathouse next to it? There are dual-cylinder hydraulic lifts in each of the four stalls of the boathouse. They operate by push-button remote for hassle-free operation. I can have one of my boats on or off the water in less than a minute. I had two of my boats delivered right after closing on the property. One's a pontoon boat, and the other is a bowrider. That's a deck boat. I also have a freshwater fishing boat and a Wake boat. They'll be delivered tomorrow. We can take the Wake boat out and do some wakeboarding before Jack goes off to Philadelphia. How's that sound?"

Mak didn't know anything about boats or wakeboarding, but it sounded like it might be fun.

CHAPTER 3

WHILE they ate a simple meal of pizza and salad that Brian had delivered, the men bombarded Jo and Mak with questions. Of course, Jack and Brian wanted to know all about the women's lives.

Jack said, "Tell us all about working on the *Rockin' R*. I have to tell you I'm in awe of the fact that two such lovely creatures do such hard physical labor every day and still retain their good looks."

Jo had everyone laughing when she told Jack that she bet she could beat him at arm wrestling, then made a muscle and told Jack to give it a squeeze.

When none of them could eat another bite, Brian stood to clear the table. Mak quickly offered to help, and he nodded his head in agreement. While Mak was loading the glasses and silverware into one of the dishwashers, she heard Jack ask Brian about sleeping arrangements.

"Your room's the second door on the right at the top of the stairs," came Brian's response.

Then Mak heard Jack ask Jo if she wanted to come to his bedroom while he unpacked, and Jo's giggled response to Jack's question.

Jack and Jo were conspicuously absent when Mak returned to the dining alcove to wipe off the table. But, of course, Mak knew what that was about. Jo didn't take long to jump into bed with a man, and Mak would be regaled with all the juicy details concerning the encounter later that night when she and Jo got ready for bed.

As Mak bent over the table to dry the surface, Brian put his hands around her waist and pulled her in tight against his hard body. "Looks like Jackie boy got lucky," Brian whispered against Mak's ear. Then, as Brian nuzzled the side of Mak's neck, his hands slipped up to graze the undersides of her breasts.

Mak gasped, but before she could respond to Brian's comment or his inappropriate fondling of her breasts, he slipped his arms behind her back and knees and lifted Mak clean off the floor. Mak was stunned at first. Before the frozen thoughts in Mak's head had defrosted, Brian had carried her all the way up the stairs to the second floor.

Finally finding the words, Mak protested, "What do you think you're doing?"

"Taking my sex slave to bed," Brian responded with a grin. "After you suck me off, I promise to pleasure you until you don't have an ounce of energy left in your body. You'll have orgasmed so many times, you'll feel like a limp noodle."

Mak blushed and started to struggle in Brian's arms. Finally, she implored, "Please, put me down. We've just met. I don't know you, and you definitely don't know anything about me."

Brian laughed, "Well, I'm just about to remedy that, sweetheart. When we're done, we'll both know each other very intimately."

At that, Mak struggled even harder. Finally, Brian was forced to set her on her feet. Otherwise, he would have dropped her on her ass on the floor. As Mak backed away, a single tear slipped down her cheek, and she managed to stammer, “I can’t. I’m still a virgin.” Then she turned and ran down the stairs and out the front door.

Brian found Mak sitting on the front stoop with her knees pulled up tight to her chest. Her head was pressed against those knees to hide her tear-streaked face.

Brian was furious at not getting what he wanted. No one had rejected him without paying the price since his first sexual encounter with one of the maids when he was fifteen. Grabbing a dishtowel from the countertop in the kitchen, Brian had cornered the girl in the pantry. First, the dishtowel was used to gag her so no one could hear her cries of alarm. Then, forcing her to her knees, he had taken her from behind. Since the girl needed her job to help support her younger sisters and brothers, she’d kept what had happened to herself. Then the maid had missed her period. Brian scoffed at her when she told him that she was pregnant with his child. So, she went to Brian’s father.

Brian Hillhouse II had told the girl not to worry and dismissed her so that she could go back to dusting the downstairs furniture. Then the billionaire had set out to manipulate the girl by having her father accused of embezzlement. It just so happened that her father worked as an accountant at a company that belonged to one of Hillhouse's frat brothers from college.

Summoned to stand before the large mahogany desk in the study of the Hillhouse mansion, Brian's father made the girl an offer. She couldn't refuse if she wanted to save her father's job and prevent him from going to prison. She would have an abortion and accept ten thousand dollars as severance pay. The frightened young lady tearfully accepted. She was promptly driven to an abortion clinic by the Hillhouse chauffer. Upon return to the study, Hillhouse had taken the document confirming that the fetus no longer existed, forced the young maid to sign legal documents preventing her from ever discussing the terms of their agreement, handed the maid a check, and dismissed her from his employ. Then she was driven by the chauffer to the bus terminal. The kindly gray-haired gentleman opened the rear door and helped the young girl step out of the limo. He apologized for the part he'd been forced to play in her dismissal and wished her luck. Then he'd handed her bus fare and told her never to return.

Brian was then called to appear before his exalted father in front of that same desk. Good old dad handed him a box of condoms, and Brian was admonished to use them if he was going to bang the hired help.

Brian never got another female pregnant, but he missed how it felt to have sex sans those latex sheaths.

If Mak indeed was a virgin, that definitely made the game more interesting. He'd never broken in a virgin. This was going to be so much fun. The hard-on he was sporting was very painful, but he could wait. He'd take his time pursuing this one. In the end, he'd get what he wanted, one way or the other. Mak would succumb eventually. Then he'd make her pay for putting him to so much trouble and for giving him blue balls.

Unfortunately for Brian Alexander Hillhouse III, falling in love hadn't been part of the equation.

CHAPTER 4

BRIAN sat down on the stoop beside Mak and placed a finger beneath her chin. The silk of her skin sent a jolt of lust to his groin, and the gold flecks in her eyes held him mesmerized. Staring into their depths, Brian realized he wanted this woman like no other. The very thought of another man deflowering Mak or ever touching her intimately made him insane with jealousy. In his mind, she was now his property, and he'd do whatever it took to prevent her from getting away.

"I'm sorry, Mak. I had no idea. Do you think you can forgive me for being so presumptuous? Let's start over. Hi, I'm Brian Hillhouse. It's a pleasure to meet you." Then he held out his hand for her to shake.

Mak stifled a giggle as she swiped the tears from her cheeks with the sides of her hands. Then she clasped Brian's outstretched hand. “Hi! I’m Makailyn Elsbeth Jamieson. People call me Mak. It’s a pleasure to meet you. Mr. Hillhouse. May I call you Bri?”

Brian had never been given a nickname before. He liked the idea very much. Brian was fascinated by the lilt in Mak’s voice as she spoke and the sound of his name from her lips. So, he told Mak that only she would be permitted such an intimacy. He stood and used their handshake to pull Mak to her feet. “Very good. Let’s go unload some boxes. While we do that, you can tell me all about your current boyfriend.”

“Umm…no boyfriend,” was Mak’s chagrined response as a blush stained her cheeks.

“Good. That’s very good,” Brian returned. “You have one now. Tell me, Makailyn Elsbeth Jamieson, what are the terms of our new relationship? Is your new boyfriend allowed to at least kiss you?”

Brian was 6’4” tall, so even though Mak was taller than the average woman at 5’8”, she still had to tilt her head to see his eyes when she responded. “I think kissing would be permissible.” Then stood there expectantly.

"I'll take that under advisement," was Brian's response. Then, he turned away and opened the door to the garage. By Mak's stunned expression, she was undoubtedly expecting instant gratification in the form of a kiss. Instead, Brian would keep her off-kilter by ignoring her and denying her that kiss. Maybe next time, she'd be a little more willing to accede to his demands regarding the sexual relationship they were definitely going to be sharing.

Confused, Mak followed Brian into the garage. Having little experience, Mak wanted the opportunity to learn the proper technique for kissing a man. Apparently, Brian wasn't interested in kissing her again, however, since she'd denied him at least twice already. As a flush stole over the delicate plains of her face, she dipped her head to hide her embarrassment. But, of course, it was presumptuous of her to think that he might, and he'd put her in her place by walking away.

Brian indicated a pile of boxes labeled "**KITCHEN**" in big block letters. Together, they transferred the boxes to the appropriate room, where they stacked them in a neat pile out of the way. As Mak opened the first box that said it contained dishes on the flap, Brian went into the study. Soft music began to emanate from hidden speakers before he rejoined her. Mak recognized the tune playing as *Can't Help Falling in Love* by *Elvis Presley*.

When Brian stepped up close and took Mak's hand in his, she looked at him questioningly. "May I have this dance?" Brian queried. Without waiting for a response, he pulled Mak in close and started to sway. "God, you smell good, Mak. You are so beautiful, sweetheart." Then he leaned down and sensually slid his lips over hers.

The walls Mak had erected around herself crumpled a little, and she kissed Brian back. Never having been kissed like that before, Despite her earlier attempts at rejection, Mak found that she enjoyed the pressure of his lips on hers a lot.

Brian ended the kiss just as the song came to its conclusion. *Unchained Melody* by the *Righteous Brothers* was the next song to play. As they continued to sway, Brian slipped his hand from Mak's waist to the curve of her ass and rubbed in slow circles. When Mak sighed and rested her head against his chest, Brian knew this game of seduction wasn't going to last long. He'd be inside Mak's tight little cunt in no time at all. Brian would enjoy breaking her in. He'd also put a ring on her finger to bind her to him, and he definitely didn't intend to use protection when he took her.

That didn't necessarily mean that he couldn't enjoy the next unsuspecting female to cross his path. He came from a long line of rogues who were total womanizers. Brian's father was the worst of the lot. So, Brian had learned from the best. Brian would have to ask the old goat if he'd ever had sex with a virgin the next time the old man graced the office with his lofty presence. Brian Hillhouse II spent most of his time playing golf, drinking and chasing tail at the country club. Brian thought that was good work if you could get it. Brian's father believed he'd put in his time slaving behind a desk, so he had earned it.

Just as Brian was planning to slide his hand up under the hem of Mak's dress, Jack and Jo came bounding into the room. Both looked rumpled, and Jack's hair was standing up on end as if someone had been pulling on it.

Brian gave Jack the stink eye before stepping away from Mak. "Did the two of you save any energy for actually unpacking some of these boxes?" he asked as he eyed the pair with disdain.

"Maybe a little," was Jack's response. "Jo is one hot woman. In more ways than one, I might add. Besides, I thought we were going out on the boat?"

"Maybe next time the girls visit. I think they've had enough for one evening. How about if the two of you come next Friday for a barbeque?" Brian asked as he turned questioning eyes on Mak and Jo. "Bring your swimwear and extra clothes so you can spend the night. We'll take the boat out then, and you can swim off the side. It is Memorial Day weekend. There'll be a huge fireworks display put on by the country club. We'll have a spectacular view from the water."

Mak wanted to say no. It felt like Brian was moving too fast in wanting things Mak wasn't prepared to give. He was well-spoken and handsome, of course, but that and the fact that he was wealthy would have no bearing on what her final decision would be. She could care less about his fancy home, car, or boats. He just wasn't the cowboy of Mak's dreams. Mak wanted to wait for that special man who would make her light up like a Christmas tree just by looking at her.

So, Mak wasn't thrilled when Jo chimed in, "We'd be happy to come for your picnic. What time do you want us again?"

Jack grabbed Jo and swung her up into his arms. "I want you again, right now." He was displeased when he had to put Jo down, however.

Mak grabbed Jo by the hand and said, "Come on, Jo, it's time to go home."

CHAPTER 5

AFTER the women left, Jack quizzed Brian about his unsuccessful attempts to get Mak into his bed. Having roomed with Brian for four years in college, Jack knew all about Brian's conquests and bad temper. Brian had a proclivity for rough sex and a love-em-an-leave-em attitude. He got what he wanted and hang the consequences if he had to use a little force to achieve his goal. He'd slept his way through all of the sorority houses on campus. While there was talk of encounters with faculty and spouses of professors, there was one scandal in junior year about the dean's wife that almost got Brian expelled. Jack seemed to remember that a new science lab now graced the college campus, donated by Brian Hillhouse II, due to that liaison.

Jack didn't believe in Brian's cavalier attitude about his failure to bed the lovely lady in question. Something was off, so he mentioned, “Jo told me that Mak is still a virgin. She believes that Mak is waiting for marriage. A rather antiquated notion in this day and age, but there you have it.”

Brian just shrugged and said, “Want to make a wager on how quickly I can divest Mak of that intact hymen she’s been guarding since puberty?”

“That’s rather crude, don’t you think?” Jack asked. “The loss of a woman’s virtue is not something I’d care to make a wager over. Why don’t you let this one go, Brian? She’s a sweet, naive woman who happens to be seven years your junior. There are plenty of women who’d jump feet first into your bed and never think twice about the fact that you’re a real prick. She’s not really your type, anyway.”

“I rather fancy the virtuous and maidenly damsel. Besides, I don’t discriminate as to type. A pussy is a pussy, as the saying goes. Let’s see how long or what it takes to win her over,” Brian smugly responded. There was no way Brian would ever admit that he’d fallen in love almost at first sight with the enchanting Mak Jamieson.

Jack laughed at that. “Man, you may just find yourself walking down the aisle, my friend. Then you can fill this big house up with miniature versions of yourself.”

Brian quirked his eye at Jack. "That's an excellent idea, you know. That's just what I was thinking, as a matter of fact. As the newest partner in the most prestigious law firm in Oklahoma City, it behooves me to appear as a settled family man with an attractive wife and accomplished children. I am thirty-five years old. It's time to settle down, don't you think? Besides, the old man has been hounding me to produce the Brian Alexander Hillhouse IV heir apparent."

Jack got a stunned look on his face at Brian's agreement concerning marriage and children. "Isn't it a little early to be considering marriage? You just met the woman. Hell, you're not even the marrying kind, Brian."

Dropping the subject, Jack said, "Okay, let's get some of this shit unpacked. Then we can go to bed. Jo wore me out with her sexual antics. That woman knows more about sex than any ten women I've slept with, all rolled up into one. And boy, can she suck cock. I think she turned me inside out. I'm going to miss her when I leave for Pennsylvania in two weeks."

"Shut up, Man. I need a cold shower after visualizing Jo with her mouth wrapped around your dick. Just for that, you can empty these boxes while I'm gone. I need to go fantasize about having Mak's mouth wrapped around mine to rid me of that vile image."

Jack laughed as Brian turned and headed for the hall. "Hey, no jerking off in the shower, Brian."

As Brian rounded the corner, he gave Jack a one-finger salute and said, "Fuck you, Jack. If you weren't my best friend, I'd toss your ass in the lake."

Jack gave Brian a parting grin and said, "Love you too, Bro. Enjoy that hand job."

Brian knew he wasn't going to win the verbal contest. So, before he walked away, Brian reminded Jack, "You're going to need to return to Oklahoma to act as my best man at the wedding ceremony. I'm going to bind Makailyn Elsbeth Jamieson to me as my lawfully wedded wife."

Jack was so stunned, his mouth dropped open. Brian laughed, gave Jack a two-finger salute, one on each hand, and left the room.

CHAPTER 6

JO started talking the minute she put the key in the ignition to start the car. "That was fun, and boy, what a house. Can you imagine owning a place like that? Jack certainly is good between the sheets."

"And here it comes," Mak thought as she tried not to visualize Jack and Jo naked in bed. Mak would be regaled with Jo's sexual encounter all the way back to the ranch. In fact, Mak's nose caught the male scent of Jack all over her best friend. "How do you do that, Jo?"

"Huh? Do what?" was Jo's response as she briefly took her eyes off the road to look at Mak quizzically.

"Get men to have sex with you so quickly, and why would you want to?" Mak asked. "Aren't you interested in finding just the right one? A guy who will love you for who you are. One who will want to be your forever and maybe make little Jo babies with you?"

"Boy, you're so silly, Mak. What do you think I've been doing? I'm interviewing those men for the part of the future, Mr. Johnston. If they don't pass my stringent list of qualifications, I dump them and keep searching for the perfect mate. One of those qualifications is compatibility in bed. Another is how many orgasms they can give me before they come. Oh, another might be staying power, and how about oral sex? Of course, they have to be really good at that, too."

Jo chuckled at the look on Mak's face. It was so much fun to tease her and make her blush. But the truth was, Jo just really liked sex. She was having too much fun and wasn't interested in settling down yet. Maybe in a few years, when her biological alarm clock went off, and she woke up to the fact that she was running out of time to pop out that kid.

"Mr. Johnston? You expect the man that you agree to marry to take your last name instead of you taking his?" Mak was stunned and confused. Here she thought her best friend was a sexaholic. But, instead, she had a master plan all along. "Is there anything on your list besides being good in the sack, Jo?"

"Yes, my list is very comprehensive. Don't you worry your beautiful head about me, my sweet sister from another Ma and Pa. I'm gonna be just fine. So, you and Brian? The two of you looked awfully cozy dancing in the kitchen. Anything you want to tell me? At the very least, is he a good kisser?" Jo probed.

"He was a little too aggressive at first, but then he apologized for coming on too strong. Finally, he told me that he's now my boyfriend," Mak admitted.

"Woo-hoo, girlfriend. Now, that's what I'm talking about. Maybe we'll get you laid yet," Jo said with a wink.

"Don't put your cart before your horse, Jo. Brian is a good kisser, but I'm still holding out for Mr. Right. And no, I won't be asking the right man to take my last name when we say our vows. Now, can we talk about something else? Tell me about your vacation. How are your parents? I miss them a lot," Mak admitted.

The rest of the ride to the ranch was spent catching up. First, Jo told Mak about her trip. Then Mak told Jo about the goings-on at the *Rockin' R*.

"You still have another week off, Jo. How do you plan to spend your time?" Mak inquired.

Jo started to chuckle. "Jack doesn't need to report to the office in Philadelphia for two weeks. I'm gonna introduce him to Chilton. That certainly won't take long, however. So, I expect we'll swim in the lake and get a nice suntan. Then we can take long leisurely naps on that big, soft mattress in the guest room at Brian's house right after an exhausting round of good old healthy sharing of bodily fluids, of course. The man likes to jog, too. Not my cup of tea, but I promised to accompany him on his treks every morning. Oh, that reminds me. Jack wants me to stay there with him all week. So, I'm gonna pack up some duds and meet up with him in the morning. I'm taking him out for breakfast. I'll come to pick you up on Friday for the barbeque. Okay?"

"That sounds like fun, Jo, but I don't know about the picnic. I'm really not comfortable staying at Brian's house overnight, either, because I need to be at the ranch on Saturday morning. Even though it's Memorial Day weekend, I still have clients coming for their lessons. So, if it's all the same, I'd rather not go. Maybe you could give my regrets to Brian and tell him I wish him the best. I'm not really looking for a boyfriend right now. Especially not one with soft hands."

Jo looked at Mak with raised eyebrows. "What do soft hands have to do with anything? What kind of hands does the man of your dreams have, Mak?"

"Don't laugh, Jo. I kinda want a man with big rough hands with calluses from workin' hard around the ranch. I'm sorta' lookin' for a cowboy."

"You'd take a poor rancher over a lawyer who can give you anything your heart desires, Mak?" Jo asked in astonishment.

When Mak nodded her head in the affirmative, Jo said, "Well, I don't see any cowboys in your immediate future. So, there's no reason why you can't have a little fun with the lawyer in the meantime—especially one that's a good kisser. You don't have to let things go any further than you're comfortable with. Come to the barbeque and hang out. Get a tan, and enjoy the fireworks. You'll have some fun and maybe get in some practice kissing. You'll want to be good at that when Mr. Cowboy Right comes along."

If only Mak had stood her ground and refused to go. But Jo was her very best friend, and Mak would do anything to make her happy, short of theft or murder.

So, after a long week of ranching and teaching little kids good horsemanship, Mak took a leisurely shower and shaved all those pesky areas on her body that needed tending. Once she'd donned her bikini under her favorite soft t-shirt and cut-off jean shorts, she put on her favorite *John Wayne* movie. Then she waited for Jo to pick her up. Will had given Mak some time off and promised to take care of the stable and horses that evening.

When she heard the car pull up in front of the bunkhouse Friday afternoon, Mak slipped on a pair of beaded sandals, grabbed her purse, and headed out the door. However, she was shocked when it wasn't Jo's car sitting in the spot in front of the bunkhouse door.

Jumping out of his red *Bentley* convertible, Brian ran around the front to open the passenger door for Mak when she exited the bunkhouse. After handing her into the seat, he leaned down to capture Mak's lips in a sultry kiss, then buckled her seat belt. "Hey, beautiful.

I've missed you all week. Can't wait to get you out of those clothes. Bet you look great in your swimsuit." Then he kissed her again before he closed the car door.

After Brian climbed in behind the wheel, he reached around for something in the back seat. When he handed Mak a bouquet of white and yellow daisies, she gasped in surprise. Daisies were her favorite flowers. They always cheered her up when she was feeling lonely or just down-in-the-mouth.

"Bri, thank you so much. They're beautiful. How did you know that I love daisies?" Mak asked.

"Well, a little Jo birdie might have mentioned it," Brian responded with a grin. "Do you really like them, sweetheart?"

Mak nodded her head and looked at Brian shyly. "Yes, I do. I don't know how to thank you. It was very thoughtful of you."

Brian looked at Mak intently. "Maybe we can think of a way for you to pay me back later." Then he pressed the start button, the engine roared to life, and they were on their way.

Mak had stiffened at the look of lust in Brian's eyes when he mentioned payback, but it was too late to change her mind. They were on their way to the lake house.

CHAPTER 7

JO looked so flushed with happiness when she came bounding out of the front door of Brian's house. She grabbed Mak in a bone-crushing hug. As she held on tight, she whispered in Mak's ear, "Girl, I think Jack's the one. I love him so much."

Mak noticed that Jo fairly glowed, which put the intensity of the rays of sunshine beating down on them to shame. Grabbing Mak's hand, Jo pulled her up the sidewalk and into the house. "I have so much to tell you," she added exuberantly.

Yanking her up the stairs, Jo showed Mak to one of the empty bedrooms. "Git out of those duds and into your bikini. Brian and Jack are on the back patio waiting on us so they can begin grilling the steaks."

"Wait a minute, Jo. You're going so fast, you have my head spinning, and you're making me dizzy. What do you mean, Jack's the one? You've only known him for a week." Mak questioned her friend's sanity at that moment.

"Sister-mine, you of all people know how many men I've been with. So, you should realize that when I say I've found the right one for me, you shouldn't worry that I'm making a bad decision. I don't want to spoil our picnic, but I need to tell you right now. Jack has asked me to go with him to Philadelphia, and I said yes."

Mak stared at her friend in disbelief. She wanted to say, "What about us?" but knew that would be a selfish thing to do. If Jo had found the man she thought was qualified for the title of "Mr. Johnston," and who would be the daddy of all those little Jo babies, then Mak wasn't going to stand in the way of that. But how was Mak going to survive losing her best friend? They'd been together since first grade. Mak wanted to bury her head under a pillow and cry her eyes out.

Instead, Mak hugged Jo tight, so she wouldn't see the tears forming in Mak's eyes. "I'm so happy for you, Jo. I'm going to miss you so much. Promise you'll text every day."

"Oh, honey. Don't be sad. You're still my sister from another Ma and Pa. That's never going to change. Jack promised me that we'd vacation in Oklahoma. After all, Brian's here, and he's Jack's best friend. Who knows, if Philadelphia doesn't suit him, maybe I can convince Jack to find a lawyering job in the vicinity."

"What are you going to do for a job, Jo? Do you just plan to sit around in an apartment all day waiting for Jack to get home from the office?" Mak asked quizzically. "You'll go out of your mind sitting around being idle."

"Actually, I'm thinking about going back to school and getting my Bachelor's degree. What do you think about that? Jack supports my decision to do that. Isn't he great?"

"Oh, Jo. I am so jealous right now. You're so lucky, and I'm so proud of you. I love you so much, Jo," Mak admitted.

"Okay. Enough about this. I'm here for another week, so we have plenty of time to discuss all the details. Let's go join the boys. I'm hungry all the time from all the sex I've been having with Jack. We've burnt a heap of calories between the sheets this week. Let's eat, then we can go out on Brian's boat. I can't wait to show you how good I've gotten at wakeboarding. It's so much fun! Hurry up and change."

All Mak needed to do was strip off her t-shirt and shorts since she was wearing the bikini underneath. Jo already had her suit on. Slipping on a pair of flip-flops, Mak followed Jo to the back patio, where Brian was operating the grill.

"About time, girls. The steaks are just about ready, and Jack has the table set. What would you like to drink, Mak? Your choices are beer, wine, soda, and water," Brian offered.

When Brian handed Mak the bottled water she'd requested, he leaned in and nuzzled the side of her neck. "You look amazing in that suit, sweetheart, and I love the tattoo. I'm having trouble keeping my cock under control, so I don't embarrass myself. Are you okay, Mak? You look like you're trying not to cry."

Mak set the bottle on the picnic table and scrubbed at her eyes with her fists. "I'm sorry. I don't mean to put a damper on your lovely barbeque. I'm just sad. Jo told me that she's moving to Philadelphia with Jack. Jo and I have been together so long, Bri. I'm going to be lost without her. I'll be all alone in the world."

Gathering Mak tight in a hug, Brian pressed her face to his chest. This was the perfect opportunity to put his plan into action. It was a good thing he'd come prepared. Tilting Mak's face up, he leaned down and kissed her gently in mock sympathy. Then, he ran his lips over the side of her neck, starting at her shoulder. When he reached her ear, he whispered, "Marry me, Mak. Then you won't be all alone in the world."

Mak's breath hitched, and she was having trouble breathing. This man was almost a complete stranger. All of the world's sounds disappeared as Mak tried to process what this man had asked her. Then, when Brian dropped down on one knee and pulled a ring out of his pocket, the sound came crashing back like a monster wave battering a rocky shoreline.

Mak heard Jo let out a squeal of joy and then say, "OMG, Jack. Brian's proposing to Mak. That makes me so happy. Now I don't have to worry about her. Brian will take good care of my best friend."

As Brian stared up at Mak with a hopeful expression on his face, she worried that he was waiting for an immediate answer. Confused, Mak wanted to say no, but then looked at the joy on Jo's face and knew she couldn't disappoint her. Jo wouldn't worry about Mak if Mak was being taken care of. So, after closing her eyes for a moment, Mak looked at Brian and gave him her answer.

“Can I add a couple of stipulations to my answer?” Mak requested.

There was that brief flash in Brian’s eyes that looked like anger. Again, it disappeared as quickly as it had appeared. Taking Mak’s left hand in his, Brian responded, “I love you, darling. So, what will it take to get you to say yes?”

“I’ll only say yes if you agree to a long engagement. That way we can get to know each other better. Also, no intercourse until our wedding night,” Mak murmured nervously so that only Brian could hear. She knew she was pushing Brian’s patience to the limit. Still, she wasn’t comfortable being coerced into a hasty marriage that might turn out to be a huge mistake.

Brian had to school his features to ensure that Mak wouldn’t see that he was seething with rage. Fuck! This woman was going to be the cause of him dying of blue balls. However, he’d play the game. He’d get that “Yes” answer out of her and his ring on her finger. He’d call one of the women he had an understanding with later that night. It was just a friend with benefits arrangement, but at least it would soothe the perpetual hard-on he’d been sporting since Mak stepped into his life a week ago. He was going to make her pay dearly when he finally got her into his bed. He was going to fuck her so hard she'd pass out from the force of her orgasm.

"Honey, how long of an engagement are we talking about here?"

Mak closed her eyes so that she could think. Then when she reopened them, she said, "Would a year be asking too much, Bri?"

"I already know what's in my heart, Mak. So, I'll agree to three months."

Mak rejoined, "I need at least six. That's not unreasonable."

"Okay, six it is. If those two caveats are what you need to accept my proposal, I'll acquiesce to your demands. So, are you saying yes?" Then he gave her a brilliant smile.

As Mak nodded her head in agreement, he slipped the ring on her finger.

Brian had been on his knee for almost ten damn minutes, waiting for this stubborn woman to say yes. It was a guarantee that the steaks were now overdone. Was she stupid or something? She was a nobody who worked with animals. Didn't she realize what a catch he was? By the time Brian could stand up, his leg had gone to sleep. But he'd gotten what he'd wanted, or partially, anyway. She still wouldn't let him fuck her, and Brian was out of patience. He'd bide his time. There was no way he was waiting. In the meantime, his ring was on her finger, so other men better keep their hands off his property.

Brian took his fiancée's delicate face in the palms of his hands and gave her a kiss he hoped she wouldn't soon forget. Fuck that six-month waiting period.

After Brian had turned Mak loose, Jo wrapped her up in a fierce hug and grabbed Mak's hand so that she could examine the engagement ring. "Oh, Mak, it's beautiful. You lucky girl!"

Brian wasn't confident that Mak liked the ring or if she'd even looked at it after he'd placed it on her finger. The engagement ring had belonged to Brian's grandmother. It was a 2-carat Pavé infinity diamond ring set in platinum. Brian had the wedding band to match stashed away in the wall safe in the study. He'd have to remind Mak to put the engagement ring in a safe place while doing her chores on the ranch. It wouldn't be for long. He had no intention of allowing his bride-to-be to do such menial labor.

Jack grabbed Brian's hand and pumped it enthusiastically. "Congratulations, Man. I guess I'll have to convince my new employer that I need some time off in six months. My best friend's getting married." Then he leaned in and said, "Good luck with the six-month no-sex clause."

Brian wanted to punch his best friend in the face.

CHAPTER 8

AFTER the couples finished eating, Jo and Mak offered to clean up the dishes. At the same time, Jack and Brian went down to the boathouse to lower the pontoon boat into the water.

"Oh, Mak, I'm so happy right now I'm fit to bust. Who would have thought we'd both find the man of our dreams, and they'd be best friends, too. Maybe I can convince Jack to make it a double wedding. Wouldn't that be amazing? Then we'd have the same anniversary date," Jo squeaked.

"Did Jack propose, Jo?" Mak probed.

"No, not yet, but I'm certain that it's just a matter of time. Why else would Jack want me to go with him to Philadelphia?" Jo asked doubtfully.

“I guess you’re right, Jo, but promise we’ll be there for each other. If either one of us is in trouble, promise we’ll drop everything to get to the one of us who is in need. Promise me, Jo.”

“Oh, honey, I promise. I’ll always be there for you, just like I know you will be there for me. Okay, the dishes are done. Let’s go see the fireworks. I’ve been looking forward to them all week. I’ve never seen any from the water.”

“Wait!” Mak grabbed Jo by the hand. “You remember our secret text word if we’re in bad trouble, right?”

“Yes, Mak. How could I forget? Those boys were going to rape you, sure as I’m standing here. It’s “Savior.” Jo squeezed Mak’s hand tightly. “I’ll never forget it.”

Even though Memorial Day wasn’t until Monday, the Memorial Day Fireworks Spectacular would be held by the Lake Eufaula Country Club from 8:00 p.m. to 9:00 p.m. that evening. Brian took Mak by the hand at seven o’clock and helped her board his Excalibur pontoon boat. Jack and Jo were in Jack’s room doing God only knew what. Brian knew what that something was, though. He’d had to listen to Jo’s screams of pleasure all week. She was the most vocal woman he'd ever heard when she was in the throes of an orgasm. Brian had spent each night jacking off to thoughts of Mak because of Jack's and Jo's sexual antics.

Brian led Mak to one of the upholstered seats near the dash. As Mak eased into the comfortable leather chair, Brian slipped his hand inside the waistband of her bikini bottom. As he began to stroke the tiny bundle of nerves at the apex of her sex, Mak's eyes went wide.

Mak tried to remove Brian's hand as she said, "You promised, Bri."

"Sweetheart, I promised no intercourse. I did not promise that we wouldn't touch each other. Now, let go of my hand. I only want to bring you some pleasure. You belong to me, now. Don't do anything to forget that and make me angry," he admonished.

Mak lowered her head so that her long silky hair hid her face as Brian continued to stroke her clit. Mak could hear Brian moaning softly. Peeking out from behind the curtain of her hair, Mak could see that Brian was stroking his cock with his other hand. The thing was huge. Mak winced and swallowed convulsively. It took Jack and Jo climbing onboard to break Brian's concentration. Mak could hear the anger in his voice when he whispered, "We aren't finished, sweetheart. You're going to suck my cock later tonight, and you're going to swallow every drop when I come. Is that understood?"

When Mak only nodded her head, meekly, Brian said, "I didn't hear you. What did you say?"

Trying not to cry, Mak stammered, "Yes, Brian."

Brian said, "That's my sweet girl. We're going to get along just fine. You'll make me very happy if you do as you are told. Be a good, obedient wife, and we won't have any problems in our marriage. I'll give you as many children as you want. Sound like a plan?"

Again, Mak responded, "Yes, Brian."

Brian smiled. Just what he wanted. A pliant wife who knew her place. "Good girl," he replied, then bent down and nipped her hard enough on the neck to bruise the delicate skin. After biting Mak, Brian kissed the spot to ease the pain. He intended to mark her repeatedly to prove his ownership of her body.

When Brian had control of his erection, he declared, "Let's get this boat underway before we miss the show."

There were already numerous watercraft anchored as Brian eased the pontoon boat into a spot with a good view of the cove. Brian shut down the engine and anchored the boat, then went to squeeze in close to Mak. Jack handed each of them a bottle of water, then went to snuggle up to Jo.

Placing his arm around Mak's neck, Brian pulled her close and nuzzled the side of her neck. "Are you cold, sweetheart? I can warm you up if you are," he said with a grin.

Removing his arm long enough to grab a blanket, Brian spread it over their laps. It was dark now, so he wrapped his arm back around Mak's neck. Dangling his forearm down the front of her chest, Brian eased his fingers inside the cup of her bikini top and pinched her nipple until it formed a stiff peak. Grabbing Mak's left hand, he eased it down the front of his swim trunks. Leaning in close, he whispered, "Wrap your hand around me, sweetheart, and stroke me. That cock is yours to pleasure, now. Do a good job of keeping it happy."

Mak realized that she'd messed up when she said yes to Brian's proposal, just to ease her friend's distress. Now Mak just wanted to go home. How was she going to get out of this engagement? She wasn't ready for Brian's sexual advances, and he frightened her terribly.

As Mak did as she was told, she could feel Brian's body stiffen, and then hot cum shot out and covered her fingers. When Brian was finished, he pulled Mak's hand out of his trunks and brought her fingers to her lips. "Lick them clean, sweetheart. That cum belongs to you. In the not-too-distant future, that's going to be inside your sweet pussy. Then we're going to make a baby."

When Mak was finished licking off her fingers, Brian kissed her on the lips and said, "That's my good girl."

Just then, the first fireworks shot up into the sky, and the sonic boom startled Mak. The next hour was filled with a display of bright bursts of color, loud booms, and eardrum rupturing bangs. It was an impressive show, but it wasn't the reason Mak would never forget this night. Instead, she would remember it as the night a wealthy, entitled, arrogant, and abusive bastard began to subvert her will to his.

CHAPTER 9

WHEN the show was over, Brian took Mak by the hand and made his way to the captain's chair. Mak could just make out the shapes of Jack and Jo as she was pulled along behind the man she was now betrothed to. Jack was lying on the mid-bench with Jo poised above him. They had a blanket thrown over them to hide the fact that Jo was riding Jack, but the blanket had slipped. Mak could see her best friend sliding back and forth along the length of Jack's cock. Mak knew her cheeks were flaming.

When they got to the cockpit, Brian yanked his trunks down before sitting. Then he grabbed Mak by her hair and forced her onto her knees between his legs. Brian pushed her head down until Mak's lips were pressed to the length of his dick. Then, leaning in close, Brian whispered, "I know it's your first time, so I don't expect you to know what you're doing. I'm close to going off like one of those firecrackers, so it won't take much anyway. Just remember, you're going to swallow every drop, just like the good girl you are."

Then he pried Mak's mouth open and shoved his cock inside. Mak tried to think of other things to keep from gagging as Brian rode her mouth. She thought about growing up in the Johnston household, about her love of horses and cattle, and about the litter of Australian Shepherd puppies that had just been born. When her stomach started to churn, Mak let the world around her go blank, and her focus became the handsome cowboy who was going to rescue her from this nightmare. As a load of hot, salty cum hit her in the back of her throat, she fought her gag reflex and swallowed it down, just like she was told to do. When Brian was finished, Mak passed out. The nightmare that was now her life became a deep void as black as the lake's bottom beneath the boat she was adrift in.

When Mak came to, she was lying naked on the large bed in the master bedroom. Her first thought was, "Oh, God, please don't tell me that Brian raped me while I was unconscious?" Mak didn't feel any different. Wouldn't things hurt if she'd been violated?

She was just considering making a run for it when Brian came out of the bathroom naked as the day he was born. Seeing the look on Mak's face, he promised, "I didn't rape you, Mak, if that's what you're thinking, because I want you fully aware of what's happening when we come together. Believe me, I'm going to pleasure you until you scream my name. Come here, sweetheart. I've drawn us a bath in the clawfoot tub. I noticed you admiring it when I gave you a tour of my home. It's your home, now, too, Mak. After we get out of the tub, I will give you several orgasms, but I intend to keep our agreement. No actual intercourse until the wedding night. Okay?"

Mak nodded her head and said, "Yes, Brian." Then she let him lead her to the bathroom.

"Climb in, doll face. I want to wash your beautiful body. Then you can do me. When we're both clean, I want your lips wrapped around my dick. You can bring me to orgasm, and then I'm going to return the favor. I'm going to lick every inch of your body and make you tremble. Just let me know if you change your mind about that six-month no intercourse rule you made me agree to. I'll allow you to change your mind if you want my cock inside you."

Mak prayed she'd never beg for that.

After Brian came in her mouth and she swallowed it all down, he kept his promise about licking every inch of her body. He used his tongue and fingers to bring her to orgasm three times. Brian seemed to have plenty of experience and had very talented fingers. If only he was the man Mak had been dreaming of, but she was positive that he wasn't. The man in her dreams had light brown hair and blue eyes that twinkled when he grinned mischievously. He wasn't Brian.

Mak was worn out from the stress of the situation and the force of her orgasms. She'd never experienced any before. So, when Brian tucked her up under the quilt and climbed in beside her, Mak fell asleep instantly.

When she woke up at her usual time of 5:00 a.m., Mak slipped out of bed. Tiptoeing to the room where she'd left her purse and her work clothes, she gathered her things and slipped into the hall bathroom to get dressed. After brushing her teeth several times to rid her mouth of the taste of Brian's cum, Mak made her way to the kitchen. She remembered that a pad and pen were lying on the countertop. Mak quickly scribbled a note saying that she was taking Jo's car because she needed to get back to the ranch. Clients were booked back-to-back until the middle of the afternoon. Then Mak made a beeline for the front door. Thankfully, Jo had a terrible habit of leaving her keys in the ignition. Mak didn't stop shaking until she'd made it safely to the main road that would take her home where she belonged. Then Mak took a big gulp of air, not realizing until that moment that she had been holding her breath to the point where she was ready to pass out. Merging into the flow of traffic, Mak sighed in relief.

CHAPTER 10

A familiar red convertible pulled up next to the corral where Mak worked one of the new trail horses on a lunge line several hours later. Mr. Riordan had purchased the animal at auction for the trail rides the ranch would soon be offering. This particular animal was a gentle sorrel gelding quarter horse. At a little over fifteen hands, he had a steady, quiet personality. Mak had taken him out on the trail a couple of times during the week, and the horse had performed well on a loose rein and handled obstacles like a pro. Used by the previous owner for gathering and sorting calves, the animal was also supposed to be fun to ride and quiet enough for use as a guest horse. So far, Mak was pleased with his behavior.

Jo, Jack, and Brian emerged from the car and made their way to the corral fence. Jo climbed up on the lower rung, and Mak led the horse over to her.

Jo reached out her hand to stroke the animal's neck. "Oh, he's a beauty, Mak. I'm going to miss working with the horses. As soon as I get my Bachelor's, I'll go looking for another position working on a ranch. Maybe some rich muckety-muck will want to hire me on a breeding farm if Jack and I stay in Pennsylvania. Who knows, maybe someday we'll own a place of our own."

Jo had her back to Jack, so Jo didn't see the look that passed between Jack and Brian. But Mak did, and she didn't like it. She bit her lip, now worried about the fate of Jo's relationship with the man she thought was her ever after. Should Mak say something to keep Jo from getting hurt? When Jo jumped down off the fence, ran to Jack, and wrapped herself around him, Mak knew Jo would never believe her. So, she locked her lips and threw away the key. Mak wouldn't be the one to dash Jo's hopes and dreams.

After nuzzling Jack's neck, Jo returned to the fence. With sad eyes, she informed her best friend that she'd come to give her notice to Will and to collect her belongings.

Mak swallowed convulsively to prevent the sob that was threatening to escape. "Let me turn Maverick loose, then I'll come help. Do you have boxes to put your clothes in? We live light, so I don't think it will take very many."

"Well, Jack and I thought maybe just grab what I could fit in a couple of suitcases, and maybe you could ship the rest for me? That's if you don't mind. You can always go through my things and keep what you like. I'd be pleased knowing you're wearing some of my clothes."

Mak cast her eyes down and just nodded her head. "I can do that for you, Jo. That wouldn't be a bother. Do you want to talk to Will alone? Then I'll help you pack."

"Jack can come with me while I give my notice. That way, you can spend some alone time with your fiancé," Jo responded. "Is Will in the house?"

When Mak nodded her head in the affirmative, Jo grabbed Jack's hand and headed towards the house. Mak watched her best friend in the whole-wide-world walk away. Jo wasn't even going to be around this coming week before she and Jack left for Pennsylvania. With tears blurring her vision, Mak turned and walked right into the solid wall of Brian's chest. As she looked up at him, she could see the swirl of anger in his eyes. As he gripped her arms with an iron grasp, he said, "I know that you're sad right now at the loss of your friend, so I'll go easy on you. All I'm going to say is that I'm agitated at how you took your leave this morning. There'll be a need for punishment. I just haven't decided what form that chastisement will take. What I will say is that from now on, as your fiancé and soon-to-be husband, I expect to know where you are at all times. I want you to be safe, and I don't have time to spend worrying about you. Do you understand, Mak? If you can't listen, there will be reprisals. What is your response? Are you going to behave and do as you are told?"

Mak cast her eyes down again. Then, with trepidation, she whispered, "Yes, Brian. I understand, and I'm sorry for worrying you. I promise never to do it again. I know you are an important man, so have little time to be spent worrying about where I may be or what I might be doing."

Brian tipped Mak's head up so that he could look into her eyes. "That's my good girl," he said before he took her lips in a punishing kiss. "We'll talk about your punishment later when we're alone. I believe I'll place you over my knees and spank your bare ass and then let you suck me off. That sounds like a suitable form of discipline. Don't you think?"

Terrified, Mak squeaked out, "Yes, Brian. May I go now? I need to help Jo pack her suitcases."

Brian kissed Mak gently then said, "Run along. I'll take a tour of the stable. I have no experience with horses. Maybe I'll let you teach me how to ride. Would that please you, sweetheart? If I do well, I might consider purchasing a couple of horses that we could keep stabled close to our home and ride when time allows. Then, later, when our children are older, you will be able to teach them as well. That sounds like a good plan. But, of course, I want my wife to be happy, so she doesn't have any reason to disobey me."

Mak was positive that her mouth was hanging open in astonishment as she watched her future husband walk off toward the stable. When she disrobed later to take a shower, she would find bruises on her forearms in the shapes of Brian's fingers where he had gripped her in anger.

CHAPTER 11

AS Mak folded the pieces of clothing that Jo had decided to take with her and placed them in the waiting luggage, Jo chattered away about all of her big plans for her future with Jack.

When Mak could get a word in edgewise, she asked, "Are you absolutely certain this is what you want, Jo? It's only been a little more than a week since you met Jack. I know he seems like a nice guy, but how can you be sure?"

"I knew the minute I laid eyes on him, Mak. And the first time he touched me, I swear I could see sparks of electricity shooting out between us. I want him so much. It makes me ache. I don't want you to worry about me. Remember, we promised each other that we'd come running if one of us got into trouble. I intend to keep my side of the bargain. But I'm not going to worry. I know my best friend in the whole-wide-world will be safe and happy. Brian will see to that. Okay, I think I have everything I need. Brian said he'd drive Jack and me to the airport on Friday. Will you come with us to see us off?"

"I'll tell Will I need a few hours off on Friday so I can be there, Jo, but I can't promise that I won't cry as I watch you walk away."

Entering the cabin, Brian and Jack caught the tail end of the conversation. Brian said, "Good, we'll pick you up on the way to the airport. Tell your boss you won't be back until Sunday, however. Since we'll be in the city anyway, I'll arrange a dinner meeting with my father after Jack's and Jo's departure. I want him to meet the future Mrs. Brian Hillhouse III. My mother's at our country estate, so you can meet her another time. The restaurant is rather lavish, so bring along appropriate dinner attire. Saturday, I'll take you to see some of the sites of the city."

"Umm…I'm not certain I have anything appropriate to wear for a fancy dinner, Brian," was Mak's timid response.

"Well, then we'll need to go shopping, won't we? I can't have my intended running around in rags, can I, sweetheart? We'll spend the night at the *Colcord.* We can take care of that little matter I discussed at that time and clear the air. Our relationship will be smooth sailing going forward."

Mak could only respond, "Yes, Brian. I believe that would be lovely. I look forward to it."

Grabbing one of Jo's suitcases, Brian paused long enough to graze Mak's lips and whisper, "Good girl," for her hearing only. Then he turned and headed out the cabin door. "Let's get this show on the road, shall we."

As Jack grabbed the other piece of luggage, Jo wrapped her arms around Mak and hugged her tight. "I love you so much, Mak. My parents giving you a home was the best thing that ever happened to me. You've been the very best friend a girl could ever hope to have. I will miss you like the dickens, but we'll text every day, and we can *FaceTime*, too. It'll be like I'm right here. You'll probably get sick of me botherin' you for advice and such. Plus, you'll be busy gettin' to know your sexy fiancé. You'll be so busy, you won't even notice I'm not around." Then Jo kissed Mak on the cheek and ran out the door, closing it behind her.

Mak was grateful that no one was around to watch as she slumped to the floor in a heap and started to sob. A massive hunk of her heart had just left the building.

CHAPTER 12

THAT week seemed like the longest of Mak's life. She was lonely without Jo there to pal around with as they worked. Even the horses seemed to pick up on Mak's melancholy mood. One of the bay horses nuzzled Mak while she was trying to brush him and looked at Mak with sad eyes.

"I know, boy, I'm not very good company, am I? Do you miss Jo, too? You're one of her favorites. I'll have to remember to bring you your carrot before I turn in for the night. Jo always had a treat for you. I don't want you thinking you've been abandoned. I know just how that feels."

"Hi, Mak," Willis Riordan greeted Mak as he sauntered into the stable.

"Hey, Will! What's up?" Mak returned.

"Just came to check on one of my favorite employees," Will said.

Mak laughed. "You're funny, Will. Now that Jo's gone, I'm your only employee. Is there something wrong? I know I haven't been my usual energetic self so far this week. I promise it'll get better. I just need a few days to adjust to my new reality."

"Don't you worry your pretty little head, young lady. You're the best thing that ever happened to this ranch. I don't have any complaints. I know you're grievin' over losin' your friend. It'll take time, I'm sure. I just wanted to let you know I have a young man comin' tomorrow to interview for Jo's job. It's not like you can be expected to handle your chores and Jo's too. The ranch is doin' so well, I'm thinkin' maybe we could actually use two more hands. What do you think?"

"I think that's a splendid idea, Will. However, I also need to tell you something," Mak confessed.

"What's that, Mak? I know somethin's been botherin' you, and I don't just mean about Jo leavin'. What's got you down, girl? I hope you know that I've tried to look out for you and Jo like I knew your daddies would if they were around. Believe you me, I know some of the rich men who drop their kids off have tried to compromise your integrity. But I've admired how you handle the situations when they occur without losin' the business. Fess up. What's goin' on?"

"Well, I don't know if you've noticed the blond-headed man with the fancy convertible that's come by a couple of times?" Mak questioned. "Anyway, I kinda' agreed to marry him just so Jo wouldn't worry about leaving me behind."

"That's no reason to agree to marry a man, Mak? Where's your head, girl? Off in that fog, Jo was always kiddin' you about? If you don't love the man, then I'll git my gun and run him off."

Mak laughed. "I don't think you better mess with him, Will. He's a high-powered attorney from a wealthy family. He'd sue your ass and win, too. Then where would you be? He'd own your ranch, and you'd be living off the state in some old folk's home in Oklahoma City, that's where. It will be okay, I hope. I put a stipulation on my answer to his proposal. No wedding or hanky-panky for six months so we can get to know each other better. If, at the end of that time, I'm not madly in love, then I'll hand him back his ring and send him packing. I'm sure there's a long line of women hoping to sink their hooks into Brian Alexander Hillhouse III. Ones with lots better pedigrees than this poor girl with no daddy, a footloose mother, and no two nickels to rub together. I don't even know what he sees in me."

"Woo Wee! That's quite a handle that boy's parents hung on him. As to what he sees in you, the man would have to be blind and dumber than horseshit not to realize what a gem you are, Mak. Okay, just remember, I keep my shotgun loaded and ready for any kind of trouble. Just let me know if you need me. Oh, and Mak? If you do decide to marry the fancy pants, give me a little more notice than Jo did, please."

"I'll be sure to do that, Will. Thanks so much for listening. I appreciate your concern and support. I really do!" Mak leaned in and placed a gentle kiss on the old man's grizzled cheek.

Will blushed. Mak could hear Will mumbling about pretty young girls bein' nothing but trouble as he walked on back to the house. Probably to take a nap.

After all the horses were bedded down for the night, Mak got cleaned up. As she settled down for a viewing of her favorite western, there was a soft tap on the door. When she opened it a crack, she was surprised to find Brian standing there holding a garment bag.

"Hello, sweetheart. Are you going to invite your fiancé in or leave me standing out here in the cold?"

That got a giggle out of Mak. "You're funny, Bri. It may have cooled off a mite, but it was almost ninety degrees today. So, what brings you all the way out here? Have Jack's and Jo's plans changed? I haven't heard from her since she quit her job. Please come in."

Once Brian had his foot in the door, he hung the garment bag on the hook meant for Mak's coat when the weather was cooler. Mak stood there expectantly, waiting for a response to the question she'd asked.

So, she wasn't prepared when Brian grabbed ahold of her. After kissing her senseless, he pulled her towards her bed. Mak could feel that Brian was vibrating with sexual tension. After taking a seat on the edge of the mattress with Mak standing before him, he slid her pajama shorts down her legs. "Step out, sweetheart. It's time for your punishment."

All Mak got out was a "But" before she was lying across Brian's knees with her exposed rump in the air. The next thing she knew was the stinging slap of Brian's hand as it connected with the tender skin of her behind. Brian rubbed his hand over the surface between each slap to mitigate the pain. Mak lost count of the number of times Brian hit her, but she could feel that he was aroused by what he was putting her through. Mak knew what would be happening when Brian was finished disciplining. She was also sure that she wasn't going to be able to sit down anytime soon.

Intervals between the slaps lengthened as Brian began to alternate them with rubbing her clit. Mak was to the point where she was fully aroused and starting to squirm. Finally, when Brian pushed two fingers into her pussy, she was so primed, she bore down, and her orgasm ripped through her.

Physically drained from the force of her release, she just flopped over Brian's lap like a limp noodle. She didn't have the energy to protest when Brian laid her on the bed and began to disrobe. His shaft jumped to attention when he lowered his boxer briefs, and Mak could see the bead of pre-cum leaking from the slit. Bringing his cock to Mak's mouth, Brian said, "Open up, doll face, so you can finish your punishment. Unless you'd like me to put this to better use. We could start on our family tonight if you want to forego the rest of our agreement."

Mak shook her head no and took Brian's cock into her mouth.

When Brian was spent, he flopped down beside Mak and pulled her in close. Brushing a piece of her hair behind her ear, he said, "Sweetheart, you are so determined to make me wait, aren't you? I don't know how much longer I can hold out, Mak. We could be making beautiful babies right now instead of playing games. I'd love to be able to tell my father that we're expecting. What do you say, Mak? Will you let me make love to you? The first time will hurt, but then I promise to bring you a lot of pleasure."

As a single tear slid down Mak's cheek, she said, "I'm not ready yet, Bri. I need the next six months to get to know you better so that I know I am making the right decision."

There was that brief glimpse of anger in Brian's eyes as he responded, "Six days or six months, it doesn't matter. You belong to me, and I'm never letting you go. So, you'd better get used to the idea, and the sooner you do, the better off things will be. I'm not a patient man, Mak. I want our first time to be special. I don't want to force myself on my intended because she doesn't know a good thing when she sees it. Until you submit, you'll receive another spanking every week. Is that understood, Mak?"

Mak made the mistake of looking at Brian defiantly. When his hand connected with her cheek, she cringed and tried to pull away.

Brian got a horrified look on his face. Cupping her jaw, he kissed her cheek tenderly. "I'm so sorry, baby. I lost my temper. It's your fault for making me angry. I've brought you a present, Mak. I picked up a dress and shoes for you to wear tomorrow night when I introduce you to my father as my betrothed. You're going to look so beautiful in it, sweetheart. Say you forgive me, Mak."

Terrified of the consequences, Mak could only respond, "Yes, I'm sorry, Brian, for making you angry. I'll try to do better from now on."

Brian smiled, kissed Mak tenderly on her bruised cheek, then removed her sleep top. After licking along the line of Mak's butterfly tattoo, Brian began to suckle on her breasts. As he made love to one nipple, he pinched the other. Then Brian started to nip Mak's tender flesh, leaving marks on her breasts and belly. After each bite, he licked and kissed the spot to soothe it. Mak moved restlessly under Brian's assault on her body. She didn't know how to react. At once, it was both painful and also arousing. What did that say about her that she would be turned on? It wasn't so much the pain but how Brian tried to take away that pain that had her blood humming. That frightened Mak even more. This man knew how to play her body like a finely tuned instrument, but he scared her so much. As she began to rub her legs together, Brian slipped two fingers inside her and began to pump them in and out furiously. Mak orgasmed so hard she thought she must have blacked out. When she could see clearly again, Brian was staring down at her with a smug look on his face.

"That's my good girl," was his response. "Go to sleep, Mak. I'm going to stay. But don't be surprised if I wake you in the middle of the night. I can't get enough of you, and the small amount of physical contact you allow me only whets my appetite for more. I'm horny as hell, and I want you so much, baby."

CHAPTER 13

BRIAN left early the following morning, but not before bringing Mak to orgasm several times. At this rate, Mak was positive her vagina would be all worn out before she actually allowed Brian to penetrate her on their wedding night. But at least she'd be good at sucking a man's dick by the time Brian got done punishing her.

Exhausted, Mak dragged herself out to the stable and got to work on mucking out the stalls. She'd promised Will that she would work until 11:00 a.m. Brian would be back to pick her up at noon, so she'd need to hustle to get ready to go. It was a two-hour drive to the airport. The flight was scheduled for 4:00 p.m. Mak and Brian would have to say goodbye to Jack and Jo before they went through the metal detector so their parting would be very public. Mak wanted a few minutes alone with Jo before she was forced to acknowledge that she wouldn't be seeing her best friend again for a long time.

Promptly at 11:00, Mak went into the bunkhouse, stripped out of her work duds, and hopped in the shower. After she'd shaved the necessary body parts, she stepped in front of her full-length mirror. Brian had left numerous bruises and bite marks on her torso, and some of the areas looked inflamed. Sighing, she grabbed the peroxide and some cotton swabs from the tiny medicine cabinet and set about trying to prevent any infection. Then Mak applied some antibiotic ointment. She hoped the marks wouldn't result in any scarring. While she worked, Mak puzzled over why Brian felt the need to hurt her. The only conclusion she could come up with was that she must be doing something wrong. Not having any experience with men, there was nothing to measure her new relationship against. She would have to guard herself against doing or saying anything that would precipitate Brian's need to punish her. By the time that damn cowboy showed up to rescue her, there wouldn't be anything left of her body to save. Brian would have nibbled it all away.

Thinking of the cowboy jogged Mak's memory about the strange dream she'd had during the night. Mak wasn't positive, but it might even qualify as a nightmare of sorts. While she recalled the details of her dream, Mak slipped into the tiny bathroom to dry her hair and finish dressing.

Mak dreamed that she awoke bound hand and foot to a narrow bed in a rough-looking cabin of sorts. The place reminded her of the cabins portrayed in the *John Wayne* movies she was addicted to. Besides the two cot-sized beds that consisted of head and footboards of rough-hewn logs and thin mattresses, the only other furniture was a small table and two chairs. Rough shelving lined one wall with a porcelain sink suspended beneath. The sink was the old-fashioned kind with the built-in drainboard. A hand pump brought water to the sink, so there must be a well or water source for that. A window separated the wall space between the sink and a cabinet supporting a hot plate.

Mak wondered if she'd fallen down the rabbit hole and become a cast member of one of those movies she loved. Maybe she'd been billed as the fair damsel in distress? She'd better stop watching those movies if she was going to have surreal dreams like this one.

In the dream, Mak struggled with the cords that bound her wrists. It didn't last long. Her body and head hurt so much. As she glanced down, she realized that her left eye was swollen shut which accounted for her visual distortion. Licking her lips, she winced when she ran her tongue over a split on the left side. The coppery taste of blood from the cut coated her tongue. Raising her head slowly to mitigate the pain, Mak could see that she was covered in bruises and bite marks which made her think of Brian for some reason.

Mak started to sob just the way she had in her dream. She remembered that she'd tried to call out for help but cowered in fear when the door to the cabin flew back against the wall. Then her dashing cowboy hero had barreled into the room. He quickly made his way to her side and cut the cords that bound her to the bed. When she was free, he gently cupped her face and grazed her lips in a gentle kiss.

Then Mak remembered the most crucial facet of the dream. She had reached up to touch the handsome face of her rescuer. When he lifted her gently into his arms, she sighed. Then as she rested her aching head against the broad expanse of his muscular chest, she had murmured, "I love you so much, Sean."

Then Mak had jerked awake to find Brian sleeping beside her.

Mak gasped. Her handsome cowboy was named Sean. Thankfully, she hadn't said his name out loud. That certainly would have angered Brian, and then he'd feel the need to punish her again.

Hair and makeup complete, Mak stepped out of the bathroom to find Brian seated in the room's only chair, and he was scrolling through the messages on her phone. When Brian realized he'd been caught, he downplayed the invasion of Mak's privacy by telling her, "You're my wife, so there will be no secrets kept from me. Is that understood, Mak? If I even suspect that you have any inappropriate contact with another man, punishment will be exacted. I don't expect we'll have any problems, however. I know you are my good, sweet girl."

Mak wanted to remind Brian that she was not his wife yet, but thought better of it.

Brian handed Mak her phone, then stood to embrace her. "You look beautiful and smell wonderful. It's too bad we have to get going so that Jack and Jo won't miss their flight. Otherwise, I'd take those clothes right back off you and lick your sweet pussy top to bottom. Would you like that, sweetheart?"

Mak dutifully said, "Yes, Bri, I'd like that very much."

Pleased at her response, Brian lifted the hem of Mak's dress to cup her mound. "Good girl. I love you so much, Mak."

CHAPTER 14

EXITING the main house, Jo squealed and took off, running across the yard to the bunkhouse, leaving Jack to follow in her wake. Will watched her go from the entryway, returned Jo's wave when she turned to look back one last time, then slowly closed the door. He would miss having Jo around. She was full of life.

When Jo reached Mak, she wrapped her up in a tight hug. Jack had kept her so busy all week doing vacation-type stuff that, unfortunately, there was little time for Jo to even think about Mak. Jo was sorry for that. She missed sharing every aspect of her life with her best friend.

There was little chance for alone time with Mak, then, either. Since Jack and Jo were running late for their flight's departure to Pennsylvania, the women climbed into the rear seat of Brian's convertible. Brian had been considerate enough to put the top up so that their hair wouldn't be a windblown rat's nest by the time they arrived at their destination. It also made it easier to talk. While Brian was driving, he and Jack conversed about the cases Brian was handling and the details of Jack's new position with a prestigious law firm in Philadelphia.

In lowered voices, Jo and Mak shared stories about Mak's young students and discussed Will's plan to hire two additional full-time ranch employees. However, Jo could tell by Mak's countenance that she was upset about something. Mak's facial expressions always revealed what Mak was feeling. Currently, Mak seemed distraught and acted like she desperately needed to share something with Jo. Jo tried to get Mak to voice her concerns by asking leading questions. Still, with each query, Mak worriedly glanced in Brian's direction and then refused to answer by changing the subject. Jo wasn't confident that she really wanted to know, anyway. So, she put her concerns out of her mind and proceeded to tell Mak all about the tourist sites she and Jack had visited that week. Jo wanted to believe that Mak would be just fine and prayed that her friend would be as happy with Brian as she was with Jack.

Just as Jo feared, there wasn't any privacy when it became time to part with her best friend. Jo and Mak both cried as they hugged each other when the flight was called for boarding. Then, just before Mak pulled away, she whispered in Jo's ear, "Don't forget. *Savior*."

Jo stared worriedly at her best friend's back as Brian steered Mak towards the exit. Did Mak mean that she needed saving right now?

Jo's anxiety over Mak was replaced by excitement over her future with Jack when he grabbed Jo's hand to lead her towards the line for the scanners. It would be two-and-a-half months before Jo would have reason to recall the look on Mak's face when she'd turned back that last time. Instead, Jo would have to live with the remorse she would feel over failing her friend in her time of need. If she'd only stayed, she would have saved them both a lot of heartache and suffering.

Mak managed to hold herself together as Brian led her away. He kept his hand at the small of her back as he guided Mak toward the parking lot. After opening the door, he eased Mak into the front seat and even fastened her belt.

When he slipped behind the wheel, he glanced over and took in Mak's ashen cheeks. She was definitely taking her friend's departure hard. But hopefully, Mak would enjoy dressing up and dining out that evening.

Brian had requested a formal meeting with his father. He'd told the elder Hillhouse that he had proposed to a woman and would be getting married in the foreseeable future. His father grilled Brian about the prospective bride, then agreed to the dinner plans so that he could be formally introduced to his future daughter-in-law.

Unbeknownst to Brian, his father immediately set the firm's on-staff private detective to work finding out all of the background information on one Miss Makailyn Elsbeth Jamieson. The report that the detective handed Mr. Hillhouse certainly didn't showcase the young woman in a flattering light, which led the man to assume that Miss Jamieson was a gold digger. Therefore, Hillhouse did not arrive at the restaurant for the evening's engagement with a favorable opinion of the woman he would soon meet. Nevertheless, he would do whatever it took to prevent his one and only heir from making a terrible mistake. In his mind, women, like Makailyn Elsbeth Jamieson, were good for one thing and one thing only. Maybe after his son was tired of fucking the little strumpet, Hillhouse would give her a roll in the sheets as well. It wouldn't be the first time the father and son had shared a woman, even if his son wasn't aware of that fact.

CHAPTER 15

BRIAN filled the strained silence on the drive from the airport to the 4-star hotel with details about where they would be spending the night. Mak had never been inside such a luxurious hotel before or any hotel at all for that matter. Even though she wasn't paying strict attention to his words, the drone of Brian's voice helped to ease Mak's distress. When Mak told him how much she appreciated his thoughtfulness, Brian clasped Mak's hand and placed a kiss on her palm. The gesture caught Mak by surprise, and she smiled shyly. Maybe there could be something good between them after all. The next six months would surely give her a clue.

After being shown to their suite, Mak stepped into the partially open bathroom to take another shower. The air conditioning in the airport hadn't been working, and it was extremely humid out. Hence, she was sweaty and very nervous about meeting Brian's father. What could she possibly have to contribute to their dinner conversation? Her dyslexic mouth was sure to cause her embarrassment when her sentences came out backward.

While Mak was washing her face, she felt a fully aroused cock pressed into her backside as Brian's hand reached around to squeeze her nipples until they had formed stiff peaks.

Brian nibbled at the side of Mak's neck and whispered, "I need you, baby. I'm all finished waiting. Before Mak could get the soap out of her eyes, Brian had lifted her up and carried her to the massive pillow-top bed. Heedless that they were both wet, Brian lowered Mak down and then pinned her with the weight of his body. Mak could clearly see the intent in Brian's eyes and started to struggle violently in an attempt to get away.

Crying, she twisted her head from side to side and pleaded, "Please, Bri, you promised," but it was too late. As Brian placed his hand over Mak's mouth to stifle her, he forced her legs wide and plunged his cock inside her unwilling body. Mak bucked when Brian ripped through her barrier and started to cry from the pain and alien feeling of being stretched too wide. As she cried silent tears of sorrow,

Brian bit her repeatedly across her breasts while pounding against her. Finally, with a shudder, he groaned as he emptied himself. Then he collapsed his weight on top of her.

At some point, Mak fainted. Her last coherent thought before the inky blackness claimed her was that her cowboy wasn't coming to save her. The gift she'd saved just for him had been stolen, never to be replaced.

Mak came to when she felt a warm cloth pressed between her thighs. She watched as the man who had just raped her gently cleansed her bruised flesh. When he was finished, Brian looked at Mak with sad eyes. "I'm sorry if I hurt you, baby, but now that's out of the way, and we can move forward. I've wanted so much to please you. But unfortunately, you were preventing that from happening with your silly rules about waiting until our wedding night. As far as I'm concerned, we're already man and wife, Mak. I told you that you belong to me now. Denying me what is rightfully mine made me very angry. Now that we've been mated, we can explore our sexual relationship to its fullest. But, come on, doll face, we need to get ready to meet my father. I told him that we'd meet him in the lounge for a drink before dinner."

Brian lifted Mak from the bed and carried her into the bathroom. He eased her into a warm bath that he had drawn for her. "You have a few minutes to soak, sweetheart. Hopefully, it will help to ease some of your discomfort. Leaning over the side of the tub, Brian gently washed Mak's body as she rested against the back of the tub. She was still crying silently, distressed over what had been stolen from her. Who was this man? He could be so kind and considerate at times, but the other side of him was terrifying.

After washing gently between her thighs, Brian lifted Mak from the tub and toweled her dry. "Get dressed, baby. I'll only be a few minutes. When Mak glanced down, she could see evidence of her lost virginity on Brian's penis. She gulped down a sob and left the room to give Brian some privacy and to try to get her emotions under control.

CHAPTER 16

BRIAN and Mak were running late when they finally made it to the restaurant. They found the elder Brian Hillhouse already seated at their table. The man stood to greet them as they approached.

Mr. Hillhouse held out his hand as his son made the introductions. “Father, this is my fiancée, Makailyn Elsbeth Jamieson. Mak, this is my father, Brian Alexander Hillhouse, II.”

The elder Hillhouse bowed over the young woman’s hand and placed a kiss upon it. His first thought was that she was even more beautiful than the photographs that were a part of the dossier the law firm’s detective had put together. He could see why his son was enamored.

As Brian helped Mak to sit, he leaned down and whispered in her ear, “You look beautiful in that dress, Mak. I can’t wait to strip it off you. I fully intend to enjoy fucking you later. Would you like that, sweetheart?"

Mak had been looking down at the place setting on the table before her. When she glanced up at the distinguished-looking gentleman seated across from her, she could see the smirk on the man's face. Of course, he had heard every word Brian had uttered. This was going to be far worse than Mak had imagined. They should just take her out, strip her naked, and flog her in the town square. That would probably be far less humiliating. Brian could wield the whip since he enjoyed punishing her so much.

Mak knew that Brian was waiting for an answer, so she lowered her eyes and whispered, "Yes, Bri, I'd like that very much."

She got a "Good girl" in return.

They hadn't even made it through the entrees before the elder Hillhouse began his inquisition. Even though he'd read the file on Mak several times, he wanted to see how creative or inventive she could be when she made up lies about herself to impress him.

"Miss Jamieson, tell me a little bit about yourself. Who are your mother and father? I went to school with a Jamieson from a well-to-do family in South Carolina. They have numerous holdings there. Are you one of those Jamieson's? It would give me great pleasure to know that my son has chosen well. Make me understand what Brian sees in you, my dear."

Mak kept her eyes trained towards the place setting in front of Brian's father as she began to speak. "Mr. Hillhouse, please call me Mak. There's no need for formality. I can't honestly speak to what Bri sees in me, sir, and if you think I'm after his money, I can tell you with all sincerity that I could care less about it. I don't come from any fancy, well-to-do Jamieson's from South Carolina. I'm a nobody from Oklahoma. My mom ran off with a traveling salesman when I was eight. My dad was killed in a hit-and-run when I was twelve. After my father's death, my best friend's parents took me in and finished raising me the best way they knew how. I got a degree from *Northeastern Oklahoma A & M College* eight years ago. I guess the only thing I could brag about if I were inclined to do so would be that I made high honors in high school and graduated with a 4.0 from *NOA*. I've been working on the *Rockin' R Ranch* since I got my diploma. I try to treat everyone with respect, humans and animals alike. I don't lie, cheat, or steal, and I've never murdered anyone," Mak said with a self-deprecating smile. Having glanced up towards the end of her speech, she lowered her eyes back down to the table when she ran out of steam.

Hillhouse was surprised by the young woman's candor. He fully expected to hear lies that would show her in a favorable light so that she could get her hands on some of Brian's wealth.

"Brian has told me that you insisted on a long engagement. Tell me your reasoning behind that request?" he asked her.

"Well, sir, it's a matter of trying to do what's right. Bri hasn't known me very long and vice-versa. Since we don't really know very much about each other, I'd like the chance to rectify that to be certain we're making the right decision. Brian's proposal came out of left field and kind of took me by surprise," Mak admitted.

"Everything you say is all well and good. However, would you be willing to sign a prenuptial agreement if this marriage is to go forward? By agreeing beforehand to walk away without compensation if the marriage should disintegrate, it would prove that you are sincere about not caring about Brian's wealth."

Appalled, Brian jumped in to defend Mak's honor, "Wait just one minute, Father. I won't have you impugning Mak in any way. You're treating her as if she were a common street trollop who has specifically targeted me. I'll have you know, sir, that until barely an hour ago, this woman whom I fully intend to marry was still a virgin. If I'm fortunate, she is already carrying my son or daughter. As far as I'm concerned, Mak is already my wife by virtue of the fact that we've already consummated our intentions towards each other." Of course, he didn't bother to inform his father that the reason why Mak was no longer a virgin was that he'd forced himself upon her.

Amazed that his son was finally showing some backbone, Hillhouse signaled for the waiter. When he approached, Hillhouse said, "We'd like a bottle of your best champagne, please. We have something to celebrate."

As Brian Alexander Hillhouse II raised his glass in a toast to Mak. He said, "Here's to that grandson or granddaughter you may be carrying. I fully expect Brian to continue to work on that endeavor, my dear, just in case you aren't yet pregnant."

Mak blushed furiously.

That night, in the privacy of their hotel room, Brian took Mak repeatedly until she fell asleep from exhaustion. The following morning, she was covered in bruises and marks where he'd bitten her repeatedly while in the throes of passion.

Things continued in that vein for the next two weeks. Brian stayed at the ranch several nights a week and insisted that she come to his home on Saturday nights. He would wear her out by performing sexual acts that Mak was highly uncomfortable with, and then they would spend Sunday out on the lake on one of his boats. When Mak missed her period, she knew she was trapped and that it was very likely that she had gotten pregnant the day Brian raped her. At least Brian had only hit her four times since and only spanked her twice before taking her from behind.

The only bright spot in Mak's life was her job working on the *Rockin' R*. Brian didn't know she was pregnant, and she had no intention of telling him yet. He would demand that she quit her job and force her into marriage immediately. Mak had just about made up her mind that marriage wasn't in the cards. If Brian couldn't control his anger, Mak didn't want to expose a child to the man's abuse. She started to lose weight from all the anxiety of trying to figure out what to do. If only Jo were here to advise her and offer Jo's unique form of protection. If she knew Brian had raped her and that he was abusing her, Jo would give him a taste of his own medicine.

About six weeks into their engagement, Brian pulled into the driveway of the ranch. Mak was joking around with one of the new ranch hands Will had hired a few weeks after Jo left for Pennsylvania. The guy, named Sam, was just a kid, really, as far as Mak was concerned. He was only twenty-one, so seven years, Mak's junior.

Mak could see that Brian's eyes were blazing with anger as he made his way towards them. To forestall any unnecessary confrontation, Mak excused herself and hurried towards her intended. Hopefully, to assuage Brian's anger, Mak threw her arms around his waist, pressed a kiss to his lips, and said, "Hi, Bri. I've missed you. Did you do well in court today?"

Brian's day had gone badly. First, the firm had lost its argument in court, then his father, in a fit of rage, had demanded to know why Brian's fiancée wasn't pregnant yet. The last thing Brian needed to see was some other man touching Mak on the arm and making her laugh.

Brian was seething inside, and Mak's kiss did nothing to alleviate that burning anger. Grabbing her wrist, he said, "You are done here. I'll permit you the time to say goodbye to your boss, then you are coming home with me. Until I feel that you've regained my trust, I will be hiring companions to watch over you and keep you safe. I'll send my assistant to gather your belongings. You'll need to be suitably punished for flirting with that man. I've told you repeatedly not to anger me, and at the moment, I am furious. Am I making myself perfectly clear, Mak?"

Brian had an iron grip on Mak's wrist. She'd only been sharing a laugh over something that had occurred with one of her students. Still, Mak was afraid that Brian might do something to hurt the young man if she didn't comply. So, Mak could only respond, "Yes, Brian. I understand completely."

That night, Brian beat Mak until she passed out from the pain. Then, he raped her anally, thankfully before she came to. After, Brian cried and begged for Mak's forgiveness for hurting her even though he said it was her fault for making him angry.

CHAPTER 17

MAK felt trapped in a nightmare because she was now a prisoner in Brian's home on Lake Eufaula. Brian had hired two men to carefully watch over every aspect of her life when Brian wasn't home. Her only privacy was when she isolated herself in the master bathroom.

Now ten weeks pregnant, Mak was alone, bored, and going out of her mind. Thankfully, she hadn't shown any signs yet, of her impending motherhood, so Brian didn't know that he would be a father. But, of course, he was going to be very angry that she hadn't told him when he finally found out.

Brian had been away on a business trip for two days to depose a witness and was due home that afternoon. Mak had strict instructions to be lying in bed, horny and wet for him, when he arrived. With an hour still to go, Mak was surprised to hear a tentative knock at the front door. No one ever came to the house, so it must be a delivery. Mak could hear the guards talking together in the kitchen. Assuming that they hadn't heard, she went to answer the door. She never expected to find a very pregnant young girl standing on the other side of the door who requested to speak to Brian Hillhouse.

Confused, Mak invited her in and took her to the study. That way, they could have a private conversation out of the earshot of the guards.

Once she'd closed the study door, Mak held out her hand and said, "Hi, I'm Mak. Is there anything I can do for you?"

"My name's Millie," the girl responded as she shook Mak's hand. "I was a waitress in a bar in Oklahoma City until a few days ago. It took some doing to find the man who caused this," indicating her enormous abdomen.

"Did you have an affair that went badly?" Mak questioned.

"No, ma'am. I was working the floor one night eight months ago. I had served a good-looking gentleman his drink, then gone to the storeroom to get some napkins and straws to restock behind the bar. The man I'd served the drink to followed me in and locked the door. I got scared and tried to scream, but he stuffed a rag in my mouth and forced himself on me. That's how I ended up in this predicament. I know he used a condom but apparently, it didn't work."

Mak's stomach was roiling. "How do you know you have the right man?"

"Well, ma'am, my best friend has a brother who is a private eye. He's the one who figured it out. My friend took me to the doctor for my check-up in Oklahoma City, and then we did some window shopping. I saw the man entering a building and pointed him out to my friend. The sign on the building said *Hillhouse, Bow, and Hillhouse, Attorneys at Law* on it. So, we told my friend's brother, and here I am standing in the bastard's home. I'm not here to cause any problems or even ask for anything. I just want the satisfaction of seeing the look on his face when I confront him. I know I don't have a leg to stand on, him being rich and all. I didn't tell the police about the rape, so it's just my word against his that it wasn't consensual."

Mak felt sick to her stomach. She wasn't Brian's only victim. She wondered how many more there might be. "Well, the man you're looking for won't be home for a while, so maybe you could come back, or I could take your information if you'd like?"

“No, that’s kind of you to offer to help. I’ve used up all the courage I had. I’m leavin’ and goin’ home to my Ma in Wyoming. She raised a passel of kids, but this will be her first grandbaby. I think the baby will be a whole lot better off never knowin’ who his daddy is anyway, don’t you think?”

Mak could only agree, “Maybe it would be better if Brian never knew. Being rich, he could certainly try to take the child away from you. Also, being rich, I’m positive that he would succeed and also prevent you from having any contact.”

Millie thanked Mak for her sound advice. “I sure am glad I got to meet you, Mak. I’m gonna take your good advice to heart. Nobody’s gonna take this baby away from me. Not even some scumbag who thinks he can get away with anything, just because he has lots of money.”

Mak watched as the young woman was driven away in a beat-up *Toyota Corolla* that looked like it had seen better days. When the car was out of sight, Mak turned and ran into the brick wall of the guard’s chest.

"Who was that?" he demanded to know. "I didn't hear the doorbell."

"Just someone who was looking for an address, but they had the wrong side of the lake. So, I wrote down the directions for the woman," Mak lied. It was the first lie she'd ever told. "Mr. Hillhouse should be home momentarily. Will you be leaving for the night after he arrives home?" Mak enquired.

"Yes, ma'am, same as always," came his gruff response.

After the guard went back into the kitchen, Mak raced up the stairs and locked herself in the bedroom. Frantically she began stripping the dresser drawers and closet of her belongings. As soon as she was finished facing Brian, she was getting the heck out of here. Nothing and no one was going to stop her.

Brian was in a decidedly chipper mood when he walked through the front door of his home. The trip had gone well, and he'd even gotten laid. The daughter of the witness he'd deposed was a beautiful woman who enjoyed kinky sex.

Thinking about that encounter got him all riled up, so his thoughts went to Mak. She'd better be lying naked on his bed when he went upstairs.

Brian stopped to talk to the guards he employed to get a full report on what Mak had been doing for the last two days. After showing them the door, Brian turned to head up the stairs. It was time to make love to his soon-to-be wife. Maybe this time, he'd get her pregnant. He'd just have to be really aggressive. Lost in what he planned to do to Mak, Brian almost fell over the suitcases Mak had just placed at the head of the stairs.

"What's this about," Brian demanded angrily as he stepped around the luggage and Mak to get to the bedroom. "Put your stuff away, Mak, right now, and maybe I won't be hard on you."

Mak stared back defiantly. "No, Brian. I won't. A young girl came to your home an hour ago with a story about being raped by you eight months ago. The girl was very pregnant with your child, Brian, and I believe her. We're done." Then Mak removed the engagement ring from her finger and threw it at him.

Shocked that she would have the audacity, Brian reached out and slapped Mak hard on the side of her face. The force of the blow caused Mak to lose her balance. As her body twisted, she stepped back to try to regain her balance but toppled over the luggage behind her. Together she and the suitcases tumbled end-over-end down the stairs.

When Mak came to, she was lying on a gurney in the emergency room at the hospital. After the attending physician explained Mak's injuries and told her that she'd lost her baby, Mak broke down and sobbed uncontrollably. Then Mak requested, "If there's a blond-haired man in the waiting room looking for me, please don't give him any information concerning my condition. I don't want to see him, either."

Mak was asked questions about abuse or if the blond-headed man was responsible for her injuries. Mak lied for the second time in her life and told the doctor no. She said she'd tripped over some luggage and fallen down the stairs. The doctor just nodded his head, but the nurse that was standing behind him rolled her eyes. She'd heard that story too many times to count. At least this young woman wasn't letting her abuser in to see her. Hopefully, she'd find the courage to leave the bastard.

Mak was admitted and taken to a room soon after for overnight observation. One of the night nurses, whose name was Remzie, came in to check Mak's vitals. Even though Mak denied having been abused, Remzie was very empathetic to Mak's plight. Her very best friend hadn't escaped the abusive situation she had been trapped in. So, Remzie now recognized the signs and was worried about this young woman lying in a hospital bed.

When Mak asked Remzie if she would be kind enough to do her a small favor, Remzie readily agreed. It was such a simple request, really, so the nurse was happy to comply.

Mak gave Remzie a cell number to use and anxiously requested that she send a small text to that number. That text message simply read, "*Savior* and *OSU Medical Center*."

Mak cried for a long time that night over the loss of her baby.

At the end of her shift, Remzie came back in to check on Mak one last time before going home. She found Mak sobbing into her pillow to muffle the sounds. Remzie pulled a chair up next to the hospital bed, sat down, and reached for Mak's hand.

"I just came in to check on you and to let you know that I understand," Remzie began.

"Understand what?" Mak asked. She was determined that no one would know what she had been through. Well, maybe she would be able to tell the person to whom the nurse had sent the "Savior" text if Jo actually showed up.

"I just needed to talk with someone because I still hurt and need someone to talk to. So, I was hoping that you might like to be my friend."

"Oh! I could be that for you. Would you like to tell me what is causing you so much pain? I don't know if I'll have any answers for you, but I can hold your hand and give you a hug," Mak smiled tentatively.

"I'd really like that," Remzie responded. Then, as the two new friends held hands, Remzie told Mak about the woman who had been her very best friend practically from the moment they were born. "Our mothers were best friends as well, so we were always in each other's lives. We were even roommates in college. I was taking business courses. I'd planned to take over the corporate world. But, when I lost my friend, I lost my direction in life. After a while, I realized that I'd be much happier helping people than if I were to become a corporate tycoon. That's when I changed my major so that I could become a nurse."

"Tell me about your friend," Mak requested, sensing that Remzie needed to talk about her.

Mak cried as Remzie related the details of how that woman had found herself in an abusive relationship that led to her death.

"She never told me," Remzie cried. "She hid everything behind a mask, not wanting anyone, especially me, her very best friend, to know what she was coping with. I think she blamed herself or thought that somehow, she was the one responsible for the way the man treated her. She was the dearest sweetest person anyone could ever hope to call a friend. You remind me of her a lot."

"I appreciate that you were willing to let me get that out," Remzie continued. "It's coming up on the anniversary of my friend's death. I always have a hard time with that. Talking to you really helped, Mak. I'll go now and let you get some rest. If you ever need someone to talk to, I'd be more than happy to be the person you confide in. You can find me through the hospital. Just leave a message where you can be reached."

Mak gave Remzie's hand a squeeze. "Thank you for sharing that with me. You've helped me more than I think I may have helped you. As soon as I know where I'm going to land, I'll be in touch. Thank you, my new friend."

Remzie smiled, gave Mak's hand a squeeze in return, and concluded, "You take care of yourself." Then she left.

CHAPTER 18

THE following morning, Jo stood near the luggage carousel at *Will Rogers Airport* in Oklahoma City. While waiting for her luggage to make an appearance, she pulled her cell phone from her purse so that she could text Mak that she was coming to the *Rockin' R* to see her. Jo looked at the cell phone in annoyance when she noticed that the screen was blank. Making a frustrated sound in the back of her throat, she shook her head because she'd forgotten that she'd shut the damn thing off during the flight. A ding sounded when the phone booted up to indicate an incoming text. Swiping her finger across the screen, she realized it was from an unknown number. After tapping on the message to scan it, Jo's mouth opened in shock. The text message read, "*Savior* and *OSU Medical Center*."

"Fuck," she thought. "Mak's in bad trouble." When her suitcase finally made an appearance, Jo grabbed it and raced to the car rental agency. She had to get to the friend she should never have left behind. Throughout the past few weeks and the almost five-hour non-stop flight from Philadelphia, she'd had plenty of time to dwell on her lapse in judgment.

Jo had been so happy when she'd followed Jack Hamilton to Philadelphia. He'd been attentive during the two weeks they'd spent together after meeting each other on a flight from California to Oklahoma City. She'd fancied herself in love and believed Jack loved her as well. Why else ask Jo to quit her job and move so far away so that they could continue exploring their relationship.

By following her heart instead of her head, she'd left her very best friend, Mak, behind. What was she thinking? She and Mak were like sisters.

Everything had been going so well. The apartment Jack had rented was in the heart of the city, not far from the law offices where he was working. Jo used her own savings to give the place a homey feel.

Jo did online research and signed up for classes for that fall to study for her Bachelor's degree. She'd even found a part-time job at a small coffee shop just down the street from the apartment.

Jack was very busy settling into his new position at the law firm, so Jo wasn't too concerned at first when he worked late hours. They definitely made up for things on the weekends, however. The magnitude of their seismic sexual encounters was off the charts.

Small things taken individually didn't seem to matter. Still, taken as a whole, Jo realized that she had been highly naïve. Take, for instance, the number of times that Jo had suggested visiting Jack's parents, who lived close by in Haverford. Of course, Jack always made excuses about why it wasn't a good time. But Jo began to wonder. Wouldn't you want your parents to meet the girl you were in love with?

Until two weeks ago, Jo had ignored all the signs. Then she came home from the coffee shop one day to find all of Jack's clothing missing and no note explaining why. When calls and text messages went unanswered, Jo tried to confront Jack at his place of employment. The only thing that she discovered was that he had been transferred to one of the firm's satellite offices. The receptionist refused to give Jo any information and threatened to have her bodily removed by one of the guards when Jo became very vocal.

Jo went back to the apartment and cried herself to sleep. Upon waking the following day, she went out to the coffee shop, got herself a fresh cup, and gave her notice. On the way home, the cover photo on one of the local newspapers being sold on the corner newsstand caught her eye. The caption read, "*Son of Local Philanthropist to Wed Heiress*." There was a picture of her Jack with some donkey-faced young debutante. Jo paid for the newspaper and went home to devour the details of the article. When she'd gleaned all she could, she began to plan her revenge. Jo also searched online for horse and cattle ranches in the western states looking to hire someone with her credentials. She needed to make some significant changes in her life, including no more sleeping with any man who struck her fancy. She'd behave like Mak and wait for the right one to put a ring on her finger first. The bigger the rock, the better. Then if it didn't work out, she could always sell the ring for cash.

One advertisement in Montana caught her eye, so she sent her resume to the indicated fax number. After several back-and-forth emails and a few phone calls with the prospective employer, Jo was informed that the job was hers if she wanted it. However, she wouldn't need to begin her duties until the end of September. That gave her four weeks.

With a new job waiting for her and four weeks to get there, Jo decided to take her revenge. Then she would stop to catch up with Mak in Oklahoma before flying on to California to spend some time with her parents.

On the eve of her outbound flight, Jo dressed in a sexy *Alfred Sung* V-neck, sleeveless cocktail dress that she'd purchased on sale at *Neiman Marcus*. When her cab arrived, Jo told the driver that she needed to be delivered to the *Rittenhouse Hotel.*

Tucking herself in behind some invitees, she was able to make her way into the banquet hall. The evening's honored guests would be one Jack Hamilton and his donkey-faced fiancée. After getting a good look, Jo decided the woman's name suited her appearance. Philomena Middleton was at least six feet, so two inches taller than her intended. She had an amazon shape, brassy red hair, bushy caterpillar eyebrows, and a donkey-snout nose, which was why Jo called her the donkey-faced fiancée. She was wearing an orange dress that clashed with her hair and looked like it had been sitting in someone's closet since the

1950s. The woman with a pretentious name wore bright red lipstick and way too much powder. Even the woman's laugh sounded like the bray of a jack-ass. Jo snickered to herself. She'd made a funny, "Jack's *ass*."

Jo hid behind a tall Fiddle Leaf Fig tree until all of the guests were seated. Then, after managing to snag herself a flute filled with champagne from one of the passing waiters, Jo listened as toasts were offered in congratulations to the newly engaged couple.

Jo stepped out from behind the potted plant when all was quiet except for the clink of silverware on porcelain dinnerware as everyone concentrated on their meal. Placing her fingers in her mouth, Jo gave a shrill whistle. All eyes in the room turned towards her, and Jo could see the decidedly sick look on Jack's face as if he might throw up.

Glancing around to be certain she had everyone's attention Jo raised her voice and her glass. "I'd like to offer my congratulations, as well, to the happy couple, if I may. I just want to say that Jack's fiancée, Philomena is one of the luckiest girls in Philadelphia. She's managed to snag one of the best fucks imaginable." Directing the balance of the toast to Jack's intended, Jo continued, "I should know. He's spent the last three months between my sheets and sister those sheets were hot enough to catch fire. All the while being engaged to you. Imagine how surprised I was to find out the man I loved was just using me to get his rocks off."

Jo heard a bunch of gasps, the loudest one coming from the donkey-faced heiress. Bringing the flute to her mouth, Jo said, "Cheers, everybody!" then tossed back her champagne, smashed the empty flute on the floor, and turned to flee.

She could hear voices raised in anger, demanding answers from Jack. The loudest of all was Miss Donkey-face Middleton. Her bray was harsh enough to crack the crystal goblets that sat before each place setting.

As Jo raced through the ballroom doors, she took one peek back. When she realized that Jack had ignored the angry requests for an explanation and was in hot pursuit, she redoubled her efforts to escape. Unfortunately, the spiked heels Jo was wearing didn't allow for a full out sprint, and Jack caught her quickly before she could escape. Dragging her into an empty room near the hotel elevators, he pulled Jo to him and said, "Just wait a minute, will you, damn it. God, you are so beautiful." When he tried to kiss her, Jo angrily shoved Jack away.

"Jo, I'm sorry. I fully intended to contact you as soon as I had all the details ironed out. I would buy a house for you to live in, and I would come to you as often as possible. My engagement was all arranged by my parents when I was just a kid, Jo. I don't want to lose you."

Jo bristled and demanded, "What, Jack? Was I just going to be your dirty little secret for the rest of my life? Well, it's too damn bad. You've been caught up in a deception of your own making, and by the sounds of things out there in the lobby, I think your parents' plans for your marriage to that donkey-faced heiress may have just gone up in smoke. Pre-arranged marriage or not, you should have been straight with me from the get-go Jack."

Then Jo slapped Jack's face hard enough to leave the imprint of her hand and walked away with her head held high. As she managed to pass through the doorway, a rampaging Philomena Middleton came charging into the room. Unfortunately, Jo didn't stick around long enough to hear what the woman had to say. Jo felt sorry for the girl. She'd be lucky if she and Jack ever had sex. He'd be lucky to get an erection unless his bride was wearing a feedbag over her head to hide how homely she was.

Hailing a cab, Jo gave the driver the address of the apartment she had decorated with so much love and care for the man she had wanted to be her ever-after. After stripping out of the fancy dress, she donned a pair of skinny jeans, a soft t-shirt, and comfy sneakers. Tossing the apartment's key on the counter, she grabbed her shoulder bag and suitcase. The balance of her belongings had already been shipped to Montana in the care of Eloise Whrite-Thompson. Locking the door, she slammed it closed behind her and went back out to the waiting cab. On the way, she tossed the fancy dress and shoes in the trash can by the curb.

CHAPTER 19

MAK was asleep when her best friend slipped into her hospital room and took a seat on the chair beside her bed. Jo gently brushed the sweaty hair off Mak's forehead, then kissed her lovingly. Mak sure looked like shit.

Mak hadn't slept the night before. She'd suffered from crying bouts over the loss of her baby. Plus, Mak was terrified that Brian would bribe his way into her room. The sky outside her window was beginning to lighten by the time she finally fell into a fitful sleep. The only bright spot had been her discussion with her new friend, Remzie. Mak hoped she'd get to see the woman again someday.

The doctor stopped at her room while making his rounds. It felt like only minutes since Mak had dozed off. He went over the extent of her injuries but didn't tell Mak that she'd been lucky considering the fall she'd taken. She had lost her baby, after all. Mak appreciated that he hadn't tried to minimize her feelings with such platitudes.

Mak was informed that she had bruised ribs that would take three to six weeks to heal if she was careful. The two broken fingers on her left hand had been placed in splints. Mak was kept overnight for observation due to the blow to the back of her head. She had a mild concussion, so the hospital staff needed to monitor Mak for physical signs such as vomiting, blurry vision, loss of memory, or confusion.

The doctor told Mak that she would be released that afternoon if none of those symptoms manifested. She was admonished to rest as soon as she got home and take it easy until her ribs healed. She was also told that there shouldn't be any reason she couldn't conceive again. Mak was grateful for that news.

The minute Mak opened her eyes to find Jo's eyes staring back at her, they both began to cry. Then both tried to talk at the same time.

Jo cried even harder when Mak filled her in on what life as the fiancée of Brian Alexander Hillhouse III had been like. Jo wanted to cut off Brian's dick and shove it where the sun didn't shine when Mak admitted that he'd raped and brutalized her.

Mak listened to Jo's tale of betrayal by Jack and wanted to do the same to him. That made both women laugh and then break down in tears again.

"What am I going to do, Jo? I have nowhere to go where Brian won't find me. He's not going to let me just walk away because he said that I belong to him. When Brian finds out I never told him about the baby, he will beat me again. Maybe bad enough to kill me."

That's when they put their heads together. Jo told Mak about her new job at the *Circle R Cattle Company Ranch* in Billings, Montana. The ranch was owned by a man named Roger Willis. Mr. Willis was in the process of expanding what the ranch had to offer. He was very interested in providing the same types of programs she and Mak had offered on the *Rockin' R*.

"This is what you're gonna do, Mak. You're gonna go to Montana and take my place. We look so much alike, and they've only seen one grainy photograph of me that I faxed over to them."

"We're gonna sneak you out the back door of this hospital when no one's lookin'. Take my purse and clothing. I already had the rest of my crap shipped to the *Circle R* in the care of some woman named Eloise. So, you won't lack things to wear. I know some of it is not your style, but at least you'll be set up until you get your first paycheck. Use the car I rented and pretend you're me. Nobody will be the wiser."

"What about my stuff here at Brian's and my savings at the bank?" Mak asked.

"The money can sit there for a while. If the money isn't being touched, it'll confuse anyone Brian has tryin' to get a bead on you," Jo lectured. "As for the clothes, who cares? You can always get new duds."

Jo continued, "I have my plane ticket and an extra credit card, plus my driver's license from Pennsylvania. So, I'll be able to get on my flight to California. I'll hole up with my parents for a few months. Then I'll come to find you. We'll find a job on a ranch somewhere together. Brian will never be able to find you in Montana if you're Jaymiee Joanna Johnston."

After Mak had showered and donned the outfit Jo had stuffed in her shoulder bag, the pillows and blankets on the hospital bed were plumped beneath the top sheet to make it look like Mak was asleep. Mak and Jo giggled while they worked on that together. It was just like old times when they were teenagers, trying to sneak out of the house at night to go skinny dipping in the pond.

Jo poked her head out of the room to determine if the coast was clear, then they hightailed it for the elevator. They both breathed a sigh of relief after they'd made it safely to Jo's rental.

"Is it going to be okay for me to drive this rental all the way to Montana, Jo? What were the terms of your rental agreement?"

"There you go worrying your pretty little head, Mak. I already took care of that. I called the rental agency while you were in the shower. They've agreed to allow me, meaning you, to drive the car to Wichita, Kansas. Turn the car in there. From there you'll get a bus ticket to Billings. I also nipped down to the gift shop and picked up a disposable cell phone. I already activated it and put the number on my phone. You're takin' my phone with you. It would probably be best to use cash whenever possible. There are a couple thousand dollars in my purse. If you're frugal, that should get you all the way to Billings and then some. I programmed the address where you'll drop the car in the GPS. Just follow the directions. Someone at the rental place should be able to give you directions to the bus terminal."

"Now get the heck outta here before someone recognizes you. I'll see you in a couple of months. I upgraded my ticket. My flight for California leaves in two hours. If you're fortunate, you'll never set eyes on Brian Alexander Hillhouse III ever again."

Both women hugged each other tight, afraid to let go, but the clock was ticking. So, with tears in their eyes, they both turned away. Jo turned to capture one last look at Mak before she rounded the corner. Then she said a prayer.

"God, watch over my sister from another Ma and Pa. As you guide her safely to Montana, for heaven's sake, help her find that damned cowboy she's always dreamin' about. And if you're feelin' generous, God, maybe you could find one for me, too?"

When nurse Remzie came on shift late that afternoon, she heard the gossip about a patient named Makailyn Jamieson. Some high-powered attorney was making a stink over the fact that Mak had snuck out of the hospital. Remzie thought, "Well, good for you, Mak. I think you're going to be just fine, now." Then the nurse went about the business of helping others.

CHAPTER 20

BRIAN Alexander Hillhouse III was sick of being treated like a schoolboy being called before the headmaster at the boarding school he had attended. The man had been a pompous windbag who enjoyed browbeating the young miscreants he was in charge of.

"You've managed to royally fuck up this time, Brian." His father was shaking with rage, and his face had turned a mottled shade of red. It was almost the color of a good bottle of *Château Grand Village*. The color was good for a bottle of wine, maybe, but not a good indication of a person's blood pressure. Perhaps good old dad would benefit from smashing that decanter instead to alleviate some of his anger.

"Your fiancée was pregnant with what might possibly have been your son and heir, and you pushed her down a flight of stairs?" he bellowed.

Brian hung his head in remorse. He'd lost the child that would have made his father proud of him, and the woman he loved was lying in a hospital bed refusing to see him. Brian would definitely consider it a fuck up. If he'd known about the baby, he wouldn't have hit her. Mak hadn't bothered to inform him, so now he'd have to punish her for that.

He'd almost gone out of his mind when the hospital staff refused to allow him in to be by Mak's side while she was being treated. Then, when they denied him information about Mak's injuries, he'd totally lost his temper. Finally, they actually dared to have him removed from the premises and barred from the building.

Not knowing what to do, Brian had gone straight to his father and confessed. He knew the old man would know whose strings to pull to get him back into the hospital so that he could be by Mak's bedside. She needed him, and he desperately needed her.

Brian Hillhouse II had immediately taken charge. With a few well-placed calls to people who owed him favors, Hillhouse managed to get a copy of Mak's hospital records. Totally illegal, but for the right price, anything or anyone could be bought.

Father and son were currently discussing those records and what would need to be done to return the young woman to Brian's care. Hopefully, devoid of any future physical violence, of course.

At present, they had been informed by Hillhouse's contact at the hospital that Mak had been admitted for observation.

"Go home, Brian. You aren't going to be worth a damn here at the office until you get your fiancée back. And stay the hell away from the hospital. I don't need you making matters worse than they already are. I have to tell you, son that I was beginning to see a change in you since that young lady came into your life. You were showing signs of becoming the son I could be proud of. You also seemed more focused at the office. This incident has been an unfortunate setback, however. Go home. We'll have Mak back in your bed soon enough. As soon as she'd healed, you can work on getting her pregnant again." Then he actually threw his arm around Brian's neck and gave him a hug. The unexpected gesture made Brian break down.

As Brian hugged his father back, he admitted, “I love Mak so much, Dad, and now because I lost my temper, she’s lost our baby.”

Hillhouse was uncomfortable with the show of emotions exhibited by his only child. The older man’s parents had never been demonstrative, and he’d mostly been raised by nannies. His mother had expressly forbidden those nannies to show her only child any physical signs of affection. She was extremely jealous and worried that her son might become attached. That made the position as Brian’s nanny a very temporary one because his mother fired the current nanny at least yearly, if not sooner. Thinking that was the norm, he’d employed the same practices in raising his son, Brian. Perhaps it was not too late to change that, so that father and son could develop a relationship.

Patting Brian on the back, he stepped away. “I’m sorry for your loss, Brian. I know it is of little consolation, but you can get Mak pregnant again soon enough. The file did say that she would still be able to conceive.”

“My contact will keep me posted. When the doctor plans to release her from the hospital, you can wait in the limo while my assistant handles the hospital bill. I'll have someone in place to escort Mak to your waiting arms."

Brian thanked his father and shook his hand. "Thank you, Father, for everything. I know I seem like an ungrateful prick, but I do appreciate everything you do to take care of me."

As his son walked away, Brian Alexander Hillhouse II had a suspiciously glassy-eyed appearance. Trying not to cry, he was definitely thankful that there was no one there to see it.

When Brian arrived at his now-empty house, he made his way to the room where he'd spent eight glorious weeks making love to Mak. Flopping on the bed, he pressed his face to Mak's pillow and breathed in the scent of her. Then Brian cried himself to sleep. Emotionally exhausted, he slept the sleep of the dead until well past noon the following day.

When Brian woke up, his first thoughts were of Mak. Hopefully, she would be coming home today. He had to get ready for that possibility so that he could be waiting in the limo to pick her up when the hospital released her.

Grabbing the suitcases full of Mak's clothing, he brought them to their bedroom. He carefully placed the garments back in their proper places. Getting a good look at what she owned made Brian cringe. None of it should be gracing the body of his beautiful Mak. Brian would be taking her on a surprise shopping spree as soon as she felt up to it. He'd love to sit in a comfy chair being served champagne and hors d'oeuvres while his intended put on a fashion show just for him. Brian would buy Mak only the best designer outfits and sexy lingerie. Then they would go to fancy restaurants, nightclubs, and the *Civic Center Music Hall* in Oklahoma City so that he could show her off. When they got home, he'd strip her of those garments and make passionate love to her sexy body. They'd be expecting parents again in no time at all.

Brian fully intended to be a good father to his children. He would spend quality time with them, helping with homework, and take them to their school sports activities. But, most importantly, Brian would give them the hugs and kisses they deserved even when they fucked up. Brian knew from experience that everyone fucked up once in a while.

Brian stowed them back in the closet when the suitcases were emptied of their contents. Then he went to take a shower. It would be a cold one. Brian's shaft was painfully erect due to his thoughts of Mak and her sexy body and what he wanted to do to it.

As Brian was standing under the spray, his cell phone rang, and he missed the call. When he finally heard the message, Brian screamed in rage and put his fist through the mirror hanging on the wall in his bedroom. His father's contact at the hospital had informed him that the patient known as Makailyn Elsbeth Jamieson was missing. When the nurse had gone in to advise Mak that the doctor had signed her release forms, the woman found an empty bed. Well, devoid of the patient, that is. The pillows and blankets on the hospital bed had been artfully arranged to make it appear as if Mak was asleep under the covers. The contact had apologized but informed the senior Hillhouse that he would be receiving the hospital bill for the patient's care. Prompt payment of the invoice would be most appreciated.

Brian's father's final remark before ending the message was, "Get your ass to the office so that we can have a sit down with the staff detective. He'll be assigned to find her, so you can get her back. I want a grandson, and I'm losing patience." Good old Dad. Always thinking of himself.

CHAPTER 21

BILLINGS, Montana. Mak caught sight of the big green sign on the side of the road that read "*Billings*" in white letters as the bus passed it by. Totally drained from the trip since she hadn't slept well, Mak gave a yawn and stretched to ease the cramps from her body.

A week ago, Mak had dropped off the rental car in Wichita, Kansas. Then, after receiving directions, Mak had walked several blocks to the bus terminal. Due to the injuries she had suffered, the drive had been exhausting and especially painful. So, the walk had done her good. But, then, while standing in line, the wait had seemed interminable. Stepping up to the ticket counter when it was finally Mak's turn, she was dismayed to discover no direct bus from Kansas to Montana. Instead, services departed from Wichita, Kansas, and arrived at Billings, Montana via Kansas City, Missouri, and Sioux

Falls, South Dakota. That journey, including the transfers, would take approximately twenty-five hours. But the thought of those transfers gave Mak an idea.

Instead of buying a ticket for the bus with those two transfers, Mak decided to change buses in several major cities to throw anyone off her scent. She'd paid cash for each bus fare and had been zigzagging all over the map ever since. Of course, it helped that she didn't need to be in Montana for another month, well now three weeks, so the extra time had hopefully been well spent.

Her lack of sleep had been exacerbated by the fact that she hurt all over. She had pains in places she didn't even know could ache. Bruised ribs, broken fingers, a knock on the noggin', and an empty womb had all conspired to remind her of the poor choices she'd been making lately. Those choices had revolved around one Brian Alexander Hillhouse III. The man who was responsible for her current situation. Sighing at that thought, Mak shook her head in negation and acknowledged that she wasn't being fair. She was the one who was responsible. The blame rested squarely on her shoulders.

Another problem was that Mak needed to quit thinking of herself as "Mak" before she slipped up. For the foreseeable future, she was Jaymiee Joanna Johnston. So, maybe Mak should get used to responding to the name Jo. Better yet, she could tell the ranch owners that everyone just called her "Mak" and save herself a lot of problematic confusion.

"What a cluster fuck! Oh, pardon my French," Mak giggled softly so the other bus passengers wouldn't stare at her as if she'd lost her ever-lovin' mind. Now, she was talking to herself out loud. The looks she was already getting due to her injuries were bad enough.

After Mak disembarked, she went into the bus station to get some information. She needed to find a car rental place, somewhere cheap to sleep, and directions to the *Circle R Cattle Company Ranch.* Under normal circumstances, Mak would have gone directly to the ranch to see if she could start her job early. These weren't normal circumstances, on account of all of that damage to Mak's body, of course. Jo wasn't supposed to start her new job at the ranch for another three weeks. Mak, masquerading as Jo, needed that time to recuperate from all of her injuries. She wanted to be ready to go to work when she showed up for that job and not look like a refugee from a war zone. That would elicit questions she didn't want to answer.

The petite, elderly lady seated behind the ticket counter was a fount of information. She introduced herself as Maimee Ritter. Maimee, only 4'8" tall, couldn't see over the ticket counter when not sitting on the high stool. She had curly blue-tinged hair, wore clip-on pearl earrings and rope pearls with a cardigan sweater and pleated skirt. Patent leather pumps graced her tiny size four feet. The spry woman directed Mak to the *Rent-A-Wreck* place just two blocks over. She said Mak could get a reliable car for just eight dollars a day, even cheaper if Mak rented by the month.

When Mak told Maimee that she needed a place to stay before starting her job at the *Circle R Cattle Company Ranch*, Maimee exclaimed, "Oh, you're a lucky girl. The people who own the *Circle R* are just lovely. I attended church services with the previous owners, William and Peggy Roberts. But unfortunately, they've both passed away. The Roberts left the ranch to their foreman, Mike Willis. Mike's wife, Emilia, is new to the area, but Mike has been around for a long time. You're going to enjoy working for them."

"In the meantime," Maimee continued, "I have some friends who are letting a room in their home for cheap. Their place is just down the road apiece from the *Circle R*, about five miles, give or take.

The two-story house is kind of rundown, and the furnishings are old and tired, but Martha keeps everything clean and neat. The room has an attached bath with an old porcelain clawfoot tub that's big enough for two. You'll appreciate a good soak in that tub. The hot water will ease all those bruises you're sporting. If you don't mind me saying, you look like you took a header down a flight of stairs, my dear."

Mak ignored the comment about the stairs and said she'd appreciate the name and number of the people with the room for rent. Maimee waved her hand in the air, got right on the phone, and gave her friend a call. In no time at all, Mak had a place to stay for only one hundred dollars for the next three weeks. That included electricity and hot water.

Maimee also called over to the *Rent-A-Wreck* place because her friend owned the franchise. Maimee told the gentleman that she was sending a sweet young woman over to rent a car for a few months and admonished him to give Mak a reasonable rate. Otherwise, Maimee wouldn't be making him his favorite crumb-topped apple pie for dessert when he came for their weekly date on Saturday night. But, of course, he could forget the fried chicken, too.

Mak could only hear Maimee's side of the conversation. Still, there were indications that the gentleman on the other end of the phone could put Mak in a good reliable car for two hundred dollars. Mak smiled when Maimee told him he could do better than that. The price was quickly knocked down to one hundred fifty dollars. When the telephone conversation was concluded, Maimee wrote down directions to the house where Mak would be renting the room.

Mak thanked the woman profusely for her help and gave her a hug. A gentle hug due to Mak's bruised ribs. Maimee wrote down her name, number and address and told Mak that she expected her to visit. Mak promised that she would and that she'd bring a peach cobbler when she did. Just as soon as she got settled into her new life on the *Circle R*. It was one of Jo's mom's recipes, and it was delicious.

Mak made another friend after she walked the two blocks to the car rental place, dragging Jo's suitcase behind her all the way. Thank God the thing had wheels.

The elderly gentleman behind the counter of the car rental company looked like a perfect match for Maimee. His name was Herald Cleary. Herald was only about 5'2" tall with a fringe of wispy white hair that ringed his balding pate. Mak tried not to stare. Herald's scalp was so shiny, he probably gave off a blinding glare on a sunny day.

Herald wore gray pleated trousers, a light button-down dress shirt, darker gray vest with a pocket watch chain dangling from the vest pocket. The pocket was positioned directly across from the vest's buttonholes. The other end of the chain was inserted through a hole, and a button kept it attached.

Herald got Mak set up in a tiny *Honda Civic* that was in reasonably good shape. Mak was grateful that the car sported a nice clean interior and GPS. While Herald was filling out the rental forms on his computer, he asked numerous questions about how Maimee was doing that day. Mak could tell that Herald was enamored of the little old lady.

Herald showed Mak how to program the car's GPS with the address for the rental room where she would reside for the next three weeks. Then, Herald told her that if she wanted to extend the rental beyond that point, all she had to do was give him a call. Otherwise, Herald would make arrangements for the automobile's return.

Mak thanked the kindly gentleman for his assistance, then she was on her way. Hungry, Mak planned to purchase food somewhere enroute to her destination, the rented room that would be her home for the next three weeks. Mak also longed for a nice relaxing soak in that clawfoot tub Maimee had told her about. The trip from Oklahoma had been long and tiring.

While passing through a rural town called Butler, Mak spied a sign for a small grocery store. According to the GPS, proximity to where she would be staying was convenient since there were only another five miles to her destination. Mak laughed out loud as she eased the tiny rental car into the only available space in the parking lot. It seemed that everyone in Montana drove colossal-sized pickup trucks. The lot was full of varying shapes and sizes, makes, and models. A few colors, but mostly black and silver.

Mak took her time browsing the store's aisles while picking out some non-perishable food and toiletries. Then, as Mak was leaving the grocery, she noticed that the adjacent building housed a fast-food restaurant. Called the *Panda Express,* it offered Chinese cuisine. After placing her two bags in the footwell of the front passenger seat, Mak left her rental car in the grocery store parking lot and walked over to get some take-out.

While walking back to her car, Mak was startled by a flutter of butterflies that rose from a planter. Filled with Shasta daisies, the decorative concrete flower pot separated the parking area of the fast-food joint and the grocery store parking lot. Mak marveled at the sight as the colorful insects took flight, then settled further down the row of flowers. Mak closed her eyes in silent prayer. Her good luck charm and her favorite flower. Please, God, let it mean that you have something special in mind for me. I could really use a change of luck.

Taking a deep breath, Mak rolled her shoulders back, mentally hitched up her big girl panties, and continued across the parking lot towards her car.

As she passed the entrance, she heard the whoosh of the grocery store's automatic door as a tall cowboy exited carrying a couple of bags. Boy, he was yummy-looking. Almost like her knight in shining armor come to life. The man was tall, with light brown hair covered by a cowboy hat with a wide brim, jeans, short-sleeved

Henley shirt, and scuffed boots. The jeans and shirt hugged a lean, muscular body.

Since Mak was surreptitiously ogling the man, she managed to trip over her own two feet, spill her drink and drop her purse simultaneously. As she knelt down to retrieve the items, a human-shaped shadow merged with hers on the ground before her. Mak bowed her head and squeezed her eyes in frustration. Could things get any worse? In a perfect world, the answer was no. But they could and did. Mak wanted to die of mortification when the merged shadows shifted. Then, as the tall part of the shadow hunkered down, a deep bass voice said, "Let me help you, little lady."

When Mak looked up, she stared into sparkling blue eyes the same color as the cowboy's shirt. The man's grin was mischievous until he took in the damage to Mak's face. Then, as his look turned to one of consternation, the cowboy reached out a hand. Gently gripping Mak's jaw, he tilted her face to get a better look.

It felt like Mak had been zapped with a cattle prod when the man's soft touch connected with her skin. Maybe he felt it too because his look of consternation changed to confusion as his eyes widened at that lightning charge. His expression quickly morphed to one of anger as he growled, "Who hit you, darlin'? I'll beat the crap out of him for laying a hand on you."

Mak could feel the blush that was working its way up her neck and into her face. Caught in the depths of the man's blue eyes, she didn't have a coherent thought in her head. Mak wanted to dive into the cool blue water contained in the swirling pools of his gaze. The dip would be so refreshing she'd never want to surface.

When the man's look of anger turned to one of puzzlement because Mak hadn't responded to his query, Mak finally came to her senses. Hastily grabbing her belongings, she rushed to stand up and made a bad situation even worse by cracking heads with the cowboy. Mak wished that a sinkhole would open up in the pavement beneath her feet and swallow her whole. When it didn't, the only thing Mak could manage before she beat a hasty retreat was, "Thank you for your help."

Then she ran to her car. She could see the puzzled look on the cowboy's face as her car passed him in the parking lot. He had taken off his hat and was scratching his head. He was still staring as Mak pulled out into traffic. Well, if you could call two cars traffic, she mused. Then she continued her journey to her rented room.

CHAPTER 22

SEAN Fitzpatrick Hannity sat atop the jet black stallion that the *Circle R* had recently acquired. The horse's name was "Blackie" of course. No imagination there, but it could have been worse. Blackie had a white patch on his forehead, so he could just as easily have been named "Star" or "Blaze." Sean was tasked with putting the new arrival through his paces to ensure the horse was a good fit for the ranch. Sean and the horse had instantly bonded, so Mike allowed Sean to keep Blackie as his mount.

Blackie was a five-year-old jet-black gelding that was a Friesen/Quarter horse cross. A little over sixteen hands, he was well-built. The horse had been touted as safe for advanced beginners, but he was stout enough to carry a larger rider.

Sean had taken Blackie over the roughest terrain on the ranch and out onto the main road where the stallion seemed fine when the occasional car or truck whizzed past. The animal was also calm around the dogs and cattle.

Now Sean was walking the main path utilized for trail rides. It ran out past the line cabin that the ranch hands occasionally used for camping. Sean wanted to check the cabin and note any missing supplies. He was also tasked with double-checking the lock on the gate. The gate blocked the highway entrance to the dirt path that led onto the *Circle R* property. Someone had picked that lock a while back and left the gate open. He and John had discovered the breach when they were out looking for Emilia, a registered home health care nurse hired to care for William and Peggy Roberts. Emi had gone missing on the night that the Roberts, who were the previous owners, had passed away.

Taking the time to check the gate was a better safe than sorry kind of situation and would only mean a slight detour. The ranch didn't need any cattle wandering out onto the road and causing an accident. If someone had managed to break the lock again, cattle on the highway would be a lawsuit in the making.

Sean thought it was an excellent opportunity to take a dunk in the spring-fed pond near the cabin. The water was ice cold. So, hopefully, that ice bath would erase the image of the woman he'd knocked foreheads with clean out of his mind. Because a replay of that occurrence was stuck on a loop. She was all he could think about.

That head bash had occurred when he'd picked up a few supplies from the little grocery in Butler, about ten miles from the ranch. As he'd headed back to his truck, a woman coming from the fast-food joint next door had dropped her drink, and her purse had followed. Remembering what his granny had always said about a gentleman helping a lady, Sean crouched down next to the woman to offer his assistance. She had her head tilted down, so all Sean saw at first was the top of her head. Then, as he leaned in close, the gentle scent of her perfume hit him. That sweet-smelling odor put him in mind of the honeysuckle his mom loved so much. Still, the fragrance wasn't overwhelming—just a hint to tantalize the senses and stir the blood.

When she looked up, Sean got his first glimpse of the bruising that marred the left side of her face and the black eye that was slowly turning colors. Sean was guessing the discoloration was about a week old. Even with the injuries to her face, Sean could tell she was a natural beauty. Being that close to her lips, Sean had been tempted to steal a kiss. Sean had also noticed the soft brown eyes that were flecked with gold. Those speckles matched the streaks in her long brown hair. Again, those golden streaks looked natural, not store-bought. Sean almost embarrassed himself by reaching out to run the length of that hair through his fingers. It looked like spun silk. Then there was her face. Sean had actually touched that face. He remembered the electric jolt that had raced up his arm from that touch. The greased lightning charge had traveled through his body all the way down to his cock. When that instrument started to rise, Sean had been forced to think about dirty chores like mucking out the horse stalls or castrating bulls to get himself under control to avoid embarrassment.

As Sean tilted the delicate face to examine the bruising, he'd noticed the heart shape, high cheekbones, and small nose with the slightly upturned tip. And those lips. Sean wanted to pull the plump bottom lip between his teeth and give it a nip or two before plunging his tongue into her mouth to plumb its depths.

After they'd clunked heads as she'd pushed to her feet, Sean had to keep from drooling all over his Henley. She had an hourglass figure and definitely wasn't a slouch in the measurement department. Sean was 6'3", so she was easily 5'8" tall. With years of practice in the hook-up for a one-night-stand department, Sean was good at guessing a woman's measurements. He'd place good money on a bet that she had at least a 38" bust, 29" waist, and 40" hips. Those were hips meant to bear his children. Wait! What? Where the heck had that thought come from?

Sean would put her weight at about 135 pounds, maybe 140 pounds tops, but it looked like she was all lean muscle. That meant she was good at hard manual labor or spent her life in a gym. Sean was betting on the former.

Sean had also noticed the splinted fingers and the way she'd winced when she'd gotten to her feet. Sean would place more good money on a bet that she had some busted-up ribs under that tight little t-shirt that was hugging those glorious tits.

Sean lost the chance to ask the woman on a date because he was too busy drooling all over himself at the sight of those glorious globes. Then she'd bolted away like a calf in a roping contest and left Sean standing there scratching his head. Sean guessed she wasn't from the area since she was driving a cheap rental. She would probably return home when her visit was over, so the chances of ever seeing the little filly again were slim to none. Which meant Sean was shit-out-of-luck.

Damn, he hadn't even gotten her name. It had been too long since he'd had a date. Sean needed to head to the bar he and John liked to frequent. Sean desperately needed to get laid.

After double-checking the gate, Sean gave Blackie his head. The horse went straight to the pond for a drink. After the animal got its fill, Sean turned Blackie loose to graze. The horse was good at staying put and wouldn't leave Sean stranded.

Making his way to the cabin, Sean walked the perimeter, looking for any insect or rodent infestation signs. Although rough looking, the place was solidly built. Finding no evidence of any invasive problems, Sean made his way inside.

The cabin consisted of two cot-sized beds with rough-hewn log headboards, footboards, and thin mattresses. They were better than sleeping on the rough ground on a rainy night. The only other furniture was a small table and two chairs.

Sturdy shelving lined one wall with a porcelain sink suspended beneath that was of the old-fashioned kind with the built-in drainboard. A hand pump brought water in from the pond. A window was centered between the sink and a cabinet supporting a propane hot plate.

Chipped plates and cups sat on one of the shelves, along with canned goods—nothing to draw any rodents. A few pots and pans, silverware, cooking utensils, and a spare propane cylinder were stored in the cabinet below the hot plate. But, of course, anyone expecting to spend the night would pack in perishables or boxed goods to liven up their cuisine.

Everything in the cabin looked safe and secure. Sean plunked down on one of the cots to rest for a minute or two since he hadn't slept well in weeks. Then he drifted off to sleep. He didn't know how long he'd been out, but he jolted awake from a nightmare starring the beautiful, bruised damsel in distress from the grocery store parking lot. Just like in real life, her face had been battered. In the dream, her naked body was also covered by bruises and bite marks. As the remnants of the dream faded, Sean remembered how she'd rested her aching head against the broad expanse of his muscular chest. Then she'd murmured, "I love you so much, Sean."

Sean woke up with a hard-on that you could use to pound in fence posts, so he stripped off his clothes and ran down the slope to the pond. The icy water damn near stopped his heart when he dived in, but at least his erection was gone. He'd need superhuman abilities to maintain a hard-on in the frigid temperature of that water.

CHAPTER 23

"SEAN? Get your head out of your ass. Mike asked you a question," John Marshall chuckled as he gave Sean a friendly shove.

Caught daydreaming about the woman from the parking lot, Sean glanced around him, confused. "What?"

Mike and John laughed.

"What's going on, Sean? You haven't been right for almost three weeks. If I didn't know better, I'd think you were in love, but I do know better. You haven't been off the ranch long enough to find a woman stupid enough to look at your ugly mug twice," John joked. "I just think it's been too long since you got laid. You need to find a good woman like Mike. I bet he doesn't have that problem."

Mike Willis, the owner of the *Circle R*, gave John a stern look for talking about his wife Emi and sex in the same sentence, then laughingly gave John a shove like the one John had given Sean. Mike knew it was all just good-natured ribbing. Emi was well-respected, and any man on the ranch would lay down his life to protect her from harm.

Finally aware of his surroundings, Sean turned his attention toward the two men he considered good friends. John ribbing Mike about his wife and sex got Sean thinking about Emi Willis when she'd first arrived at the ranch. Emilia was a tiny bit of a woman about 5'4" tall. She had glorious brown hair that fell to her waist and the most beautiful cerulean blue eyes. Even though she was forty-eight years old at the time, she still had nice tits, trim hips, and long silky legs. Emilia Willis was much older than Sean, but he hadn't given two fucks about the age difference. She sure was a beauty. So, he'd considered asking Emilia out on a date. Mike nipped that idea in the bud. He made it pretty clear that Emilia belonged to him and planned to marry her. It turned out that Emilia and Mike not only shared a past but already had a daughter together. So that meant Sean was shit-out-of-luck.

Still, life on the ranch had been good so far. Before Sean came to work for the *Circle R*, he was part of the *Montana Pro Rodeo*

Circuit as a bull rider. That was until he was tossed on his head and stomped on his last go-round. That incident was a wake-up call. Sean didn't care for the idea of ending up in a wheelchair for the rest of his life, so he'd quit. He figured he was at the top of his game anyway. Anything after that would have been a greased slide into oblivion. He'd had his fair share of prize winnings and buckles and trophies. Not to mention the buckle-bunnies who followed the circuit just waiting to climb into the beds of the latest round of winners. He'd had his share of them, too. So, it was way past time for him to quit, and he acknowledged that fact.

Thankfully, before that fateful head toss/bull stomp, he'd been approached by an elderly gentleman named William Roberts. The man said he owned a cattle ranch near Billings called the *Circle R Cattle Company*. He told Sean to look him up whenever he was ready to quit the circuit. Mr. Roberts thought Sean would be a good fit for the enterprise he was building.

When Sean was recovered from his injuries from that fateful ride, he packed up his trailer, hitched it to his pickup truck, and never looked back. He's been working on the *Circle R* ever since.

Sean loved his job, but he longed for a happily ever after of his own. That desire stemmed from being a spectator to all of the love shared by the couples on the ranch. First, there was Mike and his wife, Emilia. Their union had recently produced twins, plus the daughter they already shared. Second, Mike's and Emi's oldest, Elli, now lived in the main house with her husband Tyler and their ten children. Third, Tyler's father and his new bride, Anna, now lived here as well. The fourth couple was Tim Jones and his wife, Jeannie. Jeannie had a daughter, Sophie, from a previous marriage. Tim built a new house out by the landing strip for his family. In addition, he expanded his charter business to include trips to and from the area and flying lessons.

Now thirty-five, Sean thought it was long past time to be making little Hannity babies with some gorgeous woman with a hot as sin body. A woman similar to the one in the grocery store parking lot. Why the fuck couldn't he get her out of his head. That nightmare he'd had at the line cabin didn't help either. Sean had a horrible feeling deep in his gut that the little filly was in some kind of danger.

Sean stared at Mike expectantly. "Okay, I admit I was daydreaming. What did you ask me, Mike?"

"I didn't ask you anything, Sean. John's just yanking your chain. I was trying to tell you about the woman Elli has hired to head up a program she wants to incorporate to pull in more revenue. Apparently, the woman was working on some ranch in Oklahoma until a few months ago. She was helping the owner raise quarter horses, Australian Shepherds, and registered Black Angus cattle. Elli was most interested in the fact that the woman performs equine massage therapy. Plus, she gave classes for young beginner clients in roping and reining and natural horsemanship. In addition, she assisted with the ranch chores and working the small herd of cattle on the *Rockin' R*."

"Elli thought she'd be a good all-around fit. The woman's name is Jaymiee Joanna Johnston. She's supposed to start tomorrow if she shows up. Elli wants you to take the woman under your wing and work with her until she feels comfortable. She'll be bunking in the cabin next to yours."

"The woman's belongings have already arrived, and Elli, Emi, Jeannie, and Jess are working up a storm adding feminine touches to the cabin to give it a homey feel. Anna's in charge of the sewing. She's made a beautiful handstitched quilt and curtains for the window. Elli really wants the woman to be so comfortable that she'll agree to stay and make a life here."

Sean's thought on the subject of Jaymiee Johnston was, "Fuck! Now I'm a babysitter. Can't John do it?"

Mike shook his head. "Nope, Elli was insistent. She wants it to be you for some reason. Some fool nonsense about a dream she had. Women and their dreams. I don't put any stock in that shit. Well, not usually. I did dream about Elli, Rick, and Tyler, and that came true. Anyway, stop whining. You're it. Hopefully, the woman won't look too much like one of our horses."

Sean groaned, which made the other two men laugh at him again. He'd definitely be spending some time at that barroom tonight. Drowning himself in a glass of top-shelf whiskey sounded like a good idea at the moment, maybe more than one glass. He'd rent one of the tiny rooms above the bar for the night. If he was lucky, he wouldn't be sleeping alone. Then he could deal with the horse-faced woman he would be partnered with come sunrise.

CHAPTER 24

THE past three weeks had passed quickly and quietly. It was the first actual downtime that Mak had enjoyed since the summer after high school graduation.

It was now the end of September. Four months since her life had changed so dramatically and entirely that Mak was sure she wouldn't be able to recognize her old life or her old self. She also believed that she would need to avoid the Friday before Memorial Day for the rest of her life. It was the defining day of this year that caused the split between the before and after Mak.

Mak had spent the last three weeks trying to recover from her numerous injuries by resting. She'd removed the splints from her fingers a week ago and was working on small finger exercises to get them limbered up. Her bruised ribs only caused a minor twinge when she did her pushups and sit-ups, so Mak was good in that department, as well.

Even though the weather was turning cooler, Mak had rested on a chaise lounge under the shade of an old tree in her landlord's backyard for the first two weeks. Finding that room in the Gormley's home had been a godsend. But, of course, Mak had Maimee Ritter to thank for that.

While Mak was sunbathing, Martha Gormley kept her husband Charlie occupied well away from the windows overlooking the backyard. The tiny bikini that Mak was wearing left little to the imagination. Martha didn't need her crotchety old husband dying of a heart attack because he'd caught a glimpse of Mak's shapely body.

Since they had taken a liking to Mak, the Gormleys invited her to share their evening meals. Mak offered to help Martha prepare each meal while Charlie sat at the table reading the evening paper. While they ate, Mak enjoyed listening to the couple's easy banter and stories of their life together.

Martha was a plump woman about 5'4" tall with short grayish-white hair worn in a bun. She had rosy apple cheeks and faded blue eyes. She liked to wear housedresses that buttoned down the front to the waist and the type of shoes that nurses usually wore.

Charlie Gormley had a fringe of greyish-brown hair kept in a crew cut, sagging jowls, a bulbous nose, bushy eyebrows, and hazel-colored eyes. Charlie was also plump around the middle. But like most men, he didn't have much in the way of a butt. He wore *Dickie* work pants, a pocket t-shirt, and Velcro sneakers.

Charlie had been a bronc rider on the rodeo circuit in his younger years before he met and married Martha. After getting a diploma from a vocational-technical college, Charlie worked as an electric motor mechanic in Billings. Then a freak accident involving a crane failure caused a fractured arm that ended his career.

In between, Martha and Charlie had raised two sons and a daughter. All three were now so engrossed in their own lives that the couple may as well have been childless.

In his early seventies, Charlie spent his time tinkering around his collection of antique tractors. He also made a little side money to supplement the couple's social security checks by repairing farm equipment for the local ranchers. Paid in cash under the table, of course, and sometimes produce, chicken, eggs, and beef. Martha had a whole pantry full of jarred goods that the neighbor women had put up and a full freezer chest of meat. All thanks to Charlie's skilled hands.

The Gormleys' two-story home was sided with chipped clapboard painted a faded tan with brown trim. The windows were adorned with wooden shutters. The front porch steps sagged a little leading up to the covered porch that was home to a couple of brown-stained log rockers and a heavy-duty roll back porch swing. The requisite worn-down bloodhound, named Rufus, loved taking naps in the shade afforded by the porch roof. The home might look tired, but the yard was neatly trimmed. Brightly colored chrysanthemums were newly planted in front of the shrubberies along the house's foundation.

Martha kept the Gormley's home neat and clean. Her spare time in the afternoons was spent watching her favorite soap operas. That was a new addiction. The couple had only recently installed a television in their living room. Before that, they had listened to the radio in the evening.

Martha also took in sewing and mending for ladies at church to earn pin money, as she called it, and loved to read sexy romance novels. Hard emphasis on the sex part. She giggled like a teenager when she said that. According to Martha, a person never got too old to think about a good tumble in the hay with a handsome cowboy. Mak had to agree with Martha. She'd enjoy rolling around in the hayloft with the cowboy from the grocery store parking lot.

Martha helped Mak make a peach cobbler using Jo's mother's recipe. The three of them, Martha, Charlie, and Mak, paid a visit to the home of Maimee Ritter for dinner one evening. Of course, Norman from the *Rent-A-Wreck* was there as well.

After polishing off a good meal of fried chicken, biscuits and gravy, corn-on-the-cob, and Mak's peach cobbler, which was a big hit, everyone laughed as they tried to teach Mak the card game of poker. Everyone teased Mak about her facial expressions as they played.

Charlie winked at Mak and pronounced, "It's a good thing we aren't playing strip-poker. You'd lose your shirt."

That pronouncement earned Charlie a swat upside the head from Martha, or maybe it was because of the wink.

Mak's nights were now filled with dreams of the yummy cowboy from the grocery store parking lot. The man had become an excellent substitution for Mak's knight in shining armor. He was stuck in her mind, like a grain of sand in the shell of an oyster, a slight irritant that might eventually lead to a beautiful pearl. Mak hadn't run into the cowboy again, so that was never going to happen. Mak was most definitely shit-out-of-luck in that department.

Mak was due at the *Circle R Cattle Company* ranch in the morning to star in her masquerade performance as Jaymiee Joanna Johnston. It was Jo's new job, but she'd convinced Mak to take it so she could hide for a while. The last thing Mak needed was for her ex-fiancé, Brian Alexander Hillhouse III, to find her. Mak's bruises had all faded away, and she didn't need Brian inflicting any additional damage. Mak was mainly healed from the loss of her child, but that was only physically, definitely not emotionally. It would take a lot longer than a month to get over that loss. Mak knew she would carry that pain deep in her heart for the rest of her life.

Planning to enjoy her last night of freedom before going back to work, Mak took a long, leisurely soak in the big cast iron clawfoot tub. Unfortunately, it was a luxury she probably wouldn't get to enjoy again for some time to come. Then Mak shaved all those pesky body parts that needed tending, conditioned her hair, and ran a flat iron over it so it lay in smooth waves to her waist. Finally, she spritzed on some honeysuckle body spray which was Mak's favorite scent.

Jo had packed a very naughty red leather belted mini skirt in her luggage that fit Mak like a second skin. Mak paired it with a tiny white tank top with a built-in bra and a strappy pair of white heels.

Mak had pampered herself with a French manicure and pedicure that day. Her nails were now a perfect match to her outfit, red with white tips. But for the foreseeable future, it would be the last time for that luxury as well. Fancy-painted nails didn't fare well while doing farm chores.

After applying a minimal amount of makeup, Mak took herself off to a barroom that she'd passed on her trip from Billings to the room she was renting. Mak only planned on having one small drink. What she really wanted to do was lose herself in the rhythm of a good dance song or two. Mak really liked to dance.

The lighting in the barroom was so dim when Mak stepped through the door that she had to pause to give her eyes time to adjust. The strains of a country ballad played on the jukebox. As the song came to an end, the cacophony of voices that filled the room changed to a low murmur. When her eyes had adjusted to the gloom, she took in the scene around her. As Mak weaved her way between the tightly packed tables and chairs towards the long mahogany bar at the back of the room, she wondered what she had been thinking. This was definitely not one of her better ideas, but it was too late to back down now. So, she may as well make the most of her last night of freedom.

Mak tried to ignore the scathing looks of the other female patrons. But she much preferred those to the lecherous glances of some of the men. Mak winced when she reached the rowdy group seated at the last table. A scantily clad woman jumped to her feet and began to scold her boyfriend as she beat him repeatedly about his head with her purse. Mak knew she was to blame for the altercation. She had noticed that he was staring at her as she made her way across the room. Squeezing past, Mak made her way to the end of the bar, climbed up on the only available stool, and laid her clutch on the bar's surface.

As Mak waited for the bartender to notice her, she took in the beautifully etched mirror running the entire length of the bar. She admired how the lighted mirror helped to make the area feel larger and brighter. Lighted glass bar shelves displayed attractive bottles and glassware. Mak could see the reflection of the men sitting in a row along the bar's gleaming surface, several of whom were glancing in her direction. Mak did her best to avoid eye contact.

After ordering a Hemingway Daiquiri made from grape juice mixed with fresh lime and Maraschino liqueur, Mak sat sipping her drink as she scanned the room.

It was a Sunday night, so the bar was mostly filled with cowboys with female dates or singles looking to hook up. Mak assumed the patrons were just trying to have a good time before starting a new work week.

About half an hour after Mak arrived, a local band set up on a raised platform near the dance floor. The five-piece band consisted of drums, bass, guitar, keyboard, and banjo. Mak enjoyed her second drink as the band pumped out some of the more popular songs in vogue.

Mak realized that unless it was a slow song, the floor area set aside for dancing was mainly filled with women. So, bolstered by liquid courage, Mak asked the bartender politely if he would mind slipping her purse under the bar for safekeeping so that she could dance. The bartender was a good-looking young man who gave her a wink and said that he'd be happy to keep her property safe for her.

Making her way in amongst the other dancers, Mak soon found herself lost to the strains of the music. Time became suspended as she swayed and slid her hands along the curves of her body. Adrift in a world of her own imagination, the rest of the people around her ceased to exist.

CHAPTER 25

THE band was already playing when Sean arrived at the barroom that he liked to frequent. Going straight to the bar, he told Ted, the bartender working that night that he wanted to rent one of the rooms upstairs.

"You plan on getting drunk or just lucky, Sean?"

"Hopefully the latter, but I'll settle for a good buzz. Both if I'm fortunate. Boss has some new hire starting tomorrow. Some horse-faced woman. Guess who the lucky fuck is that gets to babysit her until she learns the ropes?" was Sean's response. Then, noticing the crowd, he asked, "What's going on over there? Why're all the guys hanging around the edges of the dance floor? Is there some kind of dance contest going on? If it's a wet t-shirt contest, I'll take my drink on over to watch."

Ted laughed at Sean about the horse-faced woman remark, then nodded toward the crowd at the edge of the dance floor. "Nope, not any kind of contest. Just some hot as fuck woman dancing by herself. Every guy that tries to get close gets the boot. The men have started placing bets to see which one of them will actually get the chance to dance with her. If I wasn't stuck behind the bar, I sure would like the opportunity to hold that body in my arms for a slow dance. I served her a drink before she went over to enjoy the music. She's a real looker."

Just then, the crowd parted, and Sean got a glimpse of the woman the bartender had been extolling the virtues of.

Sean's eyes went wide, and he said, "Oh, fuck a duck! No way am I letting that happen," as another guy tried to get close to her.

Ted looked confused at Sean's comment, then watched as Sean tossed back a whiskey, set the glass on the bar, and then made his way to the dance floor. Ted had a ringside seat as the music shifted to a slow song, and the woman taking center stage turned and walked right into Sean's arms.

Ted would have bet good money that the woman would tell Sean to get lost. He'd have lost that bet.

Sean recognized the woman from the grocery store parking lot the minute the crowd parted to give him a glimpse. He'd never forget that body or that face. She looked in much better shape than the last time he'd seen her. The three-week interval had done much to heal the damage from whatever cruelty had inflicted it. But, God, she was beautiful.

Tossing back his drink, he set the glass down and went off to meet his fate.

Making his way to the edge of the dance floor, Sean joined the other guys who were watching the woman's gently swaying hips in that tiny red mini skirt. When the song changed to a slow one, a couple of the men slapped Sean on the back and wished him luck as he stepped forward to stand behind her. But, as the woman turned to leave the dance floor, Sean spread his arms to prevent her escape, and she walked right into the solid wall of his chest.

Glancing up, she opened her mouth to rip him a new asshole for getting in the way, but her mouth dropped open in an "o" of surprise instead. While she was standing there dazed, Sean said, "Well, hello again, darlin'. I see you're all healed up. Care to dance?"

Not waiting for an answer, he took her into his arms, where she fit just like she belonged. She laid her head against him and sighed out, “I dreamed of you, Sean.”

Dumbfounded that she knew his name, Sean responded, “I dreamed of you, too, darlin’.” Then he leaned down and captured her in a soft graze of lips that set his blood aflame. It was only the slightest of touches, but it made his whole world shrink. It became just the universe of her and himself locked together in the middle of a small dance floor in a rundown bar in Montana.

When the song ended, she let him lead her to the bar, where she recovered her purse. Then he led her up to the room he’d rented on the second floor.

After locking the door, Sean kissed her gently, then lowered her to the bed. As he undressed her, kissing each inch of delicate skin that he uncovered, he asked her, “what’s your name, darlin’?”

“Everyone just calls me Mak,” she said.

Sean traced the path of her tattoo with his fingertips as it rose along her ribcage. Then guided them across the swell of her beautiful left breast to where the tattoo ended in a tiny butterfly poised on the tip of a thistle floret above her heart. Damn, that was beautiful, just like the rosy nipple that graced that luscious globe. He smiled as she sighed with pleasure as he took her lush nipple into his mouth.

Mak made the most seductive sounds as Sean worshiped her body. Then, when he had her wet and wanting, he slipped between her thighs and entered her with one long thrust of his hips. If Sean had been asked to describe his feelings at that moment, the only thing he could think was that it was like coming home where he belonged.

When Mak began to buck her hips, Sean knew she was getting close. He shifted his weight so that he could rub her clit with the pad of his work-roughened finger to heighten her pleasure. As her muscles began to contract, he said, "Come for me, darlin' but keep your eyes open."

As Mak's orgasm overtook her, Sean watched the beautiful transformation of her face. It was a look that he could only describe as profound ecstasy. Sean shifted his weight again and began to pump with deep hard thrusts. He could feel that Mak was going to orgasm again, and she took him with her this time.

After, they lay quietly in each other's arms. Sean told Mak a lie about being the owner of a big ranch full of cattle and horses, then winced at the stupidity of the fabrication. Why did he feel the need to build himself up in the eyes of this woman as if she would only be interested if he were a wealthy landowner?

They made love several times that night. Each encounter was more soul-satisfying than the one before it. The beauty of her smile and the swirl of emotion in the depths of her eyes were the last things Sean noticed as he drifted off to sleep.

CHAPTER 26

MAK awoke at her usual time of 5:00 a.m. with thoughts of needing to get to work. She wanted to spend time riding along the fence line before her first student showed up for her roping lesson. Mak kept her eyes closed. She wanted to savor the moment between sleep and work just a little longer.

Then Mak remembered that she no longer worked at the *Rockin' R Ranch* because Brian had put a stop to that. Just for being caught sharing a laugh with the new ranch hand, a young man who was seven years her junior. Someone who would never be interested in Mak if she stood there naked as a jaybird in the middle of the riding arena.

As Mak shifted her weight, she realized that she was sore in certain places. Then, everything came back to Mak, including what had happened the night before. She opened her eyes to the glorious sight of the handsome as fuck cowboy that was sharing her bed and thought, "Oh, no, no, no! What have I done?" She'd had sex multiple times with a complete stranger, unprotected sex, she might add. The guy probably thought Mak was on the pill and didn't need to use anything. She'd even been stupid enough to tell that stranger that she'd dreamt of him. Mak had to get out of here.

Slipping out from under the sheets, Mak found her outfit, which consisted of a slutty mini skirt and tiny tank top, and put them on. What had she been thinking? She'd have to do the walk of shame if anyone caught a glimpse of her making her way to her rental car.

Heels and purse in hand, Mak tiptoed across the room, eased open the door on well-oiled hinges, Thank God in Heaven for that, then shut the door with a soft snick.

Mak raced down the hall and the stairs that led to the outside. She didn't put on her sandals until she'd made it safely to the parking lot of the barroom.

When she got back to the room she had rented for the last three weeks, Mak drew a quick bath to wash away the smell of sex and cowboy that coated her body. Mak was sad to see it go.

Mak was ready to start her new job after donning some well-worn work jeans, a soft cotton t-shirt, and Jo's worn but sturdy work boots. She would be pretending to be Jo, of course. But Mak sure hoped the people liked her. Montana was beginning to grow on her. Once Jo showed up to take her place, maybe Mak would be able to find another job close by. She'd like that. Then Mak could continue to be friends with the Gormleys, Maimee Ritter, and Norman, the *Rent-A-Wreck* car business owner. Those people had become the grandparents she'd never had, and she loved them dearly.

Mak stopped to return the room key to the Gormleys and was invited inside for breakfast. Mak accepted. It was only 6:30, and she wasn't expected at the *Circle R* for her appointment until 8:00 a.m. The ranch was only five miles down the road, so she had plenty of time.

Martha made the most delicious maple pancakes that were to die for. Mak ate two, plus a couple of eggs and two slices of bacon. She didn't know what the day had in store for her or when she would have the chance to eat again. So, she wanted her body to be well-fortified with good food. After a final cup of coffee, Mak hugged

Martha and Charlie fiercely, told them how much she'd come to love them and that she'd only be right up the street. If they needed her for anything, they only had to give a holler, and she'd come running.

Then Mak loaded up her car, gave a wave goodbye, and headed off to meet her destiny.

Mak had spoken with Jo briefly the day before. Jo wanted to wish Mak luck. Jo said she'd met a woman who was a friend of Jo's older sister and that she was staying at her place. Since it was near the beach, Mak could hear the crash of the waves hitting the shore and the cries of some seagulls as they spoke. Jo sounded so happy.

"You wouldn't believe the tan I'm getting, Mak. And these California beach bums with their blond hair and blue eyes are so yummy. But I'm bein' a good girl, Mak. No more hook-ups. The next man isn't gettin' any until he puts a ring on my finger, and it better be a good one."

That made Mak laugh but also sad. "Don't go looking for some rich dude, Jo. They're not always a better choice."

Jo said, "I'm sorry, sweetie, I didn't mean to make you sad. Everything's goin' to work out, Mak. I can feel it in my bones. But, first, you're goin' to meet your studmuffin cowboy, and he's goin' to sweep you off your feet. Then you're gonna make beautiful Mak babies together."

Mak thought maybe she'd met that studmuffin cowboy in the parking lot of the local grocery but didn't tell Jo about that. The thought of babies, however, only made Mak cry harder.

"Damn me and my stupid mouth," was Jo's response.

When Mak had her emotions somewhat under control, she told her best friend not to worry. Things were looking up. She'd made several friends, and she was really liking Montana. Then she lied and told Jo she needed to go. Mak winced at that. She was getting too good at this lying business.

Jo said, "Love you sister from another Ma and Pa."

Before Mak could respond, the call was disconnected.

CHAPTER 27

The following day when he awoke and reached out for Mak, Sean found only the impression of her body where she'd lain beside him. Sean buried his face in the pillow her head had rested upon and wondered how he would be able to continue. She was now his reason to breathe, and he hadn't even learned her last name or where she lived. He was fucked again.

Pulling on his clothes, boots, and hat, Sean went off to work, knowing his day would be spent babysitting some horse-faced woman from Oklahoma. "Fuck A Duck!"

Sean got back to the *Circle R* just in time to be teased unmercifully by John for showing up late. That new woman was due at the ranch any minute. Sean was supposed to sit in on her interview before Mike made his final determination whether she'd be a good fit for the ranch. Not having time for a shower or breakfast, Sean made his way directly to the ranch office.

"I thought she already had the job, Mike?" Sean questioned.

"Yeah, well, we'll see. Elli was impressed, but it was all handled via email, fax, and telephone calls. You can't really get a feel for a person until you've looked them in the eyes."

Sean had to agree. Even then, you could never tell what the other person was thinking. That turned his thoughts to Mak and what they'd shared the night before. Sean would never have guessed he'd wake up to an empty bed. He thought that behavior was unique to men. Cut and run, or maybe he should say fuck and run. Guess women did it too. Well, live and learn. It made him feel a little bit used, however. He wondered if that was how the women he'd done it to felt when they woke up alone the following morning. That thought made him feel a little bit ashamed.

Sean would never pull another breath into his lungs without remembering the scent of Mak as he'd brought her to orgasm repeatedly. Their night of lovemaking had been life-altering for Sean. The only good thing about her taking off was that she would never know he had lied about being some wealthy landowner with a fancy cattle operation. If she'd found out, she probably would have thought it was to impress her to keep her in his bed. No doubt she would have been pissed when she found out the truth.

Mike and Sean were talking about the bulls they were considering as replacements for the herd when they recognized the sound of a car coming to a stop outside the new ranch office. Then they heard the vehicle's door open and shut. Mike said, "Well, here goes," but after a few minutes, they stared at each other quizzically when no one entered.

When Mak pulled up before the building with a small sign that read "*Ranch Office*," she stepped out of her rental and stared around in wonder. The ranch was beautiful. All of the buildings appeared to be well-maintained. What took her breath away the most was the large ranch house with a red-tiled roof. The home's walls were logs stained a honey oak color, and the main entryway was a beautiful arch surrounded by cut stone. Large arched stained-glass windows flanked both sides. Another smaller, identical house sat a few hundred feet away, plus a large barn, stable, and many outbuildings. Horses were grazing in a paddock behind the stable. Acres of Angus cattle lay resting in the sunshine in the field behind the barn. The land rolled away from the heart of the main proper, vast and golden and undulating. If it had been in Mak's nature to feel jealousy over someone else's good fortune, she would have been envious of Jo at that moment. What wouldn't Mak give to have a job on this ranch that was actually hers? "Well, it's not mine," Mak thought, "so enjoy it while you can."

Then, Mak gave herself a mental shake and went over to the office door to keep her appointment. As she opened the door, a flutter of butterflies took flight from the daisies lining the planters along the front of the building. A little late in the year for that. Mak let out a gasp.

Mike and Sean sat patiently, and after a few minutes, the office door opened. The light spilling through the doorway behind the person who entered prevented Sean from getting a good look. A hazy halo of light limned the person's body. He heard a soft gasp and was bewildered as to the reason. Sean's world narrowed down to that small moment in time after that, a moment that would delineate Sean's life as before and after.

Mike stepped out from behind the desk and crossed the room to offer the woman his hand to shake. As she stepped forward to accept the proffered handclasp, the door swung shut behind her. The dazzling sunlight was cut off, and Sean got his first good look at the woman who had entered.

Sean was confident he was now the one standing there mute with his mouth hanging open in an "o" of surprise when he realized that the woman who'd just stepped into the office was his "Mak." "His?" Where the heck had that thought come from?

As Mak gripped Mike's hand, she studied the man. Mak thought he might be in his early fifties and had to be at least 6'3" tall. He had blue eyes and a crooked smile. His dark brown hair only had streaks of gray at the temples. He was trim with a solid muscular build, broad shoulders, narrow hips, and long legs. He was wearing the typical jeans, plaid shirt, and boots. Mak bet most women would think that he looked like a real cowboy.

Finally, Mak realized she was woolgathering and said, "Hi! My name's Jaymiee Joanna Johnston, but everyone just calls me "Mak." I believe I have an appointment with a Mr. Willis?"

Mike clenched Mak's hand tightly and introduced himself as Roger Michael Willis, the *Circle R Cattle Company* owner. "Everyone calls me "Mike." It's a pleasure to meet you, Mak. I see you've come dressed for work, but I don't think that manicure is going to hold up."

Mak blushed prettily and told Mike, "I don't normally go in for such luxuries. I wanted to look nice last night when I went dancing. Last chance before the new job kind of thing, you know. Most generally, my hands look like the rest of me, plain and worked hard."

"Well, it's good to know. I'd like you to meet my ranch foreman. This is Sean Hannity." As Mike turned toward Sean, he got a quizzical look on his face. Sean was standing there with his mouth hanging open so far, he was sure to catch any flies that might have made their way into the office. A ranch had plenty of flies to go around, after all.

Sean couldn't get his mind to form a coherent thought. When Mike said that Sean was the ranch foreman, Mak had narrowed her eyes at him in anger. Sean knew he'd been caught up in a deception of his own making. One he should never have instigated. Finally, he got his brain cells to fire and offered his hand to Mak.

Pretending like he didn't recognize her, Sean said, "Mak, I'm pleased to make your acquaintance. Welcome to the *Circle R*. I know you will be happy here. It's a good place to work and is run by some amazing people."

Mak looked at Sean speculatively before accepting his handshake. Sean was sure that Mak felt the frisson of electricity that ran between them as they touched just as much as he did. As Mike took control of the interview, Sean's last thought was that at least she didn't look like a horse. Then he shook his head in disbelief. How was he supposed to work with this woman without needing to strip her naked at every clandestine opportunity? He needed to be inside her right this very minute. Where were those bulls he needed to castrate so this stupid erection would go away? He'd need to spend a lot of time at the pond if Mak got this job.

As Mike quizzed Mak about her years working for the *Rockin' R Ranch* in Chilton, Oklahoma, Sean's head was lost in a fog. His mind wandered as Mak prefaced the details of her eight years of employment. First, she told Mike that she held an Associate in

Applied Science degree from *Northeastern Oklahoma A & M College* in Equine and Ranch Management. Mak then said that she had immediately applied for employment at the *Rockin' R* upon graduation and had been fortunate to have been employed by Willis Riordan until recently.

Mike asked Mak what her reason was for leaving Mr. Riordan's employ. A blush crept up Mak's chest and neck and settled in her face. She cast her eyes down in embarrassment and admitted, "I was stupid to believe myself in love with a lawyer from Philadelphia. I met the man on a flight home from visiting my parents in California. When he asked me to go with him to Philadelphia, I was naïve in thinking that he also loved me. But unfortunately, it didn't take long to realize that his intentions were not honorable, and so here I am."

Mike knew this already, as Elli had gleaned that information from Mr. Willis Riordan himself. The only thing Mike didn't like was that Mak hadn't given any notice when she'd quit her job, but he wouldn't tell Mak that. He supposed he would have done the same thing if it meant following his Emi somewhere.

The meeting went on for several hours. Mike gleaned details about all of the programs Mak had instituted on the *Rockin' R.* Then he questioned Mak about the value of those programs. He wanted to know how successful they were in pulling in additional revenue for her employer.

"Can you explain what Equine Massage Therapy is?" Mike chuckled. "Sounds kind of ridiculous to me."

Mak responded, "Giving a horse a massage sounds kind of funny, doesn't it? It's not really, though. It's a method of increasing a horse's health and overall wellbeing that has become increasingly popular. It has some of the same benefits that massage for people does. It can increase the horse's circulation and flexibility. While building muscle, massage therapy can also relieve stress and establish trust. If you have a horse that you need to break, using massage therapy beforehand can make that task easier. It gives the horse a chance to become familiar with being touched and handled before you ever try to mount the animal."

Mike laughed, "Could have used that on the horse that tossed me on my head when I first came to work on the Circle R."

Then Mike went over what Mak's additional duties would be under Sean's tutelage. Second, she would be expected to create a business model to go over the rates they would charge and any expected business expenses anticipated. Next, Elli and Jeannie would work with Mak to deal with those aspects and then create advertising to pull customers.

When everyone was satisfied, Mak was given some documents to fill out for tax and insurance purposes, and everyone stood and shook hands. Sean got another jolt when he joined his hand with Mak's. Her eyes went wide. She blushed prettily, then dropped her hand back to her side.

"Sean will show you to your cabin, Mak. Then, after lunch, he'll take you on a tour of the ranch and get you started."

"I imagine you'll be bombarded by people casually showing up to say hello during the week. However, every Friday, we have an informal barbeque for all the family members, including all ranch employees. So, you'll get to formally meet everyone who resides on the Circle R at that time. You'll enjoy the barbeques. The guys operate the grill, and Tyler makes the rest of the food. Before marrying Elli,

Tyler studied at a culinary institute in New York City and ran his own restaurant in Stillwater, New Jersey. He gave it up after that. They have so many kids to feed, he gets enough practice just coming up with menus for them."

"You'll be expected to give a short speech including any personal details about your life that you may wish to share so that everyone can get to know you. Currently, there are thirteen children on the ranch, ten of whom belong to my daughter Elli. She gave birth to twin girls in April. My wife and I also have twins, a boy, and a girl. Then there is Sophie, who lives with her parents in the house by the airstrip."

At that, Mak said, "Wow. Elli has ten children? Just how old is your daughter?"

"Actually, Elli's only thirty-three. She has triplets, and the girls are her second set of twins, so she's only given birth six times. I'm pretty sure she and Tyler are finished after this latest batch. Tyler had to buy a passenger van that seats twelve to haul them all around, and he's working on getting his pilot's license. He's already purchased a plane for when they go on family vacations. He says public transportation with his brood is a nightmare in logistics."

Mak laughed and admitted, “I come from a family of nine children. Seven are my siblings, and then my very best friend is like another sister. I’ve known her since we were in first grade together. My parents took her in when her father was killed when she was twelve. I’d like to introduce you to her someday. As for me, I hope that I’ll be able to have a large family of my own, too. I love kids, so if anyone ever needs a babysitter, I’m your girl.”

Mike said, “I’m certain that will happen for you, Mak, and I appreciate the babysitting offer. I’m positive we’ll take you up on that a lot. You seem like a very good person. I hope you’ll enjoy working for us.”

Turning to Sean, Mike continued, “Sean, please show Mak to her quarters and see that she is fed.” Then Mike went off to his house to kiss his wife, and hopefully, if the twins were napping, he’d be able to make love to her.

CHAPTER 28

THE journey from the ranch office to the cabin reserved for Mak was filled with strained silence. Finally, Sean opened the door and briefly pressed his palm to the small of Mak's back as he showed her inside. With the warm touch of Sean's hand, a frisson of electricity shot through Mak straight to her heart. But Mak forced herself to ignore what she was feeling.

Mak took in the homey feminine touches as she entered the cabin and broke out in a huge grin. Covering the bed was a color-block quilt. A stallion was appliqued in the center with colts, horseshoes, branding irons, boots, and Stetson hats positioned around the outer edges. Matching throw pillows and curtains dressed up the bed and window. A large floor-length mirror was attached to the back of the cabin door, so she'd be able to get one last look at herself before going about her day. The entrance to an open-style bathroom on the same wall as the dresser completed the interior. The bathroom was just big enough to take care of the necessary hygiene requirements.

"This is absolutely unexpected. I don't know what to say. The bunkhouse on the *Rockin' R* was really designed with cowboys in mind. Not cowgirls." Noticing a pile of boxes beneath the window, Mak pointed and said, "I see that Jo's stuff arrived, too."

Mak froze and bowed her head, wincing at her blunder. Then, not daring to look, Mak prayed that Sean hadn't caught the slip about who the boxes belonged to. Otherwise, for her, the job working on the *Circle R* would end before it even began.

"Well, you have the ladies to thank for decorating. They all pitched in to get the cabin ready. They really wanted you to feel welcome," Sean stammered.

Terrified but thankful that he hadn't called her out on the "Jo's stuff" slip, Mak turned and stared up at him. The worried expression blanketing his face made her anxiety spike. She'd slept with this man, and she didn't regret it. But now he was her boss, so any more fraternization was out of the question. Besides, he'd lied to her for some reason. Mak didn't really care so much about the little white lie, but sometimes little lies hid bigger ones. Still, she'd do anything she could to put him at ease to make their working relationship go smoothly. She wouldn't question him about the lie because, after all, she was the biggest liar of all. Mak wasn't even who she was pretending to be, and this wasn't really her job.

"I'll be sure to thank them on Friday at the barbeque," Mak mumbled, not knowing what else to say because Sean looked really pensive.

Sean stared at Mak. He wanted desperately to kiss her or do something to put that delighted grin back on her face. Her whole countenance lit up like fireworks on the 4th of July when she smiled.

Deciding to rip the Band-Aid off and come clean, Sean cleared his throat several times, trying to work up his courage. Finally, grasping her shoulders to hold her in place, he stammered, "I'm sorry, darlin', for lying to you. I'm no wealthy ranch owner with lots of land and cattle and horses. I'm just a dumb cowboy doing his best to get by. It was stupid to lie, and I don't even know why I did it. Can you forgive me?"

Sean fought not to squirm under the intensity of Mak's gaze as he waited for her to respond. If the changing expressions on her face were any indication, it looked like a million thoughts were vying for attention in her head. Finally, she smiled shyly and said, "There's nothing to forgive, Sean. We all get caught up in a deception now and then. Most of the time, the need to lie is not of our choosing. It's a matter of survival sometimes, you know. I don't care that you aren't rich. Money doesn't mean a whole lot to me, having never had much of anything. I've learned to appreciate what's important and know that it isn't wealth or a bunch of fancy cars or boats or clothes. Some of the worse people on the planet are the ones who have everything. Having a lot of money doesn't make the person. It's the way you treat others that counts. Besides, someday you'll probably need to forgive me for a deception, too. So, clean slate?" and she held out her hand for him to shake.

Sean looked down at that proffered hand with the long slender fingers sporting a French manicure and reached out to clasp it. There was that jolt that went straight to his dick, and he couldn't help himself. He wrapped Mak up tight in a hug and kissed her silly.

When they both came up for air, all Sean could say was, "Thank you, darlin'. Let's go get something to eat. I'm hungry."

That made Mak laugh.

That laugh went straight to Sean's groin. Where the hell was that ice-cold pond water when you needed it? He was going to die of blue balls working around this little filly day in and day out. He sure hoped how he was feeling didn't show on his face. John would tease the hell out of him.

John had lunch ready when they went into the cabin, where they cooked, ate their meals, and socialized after a hard day's work. Sean was happy that making meals for the ranch hands wasn't part of his job description. The only time he cooked anything that passed for edible was over an open pit in a cast-iron skillet. He could rustle up some delicious bacon and eggs that way.

Tom and Jake were seated at the long table when Sean showed Mak into the room. Both young men jumped to their feet and took off their hats.

The first words out of Tom's mouth were, "God, you're the most beautiful woman I think I've ever seen. I thought Emi and Elli were, but you have them both beat."

Mak blushed furiously and averted her eyes.

Sean clapped Tom upside the head with his hat and said, "Didn't your brain come with a filter, you dumb lunkhead?"

Tom just grinned. "I just call 'em the way I see 'em, is all."

Sean said, "Well, watch your manners from now on and watch what comes out of your mouth. It's not just us guys anymore. We have a lady amongst us."

"Gentlemen, this is the newest addition to the *Circle R*. Meet Jaymiee Joanna Johnston. Jaymiee says everyone just calls her Mak for some strange reason. We'll have to get her to explain that one sometime. Mak, the one doing the cooking is John Marshall. The one without the filter is Tom, and this good-looking kid is Jake. Tom and Jake work for us full-time in the summer and weekends and vacations the rest of the year. They're both eighteen and seniors in high school. I think the school is having a teacher's in-service, so that's the reason they're here on a Monday. John is just like Tom and Jake. He worked for the previous owners, Bill and Peggy Roberts, as a teenager, then as a full-time ranch hand after serving in the military for four years. He's worked on the ranch for seven years since he mustered out. I've been here for ten. So, that takes care of the hands. As Mike said, you'll meet the families this Friday."

Mak, still blushing, nodded shyly at each of them and said, "Gentlemen, it's a pleasure to meet you." Then she stepped up to John and extended her hand. When he accepted her clasp, Mak said, "Thank you for your service, John," as she gave him a hesitant peck on the cheek.

Sean loved the way Mak blushed so prettily, and shit, she was shy, too. No wonder she'd acted like a skittish colt when he'd run into her at the grocery. He couldn't wait to find out what other aspects of her personality set his blood to humming.

Taking Mak's hand, Sean steadied her while she swung a leg over the bench to sit at the table and then sat down beside her. When he turned to look at John, he found the man standing there looking dumbfounded like he'd been kicked in the head by one of the horses. Sean didn't like that look. John was only twenty-nine and much closer in age to Mak. No, Sean didn't like that look at all. This little filly belonged to him. He'd already branded her once. Well, maybe more than once since they'd coupled four times the night before in that room above the bar. Sean would have made it five if Mak hadn't disappeared while he was still asleep. Anyway, she belonged to him now, and all he had to do was rope and tie her. That might be a little backward, but he didn't care as long as the end result was the same. She'd told Mike she wanted lots of kids. Well, he could handle that. Now, all Sean had to do was get Mak to go along with his way of thinking. He'd enjoy the branding part while she was making up her mind. Maybe he'd take her out to the pond. Those bunk beds were going to come in mighty handy, and they could go skinny dipping in the pond after.

"What's for lunch?" Sean asked to get John to stop staring at Mak.

John, shaken out of his Mak-induced stupor, responded with a smirk, "Slush burgers, taters, and good strong coffee. Typical cowboy grub. So, eat up!"

Mak studied the four men seated around the table as they shared an easy camaraderie borne of having worked together for a long time.

John Marshall looked to be about her age. He had sandy-colored hair and a dusting of freckles on his nose that gave him a boyish quality. About the same height as Sean, John also had a similar build borne of hard manual labor. He was a little on the quiet side but had a quick wit and an infectious laugh. Mak liked him a lot.

Tom was about 5'10" tall with blond hair and blue eyes. He was very straightforward in his comments which Mak found refreshing. A person would always know where they stood with Tom.

Tom hadn't come into his mature weight or build yet. So, he was slighter of frame than the other three men.

Jake was very handsome. Mak bet the girls at school fell all over themselves trying to get his attention. He was already over six feet tall. Jake had dark brown hair, classic features with dimples when he smiled, and a solid muscular build. What Mak liked most about him was how he treated her with deference and tried to include her when he was talking by always keeping eye contact.

Mak felt more relaxed around men than she ever had by the end of the meal. Hopefully, these cowboys would come to accept a woman in their midst and treat her as an equal.

The week went very quickly for Mak. She spent the mornings working with Sean, learning the ropes. Since she'd worked with all of the animals on the *Rockin' R*, it was only a matter of getting the hang of the way the *Circle R* did things differently. Mak appreciated that Sean didn't demand that she do things his way. Instead, he asked how she did them in her former job. If he liked what she said, he made a note of it with the promise that they'd discuss it later with Mike to see if he wanted to make the change. It made Mak feel valued as an employee and that her opinion mattered.

Elli, Jeannie, and Mak took over the office in the afternoons. They bounced ideas off each other about how Mak could contribute to the ranch's success with new programs that would draw customers and raise its revenue.

Late Friday afternoon, Mak took a quick shower and donned Jo's best pair of skinny jeans, a cable knit pullover sweater, and sneakers. She placed her long hair in a braid that hung to her waist. After adding stud earrings, Mak applied a small amount of makeup and a dab of perfume to the inside of her wrists, and she was ready to go. She was very nervous. Yes, she'd pretty much met all of the adults during the week at one point or another. But the prospect of interacting with all of them together made her nervous. Plus, the lie she perpetrated on them didn't sit well with her. How did her life go from having never lied to being nothing but a lie?

When a soft knock sounded on the cabin door, Mak was happy to be jolted out of how bad she was beginning to feel about herself. Her eyes opened wide in surprise when she found Sean standing on the other side of the door. She'd tried her darndest to avoid discussing anything personal with Sean all week. Especially anything about the night of passion they'd shared. Now, he was her boss, and a personal relationship was definitely out of the question. That meant no fraternization.

When Mak opened the door, and Sean got a look at her in those skinny jeans, he got out, "Oh, fuck me!" before he even realized he was going to say it. His body had gone on full alert. He didn't want to spend the whole picnic trying to hide the bulge in his jeans. The ladies present would probably understand since they were all married, but the kids not so much.

"Pardon?" Mak responded.

Sean ignored the questioning look on her face at his remark. Instead, he held out his hand to Mak, and she tentatively reached out to accept his grasp.

Sean smiled down at Mak and said, "Hey, ready to go meet the whole crew of the *Circle R*? I promise to protect you. There are so many of us now, it can be a little overwhelming. These family members have so much love for each other, and what's nice is that they aren't afraid to share it. You're going to be so happy you accepted a job here."

"Okay, let's do this," Mak said with a grin.

Sean kept ahold of Mak's hand as he led her toward the backyard to the main house. The Friday evening outdoor get-togethers were held during good seasons and good weather. The gatherings were held in Elli's and Tyler's place the rest of the time.

Mak felt the loss when Sean dropped her hand as they rounded the corner of the building. But, as she was met with a resounding chorus of "Welcome to the *Circle R,*" she was grateful that Sean had let go.

Elli raced over to Mak from where she had been standing next to her husband, Tyler. After working with the gorgeous woman every afternoon that week, Mak had come to admire her. Elli was about four inches shorter than Mak, only about 5'4" tall, with eyes the color of cerulean blue and long coffee-colored hair. She had a baby strapped to her chest in a special pouch and another child riding her hip. Mak was amazed that Elli had managed to keep her beautiful figure after giving birth to ten children. Still, she had to assume that having ten children to care for and chase after probably had a lot to do with that svelte figure. Elli certainly was a bundle of energy. Mak also couldn't believe how much Elli looked like her mother, Emi. The two could almost pass for twins except for the tiny lines around Emi's mouth and eyes that came with age.

Mak held out her hands to the little girl that Elli was holding and was grateful when the child came willingly into her arms. She so loved children. For a moment, Mak got a sad, lost look on her face at the remembrance of the baby she should still be carrying in her womb. She quickly hid the pain behind a bright smile and bent to nuzzle the child's neck.

"God, I love how they smell at this age," Mak told the little girl's mother.

"Mak, I'm so happy you're here. Come meet everyone and grab something to eat. Oh, and thanks for holding Lianne. My girl is getting big but not too old to want to be held," Elli greeted her.

When Elli and Mak had made their way over to Tyler, Elli said, “Okay, you know my husband Tyler,” to which Tyler nodded his head.

Mak thought about how lucky Elli was in the spouse department. Tyler was about 6’2” tall with hair so dark it almost looked black, but when the sunlight caught it just so, Mak could see red highlights in it. He was well-built with broad shoulders, what might be an eight pack of muscles hiding under his Henley, well-muscled arms, and probably legs too, by the way, he filled out his jeans. Elli and Tyler were a handsome couple. Mak suspected that they were deeply in love if their looks at each other were any indication.

“Tyler’s holding our youngest, Patricia Emilia. Patti for short. I have Annie in this snuggly,” Elli continued. “This is the best carrier ever. It allows me to nurse the baby without anyone knowing. I used it for Alex and Angus, too.” Then Elli laughed. “I digress. So, Annie’s full name is Anna Bella. You’re holding Lianne Susanna.”

Lianne patted Mak’s cheeks with her chubby hands when her mommy said her name. Mak laughed and gave the little girl a kiss on the tip of her nose.

After Tyler had rounded up the rest of his brood, Mak marveled at how the children cared for each other. They argued good-naturedly but were still very protective of each other.

Tyler took over the introductions, "Mak from left to right and by age, the oldest of the Whrite-Thompson clan is Jessica Blair, whom I'm certain you've already met. Jess is fourteen."

Jess rushed forward, grabbed Mak in a swift hug, which surprised Mak. And said, "Hi, Mak. I'm so happy you're going to be working here. I want to work with you on massage therapy for the horses. Here, let me take Lianne."

Tyler cleared his throat, and Jess got back in line. "Next are the triplets, Richard Blair, whom we call Blair, Peggy Lynne, and Tyler Logan, known as Logan so as not to confuse the two of us when we're together. They are eight years old now."

The three tow-headed youngsters all giggled a "Hello Mak" and ran off to play.

Mak watched them go. They grabbed a Frisbee and started to throw it for a beautiful golden retriever. Tyler saw that Mak was following the children as they played. "The dog's name is Toby," he told her, to which Mak nodded her head to show that she was paying attention.

"Let's see. Who do we have left?" Tyler grinned as Billy started jumping up and down and waving his hand in the air for his father's attention. Then, placing his hand affectionately on the top of the boy's head, Tyler said, "This young man is William Timothy. We call him Billy. He's now seven."

Billy ran up to Mak and threw his arms around her for a hug, gazed up with adoring eyes, and then a gap-toothed smile that made Mak laugh.

"Hi, Billy. I see the tooth fairy must have come recently," Mak teased the cute youngster.

Billy grinned and then lisped, "Yeah, I got five whole dollars. I can't wait to lose another tooth." Then he ran off to play with his siblings. He was welcomed with open arms.

"Next oldest is Lianne Susanna, whom you've already met and held. She turned two in June." Lianne waved at Mak from her sister's arms, asked to be put down, and then toddled off to chase after the older children and the dog. Blair gathered her up and rested her on his hip when she reached them.

Jess took Mak's hand as she watched the adorable little girl go. Elli and Tyler noticed the longing in Mak's eyes and wondered at the cause.

As Mak watched the children play, she marveled that the oldest four had dirty blond hair while the rest were dark-haired like their father. She would later learn about the death of Elli's first husband, Richard Blair Whrite, and how Tyler had been the man's best friend.

Jess interrupted Mak's thoughts by saying to her parents, "I can introduce Mak to everyone else. I know Patti and Annie need to be fed and changed."

Tyler nodded, "Thanks, sweet baby girl." Then, to Mak, he said, "Food's on the table. Please help yourself, and thanks for coming to work for us. I know you're going to be a great addition." Then he and Elli went into the house through the back door.

Jess led Mak over to an older couple, each holding one of a set of twin boys who looked to be about sixteen or seventeen months old.

"Grandma, Grandpa, this is our new ranch hand, Mak," Jess began. "Mak, this is my grandfather, Alastair Caelan Thompson, and my grandma, Annabelle."

The man held out a hand to Mak after shifting the little boy he was holding from one hip to the other. Then, clasping Mak's hand warmly, he said, "Everybody calls me Alex. Tyler's dad, if you didn't already guess by the fact that we look so much alike, and everyone calls my wife Anna. We're so pleased to meet you."

Mak studied Anna as the woman gave Mak a warm smile. Anna was about 5'5" tall with chestnut-colored hair and a trim figure. She squeezed Mak's hand in greeting and told her, "Okay, last two of the Whrite-Thompson brood. Alex is holding Alastair Lachlan, whom everyone calls Alex, so things get confusing when the two Alexes are together. And this young man is Caelan Angus Whrite-Thompson. He's Angus, and I think the boys are getting hungry. What say we go feed your grandsons, Alex? Jess, you introduce Mak to the Jones family? Then take her over to formally meet Mike and Emi."

Jess hugged her grandmother then led Mak away. As they walked towards where Tim, Jeannie, and Sophie talked with Sean, John, Tom, and Jake, Jess told Mak a little about Anna Thompson.

"Grandma has known my mom and dad since they were young kids. My father, Rick, too. She worked for my Great Grandma Jessica as a housekeeper for years. She then stayed on to take care of my father, Richard Blair Whrite, after Great-Grandma Jess passed away. When my father died, she stayed to take care of Mom and me and the triplets. Then my stepfather, Tyler, too, after he and Mom were married. She actually met Grandpa Alex at their wedding ceremony. She's just always been part of the family, loving and taking care of all of us. It was the best day ever when she and Grandpa got married, and she became an official member of the family. I love her a lot."

Sean followed Mak's movements with his eyes as she was introduced to everyone. John noticed, and the men were all teasing Sean as Jess brought Mak over.

"Mak, please let me introduce my cousin Timothy Jones, his wife Jeannie, and their daughter Sophie. But, of course, you already know these other laughing idiots, Sean, John, Tom, and Jake. To which the insulted men all said, "Hey, wait just one minute."

Mak noticed how Jake winked at Jessica and how Jess blushed prettily in return. Jake reminded Mak of Elli's husband Tyler in a way because of his quiet personality that exuded confidence, intelligence, and a sense of purpose in his actions and words.

Mak received a handshake from Tim and hugs from Jeannie and Sophie. Tim looked to be in his late thirties. Tall, at a little over six feet, he was well built, not muscle-bound. He had kind eyes and a sweet, toothy, lopsided smile. Mak liked his light brown hair. It stuck up in a cute cowlick that he kept trying to tame with his hand. It refused to cooperate. Jeannie was tall, about 5'10", but thin and fine-boned. She was a brunette with brown eyes and a smattering of freckles across her nose. Sophie was fourteen years old but was a miniature copy of her mother.

Mak watched as Jess and Sophie ran off to keep an eye on Jessica's younger siblings. They'd noticed that the younger children were now doing handstands, somersaults, and cartwheels on the lawn. Lianne giggled as she pushed the others over when they managed to do headstands.

Jeannie grabbed Mak by the arm and said, "Let's eat while the children are playing. It can get a little rowdy around here when you have that many children to supervise during mealtime. I don't know how Elli does it. I'd say she's one lucky woman, but that isn't it at all. She and Tyler are just excellent parents. They're warm and loving, and Elli's an outstanding teacher. She's homeschooling the kids until they are through middle school."

When Mak and Jeannie sat down at a picnic table with plates heaped high with chicken cooked on the grill and several types of salads, Jeannie indicated the couple sitting there. They held two more children about the same age as Elli's and Tyler's, Alex and Angus.

Jeannie said, "Mike and Emi, I'm certain you know already since Mike is the owner of the *Circle R*. Mike and Emi are Elli's father and mother. I don't know if anyone's mentioned, but Emi is *Circle R's* resident-certified home health care nurse. She takes care of everyone's boo-boos." Of course, that got a laugh out of the four adults, which caused the babies to laugh, too.

Jeannie continued, "Their little cuties are Roger Michael and Addison Mackenzie Willis. The kiddos were born the same day as Alex and Angus. And there you have all of the inhabitants of the

Circle R. Hope you like kids because I'm pregnant," which got a gasp out of Mike and Emi.

"Holy Hanna," Emi said. "When are you due? Does Elli know? She's going to be so excited for you and Tim."

"We're due in March. We've been trying since we got married, but we'd just about given up hope of it ever happening. So, I'm a little nervous. Sophie's fourteen now, and I'm almost forty."

Emi laughed. "Have twins when you're closer to fifty, and then we'll talk."

Mak took in the way all of the people that lived and worked on the *Circle R* loved and appreciated everyone else. And, God, all of the delightful children. What she wouldn't give to be so lucky. She looked at Sean with longing in her eyes as she thought about that. Mike caught that look and started to worry.

CHAPTER 29

BRIAN stormed into his father's office to meet with the detective assigned to find Mak. It had been almost three months since Mak's disappearance. She'd gone missing at the end of August, and it was now the week of Thanksgiving. The temperature in November usually averaged between forty and sixty degrees Fahrenheit. Still, after a brutally hot summer, it had turned bitterly cold outside. The frigid temperature may have chilled Brian on the outside, but he was boiling with anger inside. Plus, he was going out of his mind. He wanted his wife back. It didn't matter that they hadn't signed that damned piece of paper yet that made it official. In Brian's mind, it was a done deal. She was his wife, and he missed her. Mak was the only woman for whom he'd ever been able to unleash the beast in himself when he was making love. Between bouts of fierce lovemaking, her calm, quiet demeanor soothed his anger. He didn't mean to hurt her. He couldn't help himself sometimes. It was very seldom her fault when his anger struck him. Making love to her just helped to wipe it out and gave him somewhere to place the blame.

Brian was furious at the detective's seeming incompetence. It shouldn't be that difficult to find a woman with no means of support. The detective had been keeping a keen eye on Mak's only account, but no funds had been redrawn from it so far. Her social security account was being monitored as well. Totally illegal, but a person could achieve anything if he had the means. Brian's father proved that time and time again. If Brian Alexander Hillhouse II wanted something, he paid someone to make it happen.

Mak's account wasn't showing any income, so she wasn't legally employed. If she was being paid cash under the table, that was another matter entirely. There was no way to track that.

Brian went straight to his father's whiskey decanter and poured himself a double. Then, sitting in the only empty upholstered chair in front of his father's desk, Brian tossed back the liquor. He set the empty glass on the corner of his father's antique desk. Good old dad gave Brian a look that should have killed him, lifted the offending glass, and slid a coaster underneath it so that it wouldn't leave a ring.

Sitting in the other leather upholstered chair in front of the antique desk, the detective watched the interaction between father and son with a fair amount of disdain and wry amusement. He knew that both of them were wealthy, narcissistic, arrogant, entitled pricks. Still, the pay was good, plus the detective knew where all the skeletons were hidden. So, he kept his mouth shut and waited until it was time for him to give his report. He didn't blame the woman whom he'd been tracking for running off because he was empathetic to her situation. She was caught in an abusive relationship. She'd been knocked down a flight of stairs by the man who was supposed to love and protect, causing her to miscarry that man's child. If Miss Jamieson was his daughter, Brian Hillhouse III would be lying at the bottom of that lake he owned an expensive home near.

Brian studied the detective seated next to him while ignoring his father's hissy fit about a potential water ring on his cherished desk. The detective was about two inches shorter than Brian's 6'4" but in excellent shape. Brian would have expected a man who spent most of his time sitting behind the wheel of a car spying on people to be overweight and flabby. Not this guy. He had muscles to match Brian's, so he definitely spent time at a gym. That didn't make Brian admire the guy. He was clearly incompetent if he couldn't find one woman after three months of trying. Brian turned to the detective and said, "Well, Wilson? Where the fuck is my wife?"

The detective, named Steven Wilson, was not about to get into a pissing match with the bastard by pointing out that Miss Makailyn Elsbeth Jamieson was not legally Brian's wife.

So, Steven began, "We have camera footage from the hospital showing Miss Jamieson exiting the rear of the hospital. Unfortunately, there was a lapse in available camera coverage once she turned the corner. That gap allowed her to escape undetected."

"We know that her best friend, Jaymiee Joanna Johnston, assisted her in leaving the hospital. In addition, she lent her the car that Miss Jamieson subsequently drove to Wichita, Kansas."

"We assume that Miss Jamieson got into that car between the corner and the range of coverage afforded by the next available camera."

Brian, now visibly fuming, said, “I don’t give a royal rat’s ass about what you didn’t see. I asked you where my wife is currently located.”

“We don’t know yet,” Steven rejoined.

Brian jumped up from his seat, grabbed the whiskey glass off the coaster on his father’s desk, and went over to pour himself another double.

“Tell me what you do know, Wilson,” he demanded after he’d tossed back the double shot.

“We know that she boarded a bus in Wichita, Kansas, but she didn’t remain on that bus to its final destination. There is any number of places that she could have gotten off. At which point, she could have taken another bus to somewhere else or some other form of transportation. For all we know, she could have hitchhiked. It’s just a matter of time before we eliminate all of the possibilities, but we will find her.”

The detective paused, then continued, “Miss Johnston is currently visiting her parents in California. The young woman was approached but refused to offer any information concerning her friend’s current location. Nevertheless, Miss Johnston is being monitored. If she takes any trips, or if Miss Jamieson shows up, you'll know immediately."

"If Miss Jamieson slips up and uses her credit card or removes any funds from her checking account, you'll know immediately."

"We've also placed a tap on the phone of one, Willis Riordan of the *Rockin' R Ranch* in Chilton. Just in case he receives any calls from Miss Jamieson, as well," Steven concluded.

Brian's response was, "FUCK! One more question? What was the final destination of the bus that Mak boarded in Wichita?"

Taking the report from the file he'd compiled, the detective said, "Billings, Montana."

"I want someone in Billings to check the bus station camera footage and get back to you. She may not have stayed on the original bus, but that may be where she was headed. I want to be contacted the minute you find her. Is that clearly understood?" Brian demanded.

Steven Wilson just nodded, collected his briefcase, and left the room.

Brian downed another shot of his father's expensive whiskey, then stomped across the hall to his office. He told his secretary that he wasn't to be disturbed and slammed his office door in the woman's face.

Brian dialed the cell number for his best friend, Jack Hamilton, when he'd had a few minutes to calm down. When Jack answered on the second ring, Brian said, "I need to know what that bitch you were fucking was planning when she left Philadelphia, Jack. She must have left some clue."

Brian listened for a few minutes, said, "Okay, get back to me as quickly as possible," and hung up the phone.

Later that day, Brian's cell chimed, indicating that a text message had been received. A text that said Jack wanted to fax over some documents and that Brian should call if he needed anything else from him. Brian replied with the number of the office fax machine and a curt, "Thanks, Man!"

Brian waited impatiently by the office fax machine for the next fifteen minutes demanding that the machine spit out the documents he so desperately needed, a way to find his Mak. For the first two minutes, he stood glaring down at it as if willing it to give up its secrets. Brian paced the area for the balance of those interminable minutes, muttering expletives and yanking at his hair and necktie. The other office personnel avoided that machine and the surrounding area while Brian prowled before it. Some of the documents emitted in the interim were time-sensitive. Still, that paperwork ended up in shreds on the office floor. Torn apart because they didn't offer clues to Mak's disappearance.

As Brian gathered the precious pieces of paper he'd been seeking, he laughed hysterically in triumph. Brian's sanity was slowly becoming unmoored like one of his boats that he'd forgotten to tie up to the dock behind his house on Lake Eufaula. Everyone scattered as Brian strode towards his father's office, brandishing the paper in the air and laughing all the way.

The elder Hillhouse glanced up when his son entered his office, concerned because Brian was laughing like a loon. Then, sighing, he motioned for his son to take a seat.

"Brian, I think you need a vacation. Somewhere quiet. A sanitarium perhaps where you can relax. You've been under too much stress."

"Fuck that!" was Brian's response. "You can fire your fucking worthless detective. He isn't worth the fortune you are spending keeping him on the payroll. Three fucking months, Father. He's been dicking around trying to find my wife for three fucking months. Instead, I had to find her myself."

Hillhouse kept his composure as he calmly asked, "Where is she?"

Brian tossed the faxed documents on his father's desk. "She's been in fucking Billings, Montana, all this time pretending to be her best friend. Jo got a job on some ranch called the *Circle R Cattle Company*. The two women look so much alike, it was easy for them to switch places."

"I'll arrange to have someone retrieve her, Brian," his father assured him.

Brian's response was, "Fuck that. I'm tired of waiting. If you want a job done right, you need to do it yourself. I'm going to get my wife back, myself." Then Brian left his father's office, but not before knocking back a tumbler of dad's expensive Irish whiskey.

Hillhouse II sighed in resignation, knowing this would not go well. There would probably be more of his son's messes to clean up before this was over. He wondered what the cost would be this time. Cleaning up Brian's messes was always very expensive.

Brian went back to his office, just long enough to rearrange his schedule and reassign his cases to other attorneys on staff. He told his secretary he would be on vacation until further notice. "I am not to be contacted under any circumstances," he admonished.

Then Brian stood in front of his antique mirror, straightened his tie, and ran a comb through his hair, all while smiling wolfishly. He was going on a hunt to get back the sweet young woman who would bear the son that would make Brian's father proud of him.

Brian grabbed his briefcase and went home to plan his strategy. He spent the balance of that day making arrangements for his trip. First off, Brian booked the next available flight that wouldn't leave until 7:00 a.m. the following morning. He also contacted a dealership in Billings, Montana. Brian arranged to purchase a black *Mercedes-Benz G-class SUV* with blackout windows. He got lucky on that find. They would let Brian drive it right out of the building for a measly $140,000 cash. Chump change to the son of a billionaire. The money was wired from Brian's bank account with the stipulation that the dealership would deliver the car to the airport.

Brian would take immediate possession when his flight landed. Making that possible cost an additional ten grand.

Brian's third call was to the caretaker at Hillhouse Lodge. The lodge was situated in a remote location in the mountains of Wyoming. The structure had been built for Brian's grandfather, Brian Alexander Hillhouse I, in the man's younger days when he enjoyed the sport of hunting. A Hillhouse hadn't set foot in the lodge in over twenty years, and Brian had only seen photographs. Brian left strict instructions about his needs and told the caretaker that the staff's services wouldn't be needed again until further notice. The key was to be left under the mat, so to speak.

Brian would take his bride to Hillhouse Lodge and make love to her until she agreed to a wedding date, preferably within a few days, or was pregnant. He'd hide her shoes and clothing if necessary to keep her there until she acquiesced to his demands. She wouldn't be sneaking off while the mountainous terrain was covered in a deep layer of snow unless she planned to die of hypothermia. The sojourn would make for a pleasant little wintry vacation. He hadn't enjoyed one in years.

For the first time ever, Brian went shopping at a hardware store. He placed a call to the owner of a mom-and-pop in Billings. He purchased a pair of binoculars, bolt cutters, zip ties, duct tape, and the like just in case he needed to break into something or tie someone up. The owner was offered a five-hundred-dollar bonus for boxing the items up and delivering the package to the Mercedes dealer. Instructions were to be attached to the box, indicating that it should be placed in the vehicle Brian had just purchased.

Brian packed two suitcases. One for himself and one for Mak. Brian locked up the house after making arrangements for the staff members at his father's estate to clean his home at Lake Eufaula once a week. Then he visited a friend who sold party drugs to supplement his income. From that good friend, Brian added some "medicine" that he could use to knock Mak out until he could get her back where she belonged. In his bed.

Brian's friend was able to provide just what Brian needed. Not having seen each other in years, they spent some time reminiscing about the trouble they used to get into when they'd gone to boarding school together.

Promising to get together for a drink when he returned from his trip, Brian shook his friend's hand. Then he drove to a hotel near the airport. That's where Brian would spend the night. His car would be safer in the hotel parking lot while he was gone, and he could take the shuttle to the airport for his flight in the morning.

After ordering and eating a meal from room service, Brian paid for an adult's only pay-per-view channel on the television. Then, engorged shaft in hand, Brian worked himself to thoughts of Mak and what he intended to do to her beautiful body. Brian groaned as hot semen spurted out in thick ropey jets until he was utterly spent. Then, after using one of the hotel's towels to clean himself up, he threw the towel in the corner and went into the bathroom to take a shower.

CHAPTER 30

IT had been eight long weeks since Mak started working on the *Circle R*, and the weather had turned bitterly cold. Although the ranch had experienced several snowfalls, the accumulations hadn't amounted to much. Most mornings, Sean and Mak road fence line, checked on the cattle, spread hay for the animals' consumption, and ensured the waterers weren't frozen. In the afternoon, Mak worked with Emi and Jeannie on setting up the special projects Mak would be responsible for implementing. They planned to start advertising at the end of the winter season since Mak's classes were slated to begin in the spring. Emi had taken over for Elli since Elli was too busy teaching her four older children. All while caring for her five younger children, ages three and under. Elli's oldest daughter, Jessica, was the only child actually attending a public school, which meant

Elli was one busy lady. Mak admired Elli and the other women of the Circle R immensely.

Twice, Mak was asked to join the other four women for a ladies' night out while the men played poker. But, of course, the guys were also supposed to be watching the kids. Still, the women suspected that Jessica and Sophie were the ones actually handling that chore.

Ladies' night out seemed like a regular monthly occurrence, just like the Friday evening get-togethers, which were now held indoors because of the weather. Mak was going to miss the camaraderie when Jo came to take over this job that really belonged to her.

The ladies took her to the same barroom where Mak had gone to drink and dance the night before she first stepped foot on the *Circle R*. The one where Sean had made such passionate love to her.

Mak had club soda with lime both times because she'd been feeling a little off. Jeannie and Elli weren't drinking, either, since Jeannie was pregnant and Elli was still nursing her twin girls.

“Tell me, ladies, exactly why we spend our nights out in a barroom since most of us aren’t actually drinking alcohol?” Elli giggled.

Emi smirked at her daughter, “Where else can we let our hair down and act goofy?” and all of the women said, “Hell, yeah!” and started to laugh.

During the second girls’ night, the conversation somehow turned to men and their tattoos which segued to whether any of the four women had ever had their skin inked. Elli admitted to a butterfly tattoo on her left breast, which she’d had done as a personal high school graduation present to herself. Elli further admitted to having the tattoo altered when she realized that she was desperately in love with Tyler. She knew that he would always own her heart and soul.

“How did you have the tattoo changed?” Mak asked.

“I went back to the same tattoo parlor. The man that had done the original ink was an exceptional artist. He was able to delicately weave Tyler’s name into the butterfly’s wings. Do you have any tattoos, Mak?” Elli questioned.

Mak nodded, "I actually had mine done for my eighteenth birthday. It was a gift from my best friend. It's a tattoo of thistles and butterflies. I'll show you sometime when we're somewhere more private." That got the girls laughing and teasing Mak to take off her top. Mak just blushed and shook her head no.

The women ended up dancing together, but mostly the rest of them watched from the sidelines as Mak lost herself in the music.

Jeannie nodded towards Mak and told the others, "That's just wow! If I wasn't straight and married, I'd definitely be all over that. Mak almost glows like she's surrounded by a halo. Do you see how every guy in this joint is drooling so much they need bibs?" The others just sighed and nodded in agreement.

Whenever some drunken cowboy tried to get too close, Elli, Emi, Jeannie, and even Anna joined ranks to keep Mak safe.

Sean spent much of those same eight weeks with a painful hard-on and no way to relieve it other than cold showers and hand jobs, which he was getting mighty sick of. Other than the kiss they'd shared in Mak's cabin on her very first day, she'd avoided any interaction that wasn't work-related. Mak was even avoiding eye contact. But, of course, any conversation was job-related as well.

Mak was fine around John, Tom, and Jake when they all ate meals together. She would joke with the other men and share interesting tidbits about her childhood experiences and about the *Rocking' R Ranch* where she'd spent eight years working.

Sean was jealous because Mak seemed to exclude him on purpose. Also, John kept touching Mak on the arm when the two of them stood laughing together over something that had happened during the day. Sean figured he might need to take John aside and proclaim his own intentions towards Mak because that filly belonged to him. Then, John could take himself off to the grocery store parking lot and find his own woman.

The weather had been brutally cold, which was customary for the week of Thanksgiving, but that day the sun's rays were warmer. However, the sky bore wispy mare's tail clouds, which meant a change in the weather was coming. Stopping to repair some loose and popped staples on a section of fence, Sean climbed down from the saddle and went to stand beside Mak's horse. Frustrated, he held his arms up to her and said, "Come on down, darlin'. We need to talk."

Mak stared down at Sean for a long few seconds, trying to decide what she should do. Usually, when a man said they needed to talk, it didn't bode well. Mak knew what her heart was begging of her because she loved this man. But Mak didn't want to get hurt. She'd known she loved him the minute he'd touched her for the very first time in the parking lot of the grocery store on the very first day that she'd come to Billings, Montana. He was the white knight of her dreams. But she'd been hurt enough to last a lifetime. Painfully, brutally hurt. Sean wasn't anything like Brian, but Mak didn't know Sean well enough. What should she do? Follow her heart or follow her head? Should she trust Sean not to hurt her?

Sean lifted his arms up to Mak again, imploring her to come to him. At that moment, when she stared down into Sean's eyes, she could see the uncertainty there. That maybe he cared for her, too, and didn't know if she would accept him for who and what he really was instead of the wealthy landowner with the vast herd of cattle and horses he'd pretended to be.

Mak was also afraid because she was carrying a secret. A secret that she'd held once before and hadn't shared. Then it had been too late, and there was no longer a need.

Mak had woken up a few weeks ago with a queasy stomach and found herself kneeling on the floor in the bathroom praying to the porcelain god. Every morning since produced the same reaction. So, Mak had started to keep crackers by her bedside. But unfortunately, she'd also realized that she hadn't gotten her period again after losing her baby. So, either there was a complication from that miscarriage, or she was pregnant from the passionate night she'd spent in Sean's arms in the room above the bar.

The day before, she'd asked Emi and Jeannie if they would allow her an hour off to go into town to pick up a few things she needed from the drugstore. Since they were okay with that, plus gave her a list of things they needed as well, Mak found herself in the bathroom of the nearest pharmacy. It just so happened to sit opposite the grocery store where she'd run into the cowboy. He would be the responsible party if a plus sign showed up on the test strip from the pregnancy test, she'd just taken. Mak marveled over how long five minutes really were when you were waiting impatiently while sitting on a toilet seat in an unfamiliar restroom.

When the timer went off on Jo's borrowed cell phone, signaling that time was up, Mak was afraid to look. Finally, the suspense was killing her, and she took a peek. The plus sign was a glaring indication that she lacked good judgment when making life decisions. That made Mak think that her decision wouldn't be difficult to make after all. She would follow her heart.

Oh well, here goes, she thought as she slipped from the saddle into Sean's waiting arms. She wrapped her arms around his neck, raised her face, and kissed him hard on the mouth.

Sean's look of surprise made her laugh, but her laugh turned into a moan when he took her in an open-mouthed kiss that led to a tangle of tongues. Sean's mouth then moved to the side of her neck, where he left a trail of kisses. Opening the coat that Mak wore, Sean lifted the hem of Mak's shirt and ran his hands up and over her ribcage to graze the sides of her breasts. Then, whispering in Mak's ear, he said, "I need you, baby. So, much I ache with it. Let me make love to you, darlin'."

Mak just nodded her head in agreement. She wanted Sean inside her. Only he could wipe out all of the painful memories of Brian's brutality. But first, she needed to tell him.

Sean lifted Mak's shirt over her head and unfastened the hooks on her bra. Letting it slide down her arms, he captured a nipple and began to suck until it had formed a stiff peak. Then he gave the other the same attention.

Mak shivered from the cold but moaned with desire. Sean had already shucked off his coat and laid it on the ground. With less to obstruct her objective, Mak grabbed the hem of Sean's Henley and yanked upwards. She needed Sean's skin against hers.

Their jeans were quick to follow. Then, when they were standing there in all their glory just as Mother Nature intended, Sean lifted Mak, and she wrapped her legs around his waist. They should have been freezing, but their passion-fueled heat was keeping them warm.

While Sean kissed Mak with all the pent-up passion of eight weeks of denied intimacy, he slipped his fingers through her folds only to find her wet and ready. Then, lining himself up, he eased inside.

Mak moaned into his mouth. Then moving her lips to his ear, she whispered, "I have something important to tell you, Sean."

Going still, Sean looked at Mak's face. Her eyes seemed so serious. "What is it, darlin'? Am I hurting you?"

"No, I just need you to know that I'm in love with you. I've been in love with you since the moment you first touched me. But that's not the important thing."

Sean looked at Mak questioningly. "What is it, baby?"

"That's what it is, Sean. We made a baby that night at the barroom. I'm pregnant, Sean. You're going to be a daddy."

"For real, Mak? I'm going to be a father?" Sean couldn't believe it. Mak was carrying his child. "Oh, darlin', you've made me the happiest man in Montana. Do you know that? I love you too, Mak. I was afraid to tell you. Should we stop? I don't want to hurt you or the baby."

That made Mak laugh. "No, Sean. You'd better not stop. I've wanted you every minute of every day for the last eight weeks, and I'm horny as hell."

Sean said, "Good to know." Then laying Mak down on the coats he'd placed just so, he got back to work, bringing them both the pleasure they'd been denying themselves.

On the ride back to the bunkhouse, Sean started making plans. "I've money saved. I won quite a bit when I was working the circuit. I've never needed much over the years that I've been working here on the *Circle R*. I could talk to Mike and Tyler and ask them if they'll let me buy in if you'd like to stay here, or we could go find our own place. What do you think, Mak? You've been awfully quiet since we made love, darlin'. Are you sure I didn't hurt you, Mak?"

"No, Sean. You could never hurt me. I know that now. I'm just tired, baby. I think I'll skip supper and just take a shower. Then go lie down."

"Okay. I'll save something for you in case you're hungry later. We're going to need to tell Mike soon, darlin'."

Moving his horse alongside Mak's, he pulled her from her saddle to sit across his lap and took her mouth in a searing kiss. "Love you, Mak, so much."

Later that night, Sean slipped into Mak's cabin bearing a plate with some food for Mak to snack on. Laying the covered dish on the dresser, he stripped and lowered himself beside her on the bunk. "Need to be inside you, darlin'. I want to spend the rest of my life making love to you, Mak. We'll make those babies you want and build our family. I vow to always love and protect you and our children. I don't have a ring, but we'll get whatever your heart desires. Will you marry me, Mak? Bind yourself to me and be my wife?"

As silent tears slipped down Mak's cheeks, she nodded her head yes. "I love you so much, Sean. I want to be your wife and bear your children, but I need to take care of something first. Something that I left unresolved. Then we can always be together. I pledge my life, my love, and my fidelity, now and forever."

Sean looked like he wanted to ask her what she needed to take care of, so Mak kissed Sean gently on the lips to forestall his question. Then she pressed kisses over his chest, pausing to nip and lick each flat nipple. Moving further, Mak dipped her tongue into his navel. As she moved lower still, Sean's muscles tensed, needing Mak to reach what he hoped was her intended destination. When Mak finally arrived at his engorged cock, she licked the tip, and Sean groaned out his pleasure. That response was nothing compared to the intensity of his moans as Mak took him into her mouth and began to suck and lick. When Sean was so close to coming that he didn't know how much longer he could hold back, he tried to stop Mak so that he could finish inside her. Mak shook her head vehemently. Cupping his balls, she wrapped her hand around his shaft and pumped it up and down. As Sean started to come, she wrapped her lips back around him and swallowed down every drop.

When Sean was finished, he said, “Fuck, I love you, darlin’. Come here. I need to return the favor.”

When Mak was close, and Sean was confident she couldn’t take any more, he entered her in one long slide. He knew that he was home to stay. She was his Mak, and he was never going to let her go.

As Sean and Mak lay together, wrapped in each other’s arms, they discussed what they would like to do about their jobs and made plans for their future. They agreed that they would likc to stay on the *Circle R* if the Willis’s and Thompsons’ had room for them in their operation. If not, they would need to look for a home of their own somewhere.

Sean admitted, “It doesn’t matter to me where we end up, as long as I have you by my side, darlin’.” Then he kissed Mak gently and bid her goodnight. “Love, you, Mak. We’ll talk to Mike tomorrow.”

Sean left Mak's cabin with a smile on his face and hope in his heart that things would work out. Mak would now be his reason to get up every morning and his reason to breathe all day long as he worked hard to build a future for them and their child.

As Sean turned to make his way to his cabin, a voice came out of the darkness. Startled, Sean realized he recognized the voice and turned towards the source.

"Evening, Sean. Do you want to explain yourself?" Mike demanded. "You were in there an awfully long time. More time than it takes to bring Mak a plate of food. I don't want to sound judgmental, but the ranch foreman shouldn't be messing around with his subordinates. The *Circle R* could get sued for sexual harassment."

Sean swallowed hard. "I can explain, Mike. Please hear me out."

"Okay, walk with me, and we'll talk about it. Hopefully, you can give me a good reason not to fire your ass," Mike said as he clapped his hand on Sean's shoulder and turned him in the direction of the stable.

Nothing further was said until they were both wielding a brush. There was nothing more soothing than brushing a horse when your thoughts were troubled.

Sean took a moment to try to get his thoughts in order then began, "It's not what it seems, Mike."

When Mike quirked his eyebrow, Sean said, "Honest. I'm not hitting on an employee. I promise. Well, she is an employee, and it might appear that I'm hitting on her." Then he stared at his boss to see if Mike was making any sense out of Sean's ramblings.

Mike indicated that Sean should continue with his explanation without making any comment.

"Okay, this is the way it went down." Sean was beginning to sweat. He didn't want to blow this. "So, I ran into a woman almost three months ago in the grocery store parking lot in Butler. She was coming from that fast food place next door. When she dropped her drink and purse, I went over to help. She was hunkered down, so I didn't get a good look at her until she glanced up. Her face was all beat to shit, Mike. She had bruises and a black eye. When I touched her to get a better look, I got zapped like I'd touched the electric fence.

I only mention that because I think I fell in love with her that very minute."

Mike was staring at Sean as if this was the most fascinating story he'd ever heard. "Keep going. I'm listening."

Sean swallowed hard. His mouth was dry like he'd tried to eat a box of cotton. He could sure use a drink of that ice-cold water from the pond by the line cabin.

"Anyway, the woman took off like a startled deer, and I thought that was the end of it. Then about three weeks later, you and John were ribbing me about needing to mentor and babysit your new hire. Some woman named Jaymiee Joanna Johnston. The woman was supposed to start the next day."

"I remember that, Sean. You seemed distracted and none too keen on your new assignment." Mike chuckled to try to help ease Sean's obvious distress.

"Well, I wasn't, and I was distracted because I couldn't get that woman from the parking lot out of my head. I was even dreaming about her. So, I went to my favorite bar that night. I'd planned to rent a room just in case I got lucky or drunk, whichever came first. After I arrived, I went straight to the bar and ordered a shot. As I was shootin' the shit with the bartender, I noticed all the guys were crowded around the dance floor. So, I asked the bartender if they were havin' a dance contest. Nope, that wasn't the case. The men were all takin' bets on who'd be the lucky fuck to get to dance with the beautiful woman who was dancin' by herself. She was turning down every guy that tried to get close."

"Does this story have any bearing on our current situation, Sean? You're awfully long-winded," Mike teased.

"Yeah, just really nervous. Sorry! Anyway, it was the woman from the parking lot. If I'm going to make a long story short, I guess I could conclude by saying I was the lucky fuck who got the girl and got to use that rented room. She never told me her name other than that everyone called her Mak. The next morning when I woke up, she was gone, and she'd taken my heart and soul with her. So, I dragged my ass back to the ranch, and you know the rest."

"Well, so you already knew Mak before she showed up for her job the next morning, but that still doesn't give you leave to have sex with an employee, Sean. So, I might have to let one or both of you go for this."

Mike looked at Sean sadly as he said it. It really wouldn't be fair. If anything, Mike could be accused of doing the exact same thing with Emi when she came to work on the ranch as a home health care nurse for Bill and Peggy Roberts. It didn't matter that he and Emi already shared a history. Mike was the ranch foreman, and Emi was a ranch employee.

"No, please wait. There's more, Mike. Mak and I are in love, and we want to get married. We made a baby, Mike. I'm going to be a father."

Sean looked at Mike with so much hope in his eyes, Mike didn't have the heart to rib him over forgetting to use protection when he'd put that rented room to good use. Mike was guilty of failing once or twice with his Emi. That's how they'd managed to conceive the twins. So enough said on that subject.

"You know for a fact that it's yours, Sean, or are you just a convenient scapegoat?"

Sean hadn't thought of that, but he loved and trusted Mak, and he didn't care who the father was. The baby was Mak's, so that made it his no matter what. Time alone would tell, and he told Mike that.

"Alright, what are your plans?" Mike asked.

"Well, that's why I was in Mak's cabin so long." Sean wasn't going to add that Mak had given him the best blow job he'd ever had. Instead, he'd take that knowledge to his grave. "We're, meaning Mak and me, hoping that you and Tyler would consider allowing us to buy in on the ranch. We both love our jobs and the ranch. Not to mention all the good people. We'd like to make this our home and build a family here."

"Oh, Elli's going to love this. More babies for her to teach. She sure is being given the opportunity to put that teaching degree to good use, even if ten of those kids are her own. Okay, I'll need to sit down with Tyler, Elli, and Emi so they can put in their two cents worth. Tyler will need to run the numbers to see if it is a viable option. The ranch has to be able to support all the families. I think he has something in the works to expand, as well. There's the possibility of adding on by buying Ferguson's spread. It's a contiguous piece of property, which makes that acreage a good fit. If the acquisition happens, you'd be able to move your little family into Ferguson's ranch house. In the meantime, I'm certain the women are going to want to plan a wedding."

Sean just stared with his mouth hanging open. Everything had happened so fast. He was overwhelmed.

Mike laughed outright, “Close your mouth, Sean. You don’t want to swallow any of the flies that have been lighting on the horses’ poop. Now do you?”

Sean closed his mouth in a hurry at that comment, stuck out his hand, and said, “Thanks, Mike.”

CHAPTER 31

THERE weren't any direct flights from *Will Rogers Airport* in Oklahoma City to Billings, Montana. Instead, Brian had to endure one layover in Denver, Colorado. The only good part was that the flight wasn't full, so the seat beside Brian in first class was empty. Not having to make inane small talk with a stranger was definitely a plus. The other added benefit was that the stewardess made a point of flirting with Brian when she brought him his drink order. She was rather attractive.

After downing his Bloody Mary, Brian made his way to the galley with the empty glass in hand. Ostensibly and for appearances, he was looking for a refill. However, Brian had another reason on his mind. Finding the woman alone, he grabbed her hand and eased her into one of the bathroom stalls. It was a tight fit, but he managed to bend her over the sink. Then, sheathing his aching cock in a condom,

Brian took out his frustrations on her willing cunt. Joining the Mile High Club was a perk, but the woman wasn't the one he needed. Finished, Brian placed his hand on her back to move her out of the cubicle. After shutting the door in her face, he discarded the condom in the toilet and took a leak. Then he tucked his dick back in his pants, yanked up the zipper, and washed his hands.

After he'd returned to his seat, the stewardess slipped Brian a napkin with his fresh drink. Her name and phone number were written on it, complete with hearts shot through with arrows. Brian gave her a wink and made a point of placing the napkin in his breast pocket. When she turned away, he promptly threw the napkin under the seat in front of him.

Despite the layover, the trip was short. Brian's flight landed on time at the airport in Billings at 1:27 p. m. Brian ignored the flight attendant's bid to gain his attention as he disembarked.

A sign containing Brian's last name directed him to a man waiting near the terminal exit after Brian had collected his luggage. Everything so far had gone off without a hitch. The man actually grabbed one of Brian's suitcases to lend a hand. Together they exited the building and walked to where the man had parked the *Mercedes-*

Benz G-class SUV. Brian was given a tour of the vehicle to ensure it met with his approval. The salesman also showed Brian how to operate the car's various options. Then Brian signed the final documents, and they shook hands. As the salesman walked away, he had a massive smile on his face because that was the fastest and easiest sale he'd ever made.

Brian stowed the luggage in the back of the SUV. After perusing the items in the cardboard box from the hardware store, he placed that alongside the suitcases. Once the *Circle R Cattle Company* address was programmed into the GPS, he was on his way to find the woman he loved. His grandmother's 2-carat Pavé infinity diamond engagement ring and the matching wedding band were nestled safely in the inner pocket of his suitcase. The engagement ring would be placed back onto Mak's finger as soon as he found her. Brian fully intended to punish her for having the audacity to take it off. He hoped Mak enjoyed that spanking as much as he intended to. Brian's dick perked up at the thought of that encounter.

When the British accented voice on the GPS informed Brian that he would be arriving at his destination in one thousand feet on the left, Brian slowed the vehicle's speed. The road he was traveling was sparsely traveled, so Brian stopped the car to get a good look at the arched sign confirming that this was indeed the *Circle R Ranch*. Fenced fields on each side of the driveway contained only a thin layer of snow. No signs of cattle or horses grazing.

Brian pulled to the side of the road and used the binoculars from the hardware store to get a good look at the buildings that sat off in the distance. There was just enough light left from the setting sun for him to catch a glimpse of a man and a woman walking together towards some outbuildings that looked like cabins. Brian's heart raced. It was his first glimpse of Mak since the end of August. She was here. All he had to do was get her back.

Brian drove until he reached a gate in the fence that lined the field. Passing that, Brian found a turnaround and headed back. Parking on the berm, he grabbed the bolt cutters from the cardboard box and proceeded to cut the lock on the gate. Then Brian drove the SUV through the opening onto the farm road and parked. The rough dirt road was coated with snow with bare patches scoured clean by the wind. Brian locked the vehicle and started down the sloping hill past a rock outcropping to get the lay of the land. The discovery of a crude-looking cabin beside a semi-frozen pond was a welcome addition to his plan. Brian went over to check the building out. Elated, he found the door unlocked and decided to get comfortable by lying on one of the bunks. He'd wait until full dark to retrieve Mak.

Brian was pleased with himself at remembering to bring a good pair of insulated waterproof outdoor boots he'd purchased on a whim. They were going to come in handy.

Brian fell asleep for a couple of hours, so it was completely dark when he left the cabin. Hiking along the fence line, Brian finally came to a gate in the fence that bordered the main drive. Ignoring the gate, Brian climbed through the railing. He followed the fence again until he got to the outbuildings he'd glimpsed through the binoculars. He was just in time to see a man exit one of the cabins and meet up with another. Pressing against a shed, Brian eavesdropped on their conversation. From the part of the conversation that he could overhear, Brian discovered that Mak was inside the cabin that the man had just exited.

Unaware of what was happening beyond the four walls of her cabin, Mak was lying on her bunk. Worrying the skin on her thumb, she thought about the pickle she'd gotten herself into, with the help of her best friend, Jo, of course. Mak was living a lie, and the man she'd fallen in love with, whose baby she was carrying, didn't even know her real name. He thought her name was Jaymiee Joanna Johnston. She was undoubtedly caught up in a deception of massive proportions.

Mak had to get Jo to come to the *Circle R Ranch* to help her sort out this mess before things could get any worse. Sean had all these expectations for their future together. Mak could only hope that he would be able to forgive her the lie. Maybe when Sean knew all the details, he would understand. As for the owners of the *Circle R*, it would be up to them if they wanted the real Jo to continue to work on the ranch. They had been lied to as well. Either way, Mak guessed she would be unemployed, and if Sean couldn't forgive the deception, Mak would be pregnant and on her own with nowhere to go. The only ray of light in the whole disaster that was now her life was the fact that Brian hadn't found her. She could only hope that he'd given up. That would be a blessing.

If worse came to worse, Mak would rent the room at the Gormley's again and look for a job. Maybe at the grocery store. Ha! Wouldn't that be a kick in the pants?

Grabbing Jo's cell phone off the dresser, Mak sent off a critical one-word text to her best friend. That word would bring Jo on the double. Then, together they could sit everyone down and confess. That one word was "*Savior.*" Mak added "*Circle R*" to the text so Jo would know where to go.

Then, Mak cried for a while over the turn her life had taken until, exhausted, she dozed off.

CHAPTER 32

MAK was jolted out of a nightmare when a large hand clamped over her mouth. Her first thought was that Sean was playing a joke and had come back to make love again. Mak was definitely up for that. Well, maybe after she peed. She'd forgotten to go before she fell asleep.

As her fuzzy sleep-addled mind cleared, she got a good look at the hand's owner, and Mak realized her worst nightmare had come to life. With a curse, the hand was yanked away when Mak bit down. As she opened her mouth to scream, a fist connected with the side of her face. The impact caused her to bite her tongue instead. Quickly, a rag was stuffed into her mouth to gag her. A piece of duct tape was affixed to hold the rag in place. Terrified, Mak panicked and began to violently flail her arms and legs. Managing to throw off her assailant, she kicked, catching him in the side of the head. Twisting to the side,

Mak rolled off the cot and hit the floor so hard it knocked the air from her lungs. When she could take a full breath, she scrambled to avoid the hands reaching out to grab her. Managing to kick him again, this time in the legs, the intruder grunted as he crashed to the floor.

Finally making it to her feet, Mak tried to turn. Desperate now, she knew she needed to reach Sean. Only he could save her.

As the heavy weight of a body crashed into her, she pitched backward. When her head connected with the sharp edge of the dresser, all the lights went out in Montana. Or maybe just Mak's lights. She fell down a well so black, she doubted that she would ever reach the bottom.

Brian cursed under his breath. Mak had managed to catch him a good one on the side of his face when she'd kicked him. But unfortunately, she'd managed to connect with his legs too. Damn, that hurt. He'd probably have bruises. She'd need to be punished for that.

Lifting Mak, he placed her body onto the cot. When his hand came away sticky with blood, Brian checked and discovered that Mak had a massive lump on the back of her head. His thought was, "Ouch. That had to have scrambled her brains."

Brian remembered the injuries Mak had incurred in her tumble down the stairs at home and said, "This shit is getting to be a bad habit, Mak."

He had to hunt for the roll of duct tape he'd employed to keep Mak from crying out. Brian didn't need the two cowboys who had walked away just minutes before interfering with his planned abduction. Well, not really an abduction, just retrieval of his property. Yanking the bed away from the wall, he found the tape shoved into the corner.

Tearing off a length, Brian bound Mak's wrists behind her back. He'd leave her legs free just in case he needed her to walk. He should be strong enough to carry Mak back to the spot where he'd left the car, but he'd find out soon enough.

"Time to go, sweetheart. We're going to Wyoming, where I plan to take such good care of you. I love you, Mak, so much, and you've been a naughty girl. When we get to Hillhouse Lodge, I'll have to decide how to administer your punishment. Then, we'll get to work on making our baby after you've been properly chastised."

After punishing Mak's lips with a bruising kiss, Brian picked her up in a fireman's lift. He'd seen the technique employed that allowed one person to carry another person without assistance. Placing Mak across his shoulders would leave his hands free just in case.

Mak, being unconscious, never heard a word that Brian said. Nor was she aware of the icy bite of the wind as it hit her skin when they exited the cabin. Because he was in a hurry, Brian hadn't bothered to protect Mak from the elements with a coat, pants, boots, or hat. Instead, she was clad only in a nightgown and panties.

Brian kept to the shadows as he carried Mak away from the cabin. Then, reaching the spot in the fence where he'd initially climbed through, he put Mak down parallel to the railing. After rolling her underneath, he discovered that she was now wet from the snowmelt that had yet to refreeze.

Mak hadn't regained consciousness, and Brian was vaguely worried about that lump. It looked worse even than the one she'd sustained in her fall down his stairs. As he cleared a slight rise in the terrain, Brian stopped to rest by laying Mak down in the snow again. Then, figuring he was far enough away to remain undetected, he turned on the small flashlight he had hidden in his pocket. Lifting the still unconscious Mak, he continued on, weighing his options as he followed the well-worn trail. His first option was to dump her in the car and get the heck out of there. His second and most obvious choice was to use the pond's cold water to place a compress on that nasty lump that had formed. Hopefully, that would revive her.

When he made it to the cabin, Brian decided to go with option two and stop for a bit. Mak was heavier than she looked. Brian laid her on her side on the cot nearest the door. Then, after finding an empty container under the rough-looking cabinet, he tried to draw some water from the pump in the sink. Apparently, the line was frozen, so he went out to get some of that ice water from the pond.

Mak sobbed when she found that she was living her nightmare. She was lying on the cot from the dream she'd had when she was still working for Will on the *Rockin' R Ranch*. The one with the rough log headboard, footboard, and thin mattress. Mak could see the porcelain sink with the hand pump and the cabinet on the other side of the window. The hot plate was just where she'd dreamed it would be. The only difference was that she wasn't naked, and her hands and feet weren't bound to the bed. At least she was wearing the nightgown and panties she put on after leaving the text message for Jo.

Mak's head hurt, but she could see. Her wrists were bound behind her back, and she was gagged. Mak fought the urge to vomit, terrified that she'd choke to death on her own puke.

Frantic, Mak pushed her body backward until her face was close to the headboard and began to rub. The very rough texture of the wood scraped at her skin as she worked, bringing tears to her eyes. But Mak almost cried out in relief when the tape let go on one side, and she could spit out the gag. Running her tongue over her lips, Mak didn't find any split. The taste of blood was from where she'd bitten her tongue. So, at least those parts of her nightmare were wrong. Unwilling to take the time to free her hands, Mak jumped to her feet and stumbled to the door. Thankfully it had been left open. As she staggered out onto the snowy ground, she lost her balance and nearly fell. Regaining her footing, Mak took off, stumbling up the slope. There wasn't much light to guide her, but she kept going. Praying as she ran, "Please, Sean, come find me. I love you so much."

By the time Brian got back, Mak was no longer lying where he'd left her. Panicked, he threw the pot of water in the sink and went out to search. When he found Mak, she was going to be sorry. She was really pissing him off.

It didn't take long. Mak hadn't gotten far due to the snow and her bare feet. Brian caught sight of her as she tried to scramble over the small rock outcropping just up the hill from the cabin. He was thankful that Mak hadn't kept to her right in her attempt to flee because she might have been able to evade him. Mak would have discovered the path that led to the gate to the main road where he'd parked the Mercedes.

When Brian yelled at her, Mak panicked and tried to pick up her pace. Coming to a rocky ledge, she tried to clamber over the jagged terrain. It was challenging with her hands bound and everything covered with snow. So, she tried to step where the wind had blown the snow away and left bare patches. She'd almost made it to the top when her bare foot caught a sharp rock that cut deep into the tender flesh. Crying out in pain, Mak jerked back and lost her footing.

Brian watched as Mak stumbled and fell, all caught in the beam of his flashlight. Then, as he watched in horror, she pinwheeled down the outcropping, and her body came to rest against a boulder that protruded from a clump of grass. Brian heard the crack as her head connected with that rock.

The last thing Mak remembered was the impact of her head with a boulder, and everything went black again.

Rushing forward, Brian turned Mak to him and marveled that she'd managed to hit her head in precisely the same spot. That couldn't be a good thing.

Lifting Mak gently, Brian carried her back to the cabin, where he laid her on the cot. Checking her over, he found cuts and abrasions in numerous places. Removing the tape used to bind her wrists, Brian stripped Mak of her soggy, torn nightgown. Then using fresh pieces, he tied her spread-eagled to the bed. Now she wasn't going anywhere.

While Brian used the water from the pond to cleanse her wounds, his cock swelled painfully at the sight of her beauty. It fueled his blood with lust and a need to exert his dominance. Stripping out of his clothing, he punished Mak's flesh with his teeth as he rammed his cock inside her with hard thrusts.

Unaware, Mak dreamed that she'd fallen overboard while watching the Memorial Day fireworks on Lake Eufaula. As she sank to the bottom, she could see Sean's sparkling blue eyes and his mischievous grin, and then nothing at all.

When the beast in Brian was sated, he eased out of Mak. Removing her bindings from her ankles, he curled up next to her body so that he could hold her. It had been a long, emotional three months of waiting to make love to his Mak again. Brian was exhausted, so it took no time at all for him to fall asleep.

CHAPTER 33

AFTER his talk with Mike, Sean headed off to his bunk and, hopefully, a good night's sleep. It would be a first since running into a certain someone in a grocery store parking lot. Thoughts of Mak had disturbed his sleep ever since that first encounter.

Sean woke with a start. He could feel it in his gut that something wasn't right. Rolling off the cot, he scrubbed his hand over his face and fisted his eyes to rub the sleep out of them.

He didn't hear any sounds save the sigh of the wind against the eaves of the cabin. But something felt off. Throwing on a clean pair of jeans, Henley, and socks, Sean yanked on his boots, coat, and gloves and clamped his Stetson on his head. Then he went out to do a tour of the grounds. After that incident with Emi when she'd first arrived on the ranch, everything had gone back to normal. No more transients looking to inject some unsuspecting female full of a date rape drug so they could get lucky. Or so the cops had believed at the time. But unfortunately, the police never did come up with any clues or suspects.

Emi had been lucky. Jake had decided to muck out the stable earlier than usual that morning and scared the would-be kidnapper off.

Things had been unsettled after that, and all the hands had taken shifts patrolling every night.

While pondering that earlier occurrence, Sean walked the grounds and had just finished checking on the horses in the stable. The sky was beginning to lighten, so work would start soon, just like any other day. Sean met Mike in the doorway as he was preparing to check on the dogs.

"Up awfully early, Sean," Mike commented. "Anxious for that discussion we'll be having, so you can get the show on the road concerning tying down that pretty little filly that's carrying your baby?"

Sean shook his head. "Something's off, but nothing's out of place. I was just going over to double-check around the barn near the dog pen. Want to come along?"

"Well, now you've got my stomach acid churning. Let's go," Mike responded. "On the way, we can check on the other hands. Maybe one of them has seen or heard something. Probably, nothing, though."

When the two men reached Mak's cabin, Sean softly knocked on the door and waited for a response.

"Mak's a heavy sleeper if she didn't hear your rap. So, give it another go, only this time louder," Mike teased.

So, Sean pounded three good ones. Still no response. Confused, the two men looked at each other and came to the same decision. It was time to open the door. Hopefully, Mak wasn't in the shower, naked as a jaybird. The cabin was small, so the tiny bathroom was an open affair. Sean didn't want Mike getting a good look at his soon-to-be bride. That sight was for his eyes and his eyes alone.

They found a room that looked like there had been a struggle. The dresser was cockeyed, and the plate of snacks that Sean had prepared for Mak was lying smashed on the floor, crackers and cheese bits everywhere. Mostly ground into crumbs. Halfway off the bed, the bedclothes contained bloodstains, and that piece of furniture was also crooked to the wall.

Mak's boots and clothes from the day before were scattered amongst the wreckage.

Mak was missing.

"Get the men, Sean. Tell Tom and Jake where you've already checked, so they don't waste time going over the same ground twice. Then tell them to split up and check the fields to the north and east. Next, you grab Blackie and check the trail towards the line cabin. After that, John and I will grab the truck and canvas the neighbors. We'll meet you at the west gate if we don't find her. Then we'll need to call in the troopers. Damn it, I don't like this one bit. First that crazy shit with Emi, and now this. The blood on the bedding has me worried. I'm going to the big house first and check on Tyler, Elli, and my grandkids. I'll tell Tyler to rustle up enough grub to feed everybody, and he can coordinate things from here. Tim, Jeannie, and Sophie flew out yesterday for Oregon, so they aren't home."

Sean just nodded and took off. Then, after rousting the other men out of their cots, he ran to the stable and tacked up the horses so they would be ready to ride. While he was saddling Blackie his mind was a whirlwind of anxiety. Where could Mak have gone?

As he headed toward the main road, Sean found a trail of footprints along the fence that lined the driveway. A set both angled toward the farm buildings, and another pair mixed with the first leading toward the road. Sean could see areas where the person's weight had broken through the crust formed on top of the snow. When he came to a matted-down patch close to the locked gate to the trail, he climbed down off Blackie and crouched to inspect the area. His stomach dipped when he found a clump of long brown hair caught in a split in the bottom rail of the fence. A swath of snow contained an impression that looked like something had been rolled from one side to the other.

Mike and John pulled up in the pickup just as Sean was getting to his feet.

"Find anything, Sean?" Mike asked.

Sean held the strands of hair out for Mike's inspection.

"We noticed the footprints, Sean. Do you think the hair is Mak's?"

Sean's only response was a nod of his head in the affirmative.

"Okay, you go that way and follow the footprints. For several miles, the only thing in that direction is the line cabin and the gate. John and I'll take the road. We'll drive real slow, checking the side of the road. There are a couple of pull-offs along there. Good places to hide a vehicle. We'll meet you at the gate, no matter what. See ya in a few." Then Mike took off.

Sean put his foot in the stirrup and swung his leg over the saddle. Making his way to the gate, he leaned down to slip the lock and latched it behind him after walking the horse through the opening. Then Sean took off at a slow trot. He didn't want Blackie to break a leg on the slippery, uneven terrain.

The sky was beginning to lighten when Brian woke up with a start. He ached from sleeping on the too-narrow cot, but Mak was still beside him. Shivering from the chill of the cabin, Brian quickly donned his clothing and shoes and left the place to get a clean outfit from the suitcase in his car. He would dress Mak first. She must be near frozen. Then he'd consume some of the canned goods from the rough shelf over the sink. Not a healthy cuisine, but good enough until he could stop and grab some food elsewhere.

As Sean approached the cabin, he tried to be as quiet as possible. There were plenty of footprints in the snow, but he didn't know if anyone was inside or not. Blackie had spoiled any hope of surprise anyway. He'd whinnied when they'd come in sight of the pond. Blackie thought he was in for a treat, a fresh cold drink, and some of the shoots of winter-browned grass that lined the edge.

Throwing open the door, it slammed against the wall, and Sean rushed inside. The sight that met him nearly brought him to his knees. His Mak was lying spread-eagled on the cot closest to the door. Naked, her wrists and ankles were bound to the rough-hewn headboard and footboard with what looked like duct tape.

Grabbing his cell out of his pocket, he quickly called Mike. When the line connected, all Sean said was, "Get an ambulance quick. Meet me at the line cabin." He didn't wait for a response.

Dropping the phone back into his pocket, Sean rushed to Mak's side and gently took her sweet heart-shaped face in his hands. Her injuries were so much worse than the first time he'd held this precious face only three short months ago. The swollen lump to the back of her head was so huge, and her hair was matted with blood.

Her eye was black and near swollen shut. The side of her face was a mass of scrapes, and her lip was split. Dried blood coated her chin.

Sean's heart almost stopped when he took in the rest of her body. Scattered amongst the scrapes and cuts and her tattoo was bruised areas with what looked like teeth marks. Someone had bitten Mak repeatedly.

Sean almost lost what was left of his sanity as he called out Mak's name over and over. Mak never responded.

As Brian was returning from the car, he heard a horse whinny. The sound was followed by the cabin door banging open. A man's voice rang out in anguish, repeating Mak's name several times.

Brian turned and fled back up the slope to the car. Just as he was preparing to back out onto the main road, a pickup truck screeched to a halt to block his path. Two men got out, both wearing sidearms. Brian was instructed to get out of the car. Knowing his father would handle the situation for him, Brian complied with the request. Brian found it somewhat ironic when his hands were bound behind his back using his own duct tape.

Removing the tape from Mak's wrists and ankles, Sean wrapped her lovingly in the bedsheet and lifted her in his arms. As he reached the door, Mak mumbled, "I love you so much, Sean," but she never opened her eyes.

Sean cried all the way up the dirty snow-splotched path towards the gate where Mike had promised to meet him.

Two state troopers and an ambulance had joined the truck blocking the gate and Brian's escape by this point. Brian was read his rights, the duct tape was replaced with handcuffs, and he was escorted to the cruiser. He got his last look at Mak as Brian watched from the rear window. Her sheet-wrapped body was cradled in the arms of a cowboy, and it looked like he was sobbing. Then, after the rescue personal relieved the man of his burden, he slumped to the ground.

Brian thought, "What's he crying about? He doesn't have the right. Mak is my property."

Then the cruiser with Brian, handcuffed in the rear seat, pulled away.

CHAPTER 34

SEAN felt a profound sense of loss when the emergency medical technicians relieved him of Mak's unconscious body. Dropping to his knees on the hard-packed snowy scrabble of the dirt road, he hung his head as his tears turned to torturous sobs of anguish. The vision of Mak lying on the cot in the cabin was playing on a loop inside his head. Turning to the side, Sean emptied his stomach as he was tortured by the thought of all those bite marks covering her torso.

John rushed over to Sean as Mike helped the EMT load Mak's gurney into the ambulance. Mike asked and answered a few questions, shook the EMT's hand, and closed the door after the man climbed inside. Then, as the ambulance signaled to pull out onto the main road, Mike gave the vehicle a sharp slap to send it on its way.

Going to stand beside Sean, Mike glanced over at John worriedly. Then clamped his hand on his best friend's shoulder.

"Come on, Sean. We have to go, man. They're taking Mak to the Emergency Department at the Trauma Center. The EMT said it would be a good idea to grab Mak's purse before we head on over, so we'll be able to answer some of their questions, such as blood type and nearest relative. Any information we can supply will make it easier for the hospital staff to give her the help she'll need."

When Sean didn't respond, John grabbed him under one arm, Mike grabbed him under the other, and they hauled him to his feet. Then they double marched him to the truck. Finally, Sean seemed to come to his senses as John tried to help him into the cab.

Coming out of his fugue, he said, "He hurt her bad, John. He hurt her really bad."

"I know, buddy, but Mak's going to be okay. The hospital will fix her up in no time at all. You wait and see. Come on. Let's go so you can be there when Mak wakes up. I'm sure the first thing she'll want to see is your ugly mug."

When they got back to the ranch, Mike stopped at the main house to update the family while Sean ran to the cabin to retrieve Mak's purse.

As the men were preparing to leave, an unfamiliar car stopped in front of the ranch office. The driver's door opened, and a woman stepped out. She stood frowning at the ranch office door, then took a look around her. When she noticed the men standing near the truck, she made her way toward them.

"Hi, there, gentlemen. I'm lookin' for a friend of mine. Maybe you all can help me? She goes by Mak."

"Who are you?" Mike was flabbergasted. This woman looked so much like Mak. She could almost be Mak's twin.

"Well, I'd like to plead the 5th and keep that to myself until I speak to Mak, but by the expression on all three of your faces, I don't think you're gonna let me see Mak otherwise. My name is Jaymiee Joanna Johnston. Everybody calls me Jo. I'm *Circle R's* new hire. Mak's just been fillin' in." Then she held out her hand to shake.

When all three men just stood there looking stupefied, Jo lowered the proffered hand and said sheepishly, "Gentlemen, if you could see the stunned looks on your faces. Can I see Mak now? I suppose you all will have a bunch of questions for us later on, and we'll be happy to answer them after Mak and I talk privately."

Mike took Jo by the arm, turned to Sean and John, and said, "Let's take the car."

Jo tried to resist. Confused, she wasn't going anywhere with three strangers who looked like they were on a mission. "Where are we goin'? I really need to see my friend, so I can't just go runnin' off. Mak sent me a text that we only use when we're in trouble. The minute I got it I hopped on a jet. Please let me see Mak," she worriedly demanded.

"Get in the car Miss Johnston, or whoever you are. You have a lot of explaining to do. We can talk on the way. Mak's in the hospital. Let's go."

Sean was confused and getting angry. If this was Jaymiee Joanna Johnston, who the heck was the woman calling herself Mak? He didn't like the idea that he might have been played for a fool.

As Mike steered the car out of the ranch entrance and headed for the hospital, he took his eyes off the road briefly to study the worried face of Jaymiee Joanna Johnston. She looked so much like Mak. It was no wonder they were able to switch places.

"Before we start, let me introduce the three of us. I'm Mike Willis, owner of the *Circle R*. The two men in the back seat are Sean Hannity, the ranch foreman. He's the one that looks like he wants to kill somebody if he doesn't get some answers pretty soon. The other one is John Marshall."

Jo nodded at them, each in turn, and said, "How do you do, gentlemen. Nice to meet you." Her eyes lingered on John Marshall a little longer than the other two men. Then she turned her attention back to Mike Willis.

"Answer just one question, then you can explain yourself while we're waiting on word of Mak's condition," Mike requested.

"What question is that?" Jo asked. "And what the heck happened to Mak? You all are scarin' me a lot."

Sean interrupted before Mike could respond, "If you're Jaymiee Joanna Johnston, then who the heck did I fall in love with?" he demanded.

Jo stared at the man wide-eyed. “You’re in love with Mak? Well heck! God does answer prayers, Mister, and you look just like him. Which one are you, again? I’ve forgotten.”

Sean was getting angrier by the minute. “Name’s Sean Hannity. What in blue blazes are you talking about? Who do I look like, and who the hell is Mak?”

“Well, Mak’s white knight from her dreams, of course.” Jo pronounced, then looked at Sean suspiciously. “Please tell me you don’t ride a big black horse? Cause, you know, that would just be creepy.”

“Okay, sister. Leave my horse Blackie out of this. You’re really beginning to piss me off. This is the last time I’m going to ask. Who the hell is Mak?”

“Oh, my God, you do ride a black horse. Mak’s dream came true. Mak was saving herself for you all these years. She was a virgin until about six months ago, just waitin’ on the studmuffin cowboy in her dreams to show up. Then Brian dashed her dreams to smithereens. I gotta tell ya, she cried buckets when she lost her baby ’cause he pushed her down the stairs. A baby she was carryin’ because he’d raped her. Brian's a real bastard! Anyway, Mak's my very best friend in the whole wide world, Mister. She's my sister by another Ma and Pa. Her name is Makailyn Elsbeth Jamieson," Jo admitted. "Now, please tell me what's wrong with her. Why's she in the hospital?"

All three men had gone ramrod stiff when Jo mentioned that Mak had been raped. All three started talking over each other and demanding answers until finally Sean slammed his hand down on the console between the two front seats and yelled, "Enough already. Who the fuck is Brian?"

Before Jo could respond, Mike said, "Save it. We're here."

Piling out of the car, they raced across the macadam and into the hospital through the emergency room entrance. The person staffing the desk stared in astonishment as all four adults rushed her and began demanding answers all at once.

"Please, one at a time and a little less vocally. There are people here who are sick and injured," she demanded, in a pleasant tone of voice, of course.

Mike stepped forward, "A young woman was brought in by ambulance. Her paperwork will say Jaymiee Joanna Johnston, but that's not who she really is. I guess her real name is Makailyn Elsbeth Jamieson."

"Okay, if all four of you would kindly go sit quietly over there, I'll see what I can find out. Are any of you related to the patient, by the way?" she asked.

"Well, I'm the closest thing she has to a relative, really. Mak doesn't really have anyone. Her momma ran off when she was eight, and her daddy was killed in a hit-and-run when she was twelve. So, my parents kinda' just took her in, 'cause she had nowhere to go after that. Mak and I've been together since first grade, so we're like sisters."

The woman just stared at Jo with an overwhelmed expression. So, Sean stepped forward, "The patient is my fiancée. I'm responsible for her. I'd really appreciate it if you could find out the patient's condition. We'll be just over there, waiting."

Then he grabbed Jo by the arm and steered her toward a group of chairs in the corner out of hearing of the other people waiting for their turns for medical assistance. Jo's mouth hung open all the way.

She was dumbfounded over the man's admission that he was Mak's fiancé.

"Before you start from the beginning, you said Mak lost her baby? How long ago was that, exactly?" Sean needed to know. Maybe he wasn't going to be a father after all.

"Well, just before she left to come here, so maybe three months give or take. Why?" Jo asked.

"She told me she was two months pregnant. That's why. Start from the very beginning. Don't leave anything out, and I mean anything," Sean angrily demanded.

"Well, okay. You mean like from the very beginnin'? Cause this could take a while," Jo admitted.

Mike interjected, "I think we have the time."

Jo heaved a beleaguered sigh and started to talk, "Alrighty then. From the beginnin'."

So, while they waited on word of Mak's condition, Jo told them how she and Mak met in first grade and became very best friends. She talked about how Mak's mom was a real piece of work who cheated on her husband. Then how the woman ran off with a traveling salesman, leaving poor Mak motherless when Mak was at a vulnerable age. How Mak's daddy was left lying by the side of the road, and poor Mak and the school bus driver were the ones to find the body.

"The child welfare lady tried real hard to find Mak's momma, Mister, so's she wouldn't end up a victim of the system. My Ma and Pa took pity on Mak and brought her home to live with us. Even though they already had eight of their own, they took Mak in. That's how she came to be my sister from another Ma and Pa," Jo concluded.

After taking a deep breath, Jo continued with, "I did my best to look out for Mak. But she always had her head in the clouds dreamin' about her studmuffin white knight in armor ridin' that big ol' black horse."

"We graduated from *NOA* together and worked the *Rockin' R* together too until I made the mistake of thinkin' I was in love with a jackass from Philadelphia, Pennsylvania. That's how she came to be engaged to Brian."

All three men just stared at Jo with confused looks on their faces.

"Wait!" Sean demanded. "You've lost me. So, you're the one who followed some guy to Philadelphia? I gotta tell you, I'm confused."

"Well, I can see I've gone and befuddled the heck out of you all. Sorry about that. It's like this. I brought a fella home with me, by the name of Jack Hamilton. I was visitin' my folks out in California. Jack was sittin' next to me on my flight back to Oklahoma. Jack was goin' to visit his good friend Brian. That's Brian Alexander Hillhouse III. A pretentious name if ever I heard one. So, since Mak never left the ranch much, I made her go along. We were supposed to help the rich bastard unpack. He'd just bought this big old place on Lake Eufaula. That house is something else. Anyway, Mak ended up engaged to Brian after only one week."

When Jo noticed the angry look on Sean's face, she said, "Now hold up, Mister. Don't go gettin' any wrong ideas that Mak's a gold digger or anything like that. Like I said, Mak was waitin' for her cowboy from her dreams. I'm ashamed to say that the whole damn thing is my fault. I told Mak I was goin' to live with Jack in Philadelphia. I think she only agreed to the engagement because she thought it would ease my mind that there'd be someone to take care of her. But she did tell the man she'd only say yes on two conditions."

"Okay, I'll bite. What were the conditions?" Sean demanded to know.

"Six months engagement and no sex. I think Mak was still hopin' her happily ever after cowboy was coming to rescue her and carry her off on his black horse. She'd saved herself so very long for that cowboy. Mak tried to hold out for a year's engagement, but Brian wasn't havin' any of that. So, I left with Jack a week later, and I'm ashamed to say that I didn't keep my promise. Mak and I were supposed to text each day and *FaceTime* and stuff, but I was so caught up in my own plans with Jack. We kinda' lost touch. In the meantime, I found out that my happily ever after with Jack was just all smoke and mirrors. When I got my job offer from Eloise at the *Circle R* here in Montana, I left Philadelphia. Eloise told me I didn't need to be here until the end of September. So, I headed for Oklahoma to catch up with Mak, then was plannin' to visit my folks in California. I got a text while collectin' my luggage at the airport in Oklahoma City. Mak and I promised each other a long time ago that we would send a one-word text message if we were ever in dire trouble. Then the other would know to come runnin'. That word is "Savior."

"I found Mak in the hospital there. She was all beat to shit with a concussion, tons of bruises including ribs, broken fingers, and she'd lost the baby Brian got her pregnant with. She was an absolute mess over that loss. Mak loves kids so much and wants a big family. Anyway, Brian had broken his promise about the no-sex clause and raped Mak the day I took off for Philly. He'd been abusing her constantly, leavin' bite marks and bruises all over her. Brian told Mak she belonged to him like she was some kinda' property or somethin'. Mak thinks she got pregnant right then and there. That would have been the first week of June. Brian knocked her down the stairs at the end of August, so she was almost three months pregnant when she lost the baby."

"Mak was really scared. She didn't know what she was gonna do when she left the hospital. Since she'd never told Brian about the baby, she was afraid he'd beat her so bad, he'd kill her. So, I hatched a plan. She'd take my place here in Montana, so she could hide, hopin' Brian wouldn't be able to find her. Then, hopefully, he'd move on with his life. I figured you all wouldn't mind. Mak's much better at what we did for the *Rockin' R* than me anyway. So that's how she came to be workin' for you. I came runnin' when Mak sent me another "Savior" text last night. Got the last seat on the flight out, too."

"What does this guy, Brian, look like?" Mike interrupted.

"Brian's tall with broad shoulders. He has dirty-blond hair that he wears slicked back in a wave, piercing blue eyes, a patrician nose, a gently rounded jawline, and his lips are thin. They give him an arrogant appearance. Why?" Jo questioned.

John stared at Mike wide-eyed, "That's the guy the cops hauled away, Mike."

"What guy are you talking about?" Jo demanded to know. "Why are we sittin' in an emergency room waitin' to hear about my best friend's condition? Did she fall off a horse or out of a hayloft or somethin'?"

Just then, their conversation was interrupted when the lady from the admittance desk came over, "If you'll come with me, please, the doctor would like to speak with you."

Sean, Mike, John, and Jo followed and were shown to a small waiting room. They were told the doctor would arrive shortly to speak with them privately.

Sean paced back and forth across the limited floor space while they waited. When he glanced at the others' faces at one point, he noticed the way John was staring at Jo and thought, "Oh, fuck. So, here we go again."

When the doctor entered, Sean was asked to take a seat. The doctor shook hands with everyone present and introduced herself, "My name is Dr. Melinda Kurtis. Before I begin, there seems to be some confusion as to the true identity of my patient. I'm hoping one of you can clear that up?"

Jo spoke up, "Her real name is Makailyn Elsbeth Jamieson." Then Jo proceeded to spell Mak's name as Dr. Kurtis wrote it down.

Dr. Kurtis made some other notations and then continued, "Very good. I'll have her chart updated. Because of her condition, Miss Jamieson has been moved to the ICU. She suffers from a severe concussion caused by what I can only assume were multiple blows to the same region of the back of her head. The patient is currently unconscious. As to lesser injuries, she also suffers from hypothermia and a forearm fracture of her left arm. It is a stable, simple, isolated fracture of the ulna that has been treated with a cast. There are multiple cuts and scrapes which have been cleaned. Two open wounds near the knee joint required stitches, and dressings were applied. A deep laceration on her foot was treated and bandaged as well. It also appears that she had rough intercourse causing vaginal tearing. There are numerous bruised areas on her torso where she was bitten repeatedly. The bite marks were treated, and she was given a tetanus shot. Now…"

Sean jumped to his feet and interrupted, "Dr. Kurtis, are you telling us that Mak was raped?"

"It appears so. We can't be certain until we've spoken with the patient. However, we took the necessary precautions, and a rape kit was utilized. There's one other thing, however. The young lady is about two months pregnant. I was told that one of you is the fiancé?"

"That would be me," Sean admitted. "I'm the baby's father."

That got a gasp out of Jo, who looked at Sean quizzically.

"Very well," the doctor continued. "You'll only be allowed to sit with the patient for five minutes at a time. As soon as there is any change in her condition, you'll be given an update. One of the nurses will come to get you when you can see the patient. Remember, only one at a time. Thank you." Then Dr. Kurtis left the four of them sitting there.

Sean jumped back to his feet and began to pace again. "I'm going to kill the fucker with my bare hands!" he kept mumbling under his breath.

Mike stood and grabbed Sean by the shoulders so that Sean was forced to stop. "The man's in police custody, Sean. Don't do anything stupid. You have Mak to worry about, and you're going to be a father. She'll need all of your strength to put this behind her. So, get your act together. I know you. You're a good man. Be Mak's white knight on a black horse and take care of her."

Sean just nodded in understanding and sat down. Then, splaying his legs, he hung his head between them while trying to calm his raging emotions.

"Okay," Mike surveyed the others. "This is how we're going to work this. John and I'll take an *Uber* back to the ranch to update the rest of the family and help Tom and Jake with the chores. It's a good thing the boys are on Thanksgiving break and are available to help out. I'll leave the car here for you. Here's the key, Sean. Jo can stay here with you and keep you from doing anything stupid. Emi, Elli, Anna, and Jess will want to take turns coming to sit by Mak's bedside until she gets better. Jo, I'll get Mak's cabin straightened up. We'll talk about what will happen with your job once Mak is out of the woods. You can stay in the cabin and do your job until we get this mess all figured out. Sean, you're on paid vacation until Mak is ready to come home. Sound like a plan, everybody?"

When they all agreed, Mike grabbed Sean in a bro-style hug and whispered against Sean's ear, "Hang in there. Everything will work out. Go be Mak's knight in shining armor and make her proud."

Sean swallowed convulsively and said he'd try.

CHAPTER 35

THE nurse came to escort Sean to Mak's room soon after Mike and John left the hospital. Pulling a chair close to the side of the bed, Sean gingerly took ahold of Mak's right hand and kissed it tenderly. Then he began to talk to her about his plans for after they got married.

"I'm going to give you at least six babies, darlin'. They'll be the best of both of us. I promise to be a hands-on dad, except for the dirty diapers, of course. I want no part of that. Sean chuckled at the admission, "I've dealt with a lot of disgusting things working on a ranch, but I can't handle that 'cause it'll make me puke."

"I've already talked to Mike about how much we love each other, Mak. I told him about the baby, too. Then, I asked him about buying in on ownership of the ranch. He said he'd talk it over with Tyler, Elli, and Emi. Mike also mentioned Tyler's thinking about adding Ferguson's ranch to the *Circle R* holdings. That's another forty thousand acres of prime rangeland, plus the various buildings. Mike said we can live in Ferguson's ranch house if that happens. We'd have our own place, Mak. Somewhere just for our little family, you, me, and our baby. Somewhere private where I can make love to you and work on those other five kids."

As Sean continued to fill her in on all the plans he had in mind, Mak began to shake uncontrollably. Terrified, Sean raced to the door and yelled for help. Shoved from the room, Sean paced the hall while the physician and nurses stabilized her.

Dr. Kurtis guided Sean back to the waiting room, where Jo listened in horror as the female physician described what had happened to her best friend.

"We believe Miss Jamieson may have what's called an intracranial hematoma. That's a collection of blood within the skull. It's most commonly caused by the rupture of a blood vessel within the brain or trauma like the blows she sustained from her fall. The blood collection can be within the brain tissue or underneath the skull, pressing on the brain. She suffered a minor seizure, but we were able to stabilize her rapidly. She never stopped breathing, so there shouldn't be any harm to the fetus."

"How do you fix the hematoma?" Sean asked worriedly.

Dr. Melinda Kurtis placed her hand on Sean's arm to offer some form of comfort. She knew that having a loved one being unconscious was one of the most frightening things that could happen. But while a patient was in that state, their body worked to get them out of it.

So, the doctor told Sean, "With regards to a hematoma, they usually resolve themselves. Sometimes surgery is required. We'll continue to monitor her condition. Only time will tell. Try to remain positive. We're doing everything possible. You may want to go home and get some rest in the interim."

Jo and Sean said, "I'm not leaving," simultaneously.

Dr. Kurtis nodded and said, "Very well. We'll keep you apprised of any changes in her condition," before taking her leave.

After Dr. Kurtis left, Sean held Jo as she sobbed out her anguish because she considered herself responsible for Mak's current situation.

“She wouldn’t be in this fix if it weren’t for me, Sean. I’m the one who brought Jack home with me. He’s the reason Mak met Brian. It makes me sick that monster got his hands on my sister from another Ma and Pa.”

“Well, at least he can’t hurt her anymore since he’s in jail,” Sean responded.

CHAPTER 36

BRIAN had never been on this side of the booking process and didn't really handle this type of law, anyway. Brian's expertise lay in corporate law, not criminal. Not knowing what to expect, he remained calm. He wasn't particularly concerned. His father would handle everything, and he'd be out of jail in no time flat.

While the officers registered and entered the criminal charges against him, they compiled Brian's personal information by asking Brian for identification, including his name, birth date, and physical characteristics. Instead of answering, Brian handed over his Oklahoma driver's license.

Brian thought about Mak while he was being humiliated with a full-body strip search. He would punish her for this. Then a general health screening was done to be certain Brian didn't need any medical attention. DNA samples were also collected. Any personal items, including his clothing, wallet, keys, and cell phone, were confiscated. Brian changed into a jail uniform and was told his personal effects would be returned when or if he was released. His fingerprints would be cross-referenced to see if they matched those taken from the cabin by the pond.

Brian was confident his fingerprints would also be cross-referenced to the police database to see if he had any outstanding warrants. Waste of the taxpayers' time. They wouldn't find anything against him. Any trouble he'd ever gotten into had been taken care of by his father.

Then he was allowed to make his one phone call. Brian called his father and told him that he'd been arrested. Brian Alexander Hillhouse II told his son to sit tight and not to answer any questions. When his call was concluded, Brian was placed in a holding cell to wait.

Hillhouse II had a friend who specialized in criminal law who had attended the same college and belonged to the same fraternity. Being the luckiest bastard on the planet, his son only had to wait an hour for his legal representation to show up. Hillhouse II's friend just happened to live in Billings, Montana.

After being allowed to confer with his client, the police showed Brian and his attorney to a room with a metal table and very uncomfortable metal chairs. Then the officers began to ask questions about what had happened at the scene of Brian's arrest.

The attorney had already advised Brian to keep his mouth shut. Frustrated by Brian's lack of cooperation, one of the policemen showed Brian back to his cell, where he'd await a hearing before a judge the following day. Once they were alone, the attorney told Brian not to worry because he knew the judge and the prosecutor very well. The judge was a fellow fraternity member. The prosecutor was interested in running for governor and wanted the endorsement of the senator of Montana. That man just happened to be the attorney's brother.

"I'll speak to your father and arrange a conference call, including the judge and the prosecutor. I'll present our case at the hearing and argue for your release. The prosecutor will agree with the request, and you'll be freed to continue with your plans. However, I suggest you avoid any further contact with the party in question. Let your father handle the retrieval of your property once she's released from the hospital."

Brian asked the man to give his father a message thanking him for his help in this matter. "Tell him he'll be a grandfather soon."

The following day, Brian was shown to a courtroom where he was supposed to receive a hearing to arrange for bail to be set. However, after reviewing the details of the charges against the defendant, listening to Brian's account of what occurred, and the attorney's summation, the prosecutor agreed to the request for dismissal. So, the judge ruled that there was no clear evidence of any guilt, and Brian was allowed to go free.

Brian Alexander Hillhouse III descended the courthouse steps with his legal counsel by his side. They were greeted by a crowd of newspaper reporters. There was the flash of bulbs from cameras as they were bombarded by a cacophony of questions. A broad grin stretched Brian's thin lips. His father had come through for him again.

Then as Brian's attorney raised his hands to signal that he wouldn't allow any questions, two shots rang out. Mass panic ensued, and the crowd scattered like a room full of cockroaches after someone had turned on a light.

Several police officers, who were on their way to give testimony in a court trial, saw the whole thing and tackled the shooter. The young man was handcuffed and read his rights before being dragged away.

The attorney stood on the courthouse steps, stunned beyond belief at what had just happened. He'd never lost a client in this fashion. Taking a handkerchief from his suit pocket, he wiped the blood splatter from his face and scrubbed at the spots on his expensive suit.

As the scattered reporters rushed forward for photographs of the victim, the attorney stepped aside and placed a call on his cell phone to a number in Oklahoma City, Oklahoma.

When the call was answered on the second ring, all he said was, "The courthouse steps are overrun with reporters and camera crews, so I don't have much time to talk. Brian and I were exiting the courthouse when the sounds of gunshots erupted. I'm fairly certain that your son is dead." He listened and then said, "He was shot twice, once to the head and the other through the throat." Listening again, he promised to make the necessary arrangements to ship the body back to Oklahoma once it was released. Then he hung up.

CHAPTER 37

SEAN and Jo had taken turns all night and the next day sitting by Mak's bedside, talking to her, and reminding her how much they loved her.

They finally decided to return to the ranch around 9:00 p.m. for a good meal and a shower. When Sean parked in front of the office, John stepped out and helped Jo from the car. Then he escorted her to her cabin. Mike waylaid Sean and dragged him inside. Tyler and Tim were sitting there waiting for him.

"Is this a lynching party or something," Sean grumbled. "Or do you need to let me go because I won't be pulling my weight around here, Mike?" He was in a foul mood from lack of sleep and concern over Mak's continued failure to wake up.

Tyler said, "Sit down, Sean. We've something you need to hear."

When Sean didn't move to do as requested, the other three men proceeded to box him in, and Mike placed a restraining hand on Sean's shoulder. Once he'd lowered himself onto the chair beside the desk, Tyler said, "The state troopers were here earlier with some news."

Sean looked at each man in turn. What he saw in their return gazes had his stomach roiling. "Just spit it out, Tyler."

"They had to let Brian Hillhouse go, Sean. The judge said there wasn't enough evidence to hold him. Hillhouse was represented by a high-powered attorney, who made it look like his client was being railroaded. Hillhouse said under oath that the gate was already open. That Mak met him there for some consensual sex. He said they were into kink, which accounted for the duct tape and the bite marks. He said Mak was conscious when he left her. Hillhouse's attorney went so far as to suggest that it was you who hit Mak in the head when you discovered that she'd cheated on you."

Sean's vision became a red haze as the vein in his forehead began to pulse. Filled with rage, he tried to assimilate the bullshit he'd just heard. Finally, he let out a roar and pushed to his feet when Tyler told him that he was being accused of hurting Mak. He was going to hunt that bastard, Brian Hillhouse, to the ends of the earth if he had to, and the man was going to pay dearly for ever laying a hand on Mak.

It took all three men, Mike, Tyler, and Tim, to subdue Sean. He'd nearly dragged them to the door before they were able to wrestle him to the floor.

Out of breath, Mike finally got out, "Do we need to tie you up or lock you up until you come to your senses, Sean? You aren't going to be any good for Mak this way."

Sean screamed as spittle flew from his mouth, "Damn it! I can't live without her, Mike. The first time I touched her it was like I was struck by a lightning bolt. I've lived every minute of my life since for her. She's my reason to get up every day and my reason to breathe. But Mak will never be able to live another day of her life without fear of that man trying to get his hands on her so he can hurt her again. The man's a sick bastard. Somebody has to stop him."

"Well, then just calm down and listen because Tyler wasn't finished. And stop screaming, for God's sake. You're hurting our ears."

Tim gave Sean a hand up, then rested that hand on Sean's shoulder in solidarity. As the men turned to Tyler, Mike said, "Tell him the rest, Tyler."

"Quite apparently, Mak isn't the only woman Brian Hillhouse has brutalized. News of his incarceration made the headlines of the local papers while he was being held in a jail cell in Billings. The story was picked up and televised nationally and then splashed across the internet. To make a long story short, when a grinning Hillhouse posed on the steps with his attorney as they were leaving the courthouse, he was shot to death."

Sean was so shocked at the news, he gasped out, "Who shot him, Tyler?"

"Turns out Hillhouse raped a young woman named Millie Patterson about eleven months ago in the storage room of a bar in Oklahoma City and got her pregnant. The poor girl decided to go home to her family in Wyoming to have the baby. Unfortunately, Millie and her baby died during childbirth. It was her distraught twin brother who shot Hillhouse in retribution," Tyler replied.

Sean just shook his head, too stunned to comment. Finally, looking around at each of these men he considered a friend, he said, "Thanks for letting me know. I have to get back to the hospital. I don't want Mak waking up alone."

CHAPTER 38

AND so the long days of waiting began. Waiting for Mak to come back to Sean's arms where she fit just perfectly.

Sean never left her side unless chased out by Dr. Melinda Kurtis or the nurses that tended to Mak's needs. He watched as Mak was given sponge baths. After, the nurse allowed Sean to rub soothing lotions into the skin of Mak's hands, feet, legs, and arms. No inch of her skin went unworshipped if it was exposed to his touch. He ran his hands lovingly over the bite marks and bruises, praying that they would soon fade from her delicate skin.

He assisted when her bed linens needed to be changed. Then he'd plump the pillow just so, kiss Mak's brow tenderly, and place the pillow back beneath her head.

After manipulating Mak's arms and legs, the therapist showed Sean how to help. First, Sean pressed a kiss to each limb before working to keep Mak's muscles from atrophying.

When no one else was present, Sean talked. He told Mak everything. Even things about himself that he had never shared with another living soul. All the pain, sorrow, loss, love, hopes, and dreams of his thirty-five years. Mak was privy to it all.

Jo sat with Sean most evenings after work, and Sean listened to every word that Jo had to say. Sean learned all about Mak's and Jo's lives as children, about Mak's runaway mother and the loving father who had died too young, leaving Mak all alone in the world. About the two boys in high school who had tried to rape Mak in the boy's locker room and how Jo had come to her best friend's rescue. That attack was the birth of the word Mak and Jo created if one of them was ever in trouble and desperately needed the other. Sean laughed when Jo told him about how she'd berated the boy that left Mak sitting all alone at the junior prom and then slapped the girl he'd been kissing for daring to call Mak names.

Sean came to admire Jo. She indeed was Mak's "*Savior*."

Thanksgiving was a subdued affair, with everyone gathered around the dining room table in the main ranch house. Mike presided over the scrumptious meal that Tyler had prepared. A special prayer was said for the woman lying in a hospital bed. Mak had come to mean so much to all of them.

Plans for the joint anniversary party that would have been held that weekend for Mike and Emi, Tyler and Elli, and Tim and Jeannie were placed on hold. Instead, all three couples, who shared the same anniversary day, agreed to wait until Mak could be there to share in the celebration.

As the waiting continued, Elli made up an excel spreadsheet containing scheduled time off so that all of the adults at the *Circle R* could keep Sean company as he watched over Mak. It was designed to conform to everyone's ranch duties.

Alone in the office when Elli brought it in, Tyler came out from behind the desk to greet her, "What's up, sweet girl?" Then he walked over to the office door, threw the latch, and closed the window blinds.

"I just brought the spreadsheet I created to tack up on the bulletin board." When she noticed, Elli questioned, "What are you doing, Tyler?"

It didn't take Tyler any time at all to show her. Divesting Elli of her jeans and panties, Tyler lifted her into his arms. Then he eased her onto the edge of the office desk. Slipping his fingers between her folds, Tyler pleasured Elli until she was wet and wanting. After lowering his pants and boxer briefs, he entered Elli with one hard thrust. Knowing they might not have much time, his strokes continued to be hard and fast until Elli reached between them to rub her clit. Her orgasm slammed into her soon after. She took Tyler over with her, and he continued to work through her spasms until he was totally spent. Afterward, he slumped down onto his wife until their breathing had slowed to normal. Then he kissed Elli soundly before pulling out.

As Elli lay there staring up at the ceiling with her legs dangling off the side of the desk, she started to laugh.

Tyler looked at her quizzically. Then, sounding slightly offended, he asked Elli, "Am I getting that bad that you find our lovemaking amusing, now?"

Grabbing Tyler by the hand, Elli gave it a reassuring squeeze. "Oh, Tyler. I didn't mean to upset you. You're as amazing as ever. I'm laughing because you've forgotten something again. But because I've upset you, I'll be making it up to you later," she said with a wink.

"Oh, Shit!" was Tyler's response when he realized what she was referring to. Leaning down, Tyler took Elli's mouth in a searing kiss. "God, I love you so much. Are you angry with me? It's all your fault, you know. You're so damn beautiful. I really can't help myself. Every time I see you, I get as hard as a rock. You're lucky we don't have twenty kids instead of ten. And just exactly how do you intend to make it up to me?" he asked as he wiggled his eyebrows suggestively.

Elli's giggle was cut off as Tyler lifted her from the desk. The doorknob had rattled, so they scrambled to get dressed. Then, Elli ran back over to the bulletin board and busied herself straightening up the items pinned there. Tyler quickly tucked in his shirt and went over to unlock the door.

"Hey, Mike. What's up?" Tyler said as he walked back to the desk.

Mike took in the blush on his daughter's face and her slightly disheveled appearance as he closed the office door behind him and tried hard not to grin. Mike noticed a scrap of material poking out from under the desk as he walked towards it. Hiding that grin became almost impossible.

Elli greeted him, "Hi, Daddy. I'm just straightening up the bulletin board. I've added the schedule I worked out for everyone to spend time at the hospital."

Mike responded, "Um-hmm."

Tyler tried to busy himself with the contents of the desk drawer. Mike had never seen his son-in-law blush, but there was always a first time for everything. This was going to be fun. Mike leaned down and snagged the blue fabric with two fingers. Then he dangled the panties in front of Tyler's face.

"Is this what you're looking for in that drawer, Tyler?" he teased.

If Tyler had been a magician, he couldn't have made those thongs disappear any faster. He was lucky he didn't slam his fingers in the desk drawer when he slammed it shut.

Mike leaned down close to Tyler's ear so that only he could hear, "I hope you remembered to use protection this time? Oh, and don't forget to retrieve your wife's panties from that desk drawer. You wouldn't want one of the other guys to find them."

Tyler just hung his head.

Mike chuckled, went over to give his daughter a quick hug, and gave his son-in-law a salute as he left the building.

As soon as the door was closed, Tyler retrieved a specific piece of lacey blue fabric from the desk drawer. Elli eyed him as he gave the panties a sniff and then stuffed them in his shirt pocket.

"What do you intend to do with them, Tyler?" He just gave her a smile and a kiss and then sent her on her way.

He planned to carry his wife's scent with him for the remainder of the day. Crap, Elli hadn't told him how she planned to make it up to him later. Hopefully, it was one of her blowjobs. He was up for that; no pun intended.

After everyone discovered the spreadsheet, they lovingly joked about it behind Elli's back. They all knew how much Elli dearly loved her spreadsheets. However, Jo ignored Elli's timetable and spent the most time with Sean at the hospital. Mike, Emi, Tim, Jeannie, Elli, Tyler, Alex, Anna, John, Tom, and Jake, adhered to Elli's schedule unless circumstances prevented them from doing so.

Sean noticed that Jo usually arrived with John in tow and was amused by how they kept stealing glances at each other when they thought the other wasn't looking.

Jake usually brought Jessica with him, holding hands as they walked down the corridor towards Mak's room. Sean caught them kissing once. He sure was happy not to be Tyler. Then Sean remembered that Tyler had jokingly mentioned that Jess wasn't allowed to think about boys until she was at least thirty years old. Sean wondered if he should take Jake aside and say something to him.

Jessica was turning into a beautiful young woman. Intelligent and poised, she was now fourteen years old and already 5'7" tall. Sean had seen a picture of Rick Whrite with his grandmother. Jess looked a lot like her great-grandma and was probably going to be just as tall.

Jake was eighteen and worshiped the ground Jess walked on. Sean wished Tyler luck with imposing that moratorium on no boyfriends until the girl turned thirty.

Sean was finally convinced to come back to work. "You're not doing Mak or yourself any good sitting here day after day, Sean, plus we need your help," Mike told him.

As the days turned into a couple of weeks, Dr. Frank Kelly was brought in to handle Mak's pregnancy. An obstetrician who was well known for managing high-risk pregnancies, he had been practicing in Billings for over thirty years. Dr. Kelly was also well-respected in the community. Pleased that Mak's body hadn't rejected her unborn child, he spoke candidly with Sean. Dr. Kelly told Sean that Mak's body would continue to nourish the fetus. So, they discussed the possible plan to keep the baby in until full-term and then perform a C-section if Mak didn't regain consciousness.

After Dr. Kelly had taken his leave, Sean rested his hand on Mak's tummy. He was worried about how their lives would change when the baby was born. He was afraid that he might be doing it all alone if Mak didn't find her way back to him.

Nearing Christmas. Sean spent as much time as possible by Mak's side. Otherwise, he was kept busy checking, feeding, and watering the herd to ensure their wellbeing during the brutal weather.

Sean noticed that things seemed to have heated up between John and Jo to the point where he wouldn't have been the least bit surprised to hear about an engagement announcement. "Good for them," thought Sean. "Someone deserves a happily ever after."

It was late on Christmas Eve, and the hospital corridors were quiet. The nurse had already completed her rounds and was currently at the nurse's station. Sean was alone with his thoughts and the woman who held his heart and soul.

They had removed Mak's cast earlier in the day, and the physiotherapist had begun exercises to improve the flexibility of her arm. Sean was told that strength and function exercises would follow as soon as the patient was conscious.

Squeezing Mak's hand, Sean kissed her fingers tenderly. Then he started to cry, "Come back to me, darlin'. I miss your sweet smile and the way you say my name when we make love. You need to be here when our son or daughter is born, Mak. I can't do this all alone. We both need you."

Laying his head on the mattress, he planned to close his eyes for just a moment to rest. Instead, being emotionally exhausted, Sean fell asleep.

When Sean felt fingers threading through his hair, he thought he was dreaming. When the fingers snagged, and his hair was gently pulled. Sean wondered, “What the heck? Have I been coming here for so long that one of the nurses is getting friendly?”

Lifting his head, the hand fell away but then grabbed hold of his hand as it rested on the mattress alongside Mak’s body. Astonished, Sean stared at that hand, not willing to believe what he was seeing. It wasn’t possible, was it? When the fingers of that hand gave a gentle squeeze, Sean looked up in shock. Staring back at him was a beautiful pair of light brown eyes that were flecked with gold.

When Sean said, “Welcome back, darlin’. I’ve missed you so much!” Mak’s forehead creased, but she didn’t seem to be able to focus. The bottom fell out of Sean’s stomach when Mak shook her head no after he asked, “Can you see me, Mak?”

Leaping from the chair, it fell over in a crash as Sean rushed from the room. Running towards the nurse’s station, he yelled all the way. “She’s awake! She’s awake! Come quick. I don’t think she can see anything.”

It was 12:01 a.m. Mak waking up was Sean's almost Christmas miracle. Only one thing would have made it perfect.

CHAPTER 39

AND so the long hard haul towards recovery, but in one respect, Mak was very fortunate, and the doctors were amazed. Mak awoke from her slumber, fully cognitive. She knew where she was and why she was there. When able to speak, Mak said it was like waking up from a deep sleep. Nothing felt any different except that now she could only see shadows.

Not having eaten or drunk anything while she was unconscious, Mak had to be reintroduced to those things. She would later say that totally sucked.

Mak spent another week in the ICU, then was moved to a regular unit. She could now have more than one visitor at a time, even though they had been lenient in the ICU so that Sean wasn't sitting there keeping watch all by himself. However, visitation was still held to a minimum so as not to tire Mak out.

The police officers who had responded to the scene of Mak's abduction came to interview Mak when she had recovered her voice sufficiently. They needed to hear the details from her perspective.

Sean sat on the edge of Mak's bed so that he could hold her while she relayed the details of her kidnapping. She told the officers that she had no further recollection once her head was slammed against the dresser. The next thing Mak recalled was waking up on the cot in another cabin. She was able to give an accurate description of that room. Mak described how she had worked at the tape that held the gag in her mouth until it finally let go. After stumbling out the door, Mak said she'd made her way up a snow-covered slope to a rocky outcropping. Mak recalled how terrified she was as she'd tried to climb the craggy terrain. She knew that she was being pursued. The last thing she remembered was slipping as she'd pulled her foot back from the pain of stepping on a jagged edge.

One of the officers asked her if she could identify the person who had assaulted her in her room. Silent tears ran down her cheeks when she gave them that man's name. She also said that he was the one pursuing her up the slope. He had called out her name and told her she would need to be punished because she was making him angry.

Then Mak had to relive what had been perpetrated against her by that same man while still an Oklahoma resident. The police had already obtained Mak's previous hospital records from her stay at the *OSU Medical Center.* In addition, the medical personnel from the *OSU* emergency room and the night nurse named Remzie had given their depositions.

After their interview, the police thanked Mak and reminded her that this was only to conclude their case. Since her accused kidnapper was no longer among the living, there wouldn't be any need for her to appear to give testimony in a court trial.

Mak thanked the officers for their service. They wished her a speedy recovery and took their leave.

After they'd gone, Sean continued to hold Mak as she cried out her anguish over the death of Millie and her baby during childbirth. Mak told Sean that Millie was a lovely girl and didn't deserve what had happened to her.

Mak would continue to suffer from bouts of crying over the loss of Brian's baby and Brian himself. Sean couldn't understand that until Dr. Kurtis had a psychologist on staff come in to speak with Mak.

The psychologist said that Mak was suffering from survivor's guilt. The doctor suggested that Mak and Sean come for office visits to help Mak work through her feelings.

The rotation of visitors continued according to Elli's spreadsheet. Finally, however, on New Year's Day, Sean carried Mak over to her hospital windows and told her to look down. Mak did as she was told, but all she could see were shadowed shapes.

"What am I looking at, Sean?" Mak asked.

Sean began to describe the scene before them, "Well, darlin', there's snow covering the lawn, and there's a bunch of people holding a big sign. It reads, '*Happy New Year's Mak.*' There's everyone from the *Circle R* ranch, sweetheart. From right to left, Mike and Emi are holding their twins, Roger and Addie. Then Elli and Tyler are holding Patti and Annie. Alex and Anna are holding little Alex and Angus. Blair, Peggy, Logan, and Billy are being watched over by Jessica and Jake. Those two just happen to be surreptitiously holding hands. Tyler's going to have his hands full, keeping an eye on his daughter. Behind the kids are Tim, Jeannie, Sophie, Tom, John, and Jo. Everybody's waving wildly at you, darlin'."

Mak started to cry and waved back, wishing she could really see them but still thankful that she had so many people who cared about her. That would have to be enough.

Sean noticed that John grabbed Jo's hand and gave it a kiss. Sean told Mak about that, and she sighed. "Do you think they are sleeping together, Sean? Jo has such a terrible track record when it comes to men, and John's such a nice guy. I love Jo so much, but I don't want John to get hurt."

"They're both adults, Mak. I don't think we should get involved. They'll work it out. Now, back to bed with you. Dr. Kurtis said that maybe we can get you the heck out of here if you can continue to show improvement. I can't wait to get you home. Elli mentioned that she wants you to spend time with her and the kids during the day while you're recuperating. I certainly can't wait to spend our nights together."

"Elli's being very generous, but I'm just going to be in the way, you know. I'm not going to be of any assistance to her. I'll just be a burden to everyone, including you," Mak sighed and hung her head to hide the tears that were threatening to fall.

Sean tipped Mak's chin up and placed a kiss on each of her eyelids. "No more feeling sorry for yourself, Mak. Everything's going to work out. I promise. We have a baby coming, so we have so much to look forward to."

Thankfully, a physical therapist had worked with Mak to preserve her muscle tone and mobility, and Sean had worked with her daily as well while she'd been unconscious. Still, Mak had to regain the use of her legs and arms by building her muscles back up. So, throughout the next couple of weeks, the physical therapist continued to work with her, and Sean did his part to keep up her spirits.

Two weeks after the New Year, Dr. Melinda Kurtis paid Mak her final visit, squeezed Mak's hand after pronouncing her good to go, and signed Mak's release forms.

Even though Mak protested that she could walk, Sean carried her to the front door of the big ranch house when they got home. Tyler was there with both doors open and bent to kiss Mak's cheek as Sean carried her in. When Tyler welcomed Mak home, she broke into tears. Tyler was ready with a tissue.

The house seemed surprisingly quiet. Mak was just about to ask where everyone was as Sean rounded the archway to the living room. When she was met with a resounding chorus of, "Surprise! Welcome home!" Mak almost jumped right out of Sean's arms.

Everyone she had come to love and admire was there. Sean placed her carefully on the sofa, and Blair, Peggy, Logan, and Billy gathered around. They were all very respectful of her but full of questions. They wanted to know if Mak could hear what was happening around her while she was unconscious. Mak likened it to being in a very dark room where she could hear voices off in the distance. "I tried to reach those voices, but as I moved towards them, they just kept moving further away. It was very frustrating."

Sean would ask her later if Mak recalled anything he had told her about his life. Mak just squeezed his hand and said, "That's for me to know."

Sean swallowed really hard and blushed beet red. He'd spilled the beans about a lot of stuff while Mak was sleeping, including about the buckle bunnies he'd slept with while riding the rodeo circuit.

Elli and the other ranch ladies had planned a "Welcome Home" party for Mak, complete with a cake. Tyler had organized and prepared most of the dishes, of course.

While carrying on a conversation with John and Jo, Mak fell asleep on the sofa. Sean gathered her up in his arms, thanked everyone for their help and support, and carried Mak out to his cabin. They would be sharing it until the purchase of Ferguson's ranch was complete. Tyler and Mike had agreed to allow Sean to buy in on the *Circle R Cattle Company* holdings. Being part-owners, Sean and Mak would be living in the ranch house after closing on the property.

In the meantime, Sean would be helping Mak to recuperate, and there was a wedding to plan. The ladies were all excited about that.

CHAPTER 40

ON Good Friday, Tim, Jeannie, and Sophie flew to Oregon so that Sophie could spend Easter and the following week with her father and his family. Tim and Jeannie planned to spend Easter Sunday with Sam McCarthy at his home in Kirk. The balance of the week would be spent at Jeannie's parents' house while Tim worked at his satellite office at the hangar in Kirk. Sam was doing an excellent job of running the airport. Still, he and Tim needed to go over plans for expansion, improvements, and balance the books.

Jeannie's mom had planned a surprise baby shower for the Saturday following Easter. The invited guests included Jeannie's aunts, sisters-in-law, cousins, and girlfriends from high school and college.

Tim hung out with Jeannie's father and brothers, Frank, Jr., and Jason, in the rec room. While watching the sports channel on the large screen television that hung on the wall, the party was in full swing upstairs. The men could hear the women oohing and aahing over the baby clothes as Jeannie unwrapped the gifts she had received. The men were delighted that they weren't part of the festivities. However, when the sounds changed to shouting, all four men were on their feet and rushing for the stairs.

They found the women huddled around Jeannie's chair, offering words of support and encouragement because Jeannie's water had broken in the middle of a game that the women were playing.

Tim took one look at his wife, turned as white as the baby blanket she was clutching and sank onto the edge of the coffee table.

"What are we going to do?" Tim gulped. "Jeannie's doctor is in Billings."

Frank, Jr.'s wife, Karen, pressed her hand to Tim's shoulder and said, "I have a friend who runs a birthing facility in Klamath Falls. She's a midwife. I'll call her and ask if she'll be able to help."

Jeannie's father, Frank, took one look at his son-in-law and told his wife, "Looks like I'd better drive. I don't think Tim's in any condition."

Jeannie's mom, Sophie, whom Jeannie's daughter from her first marriage had been named after, started issuing orders. Frank handed Tim a glass of whiskey to fortify him as Sophie led her daughter to the guest bedroom to change her soggy maternity outfit. Jeannie's oldest brother, Frank, Jr., grabbed Jeannie's suitcase. Her younger brother, Jason, and her father supported Tim as they helped him to the family's station wagon.

Once Jeannie was safely resting in the backseat with her head in her husband's lap, Frank climbed behind the wheel with his oldest son riding shotgun.

Sophie stayed behind with her youngest son to help wrap up the party. After all of the guests had left, with promises of text messages when the baby made its grand entrance into the world, Jason drove Sophie to the birthing facility. Jeannie's sisters-in-law remained at the house to clean up the party decorations, leftover food, and dirty dishes. Since neither had children, this would be the family's second niece or first nephew. Jason was admonished to call and keep them updated.

The forty-mile trip from Kirk to the birthing center in Klamath Falls took almost an hour. Thankfully, the birthing suite and the midwife were available to assist in the baby's birth.

When they pulled up in front of what looked like a comfortable home, Tim said, "This can't be right. It's somebody's house."

Frank said, "No, this is it. The sign says it's a birthing center. Let's get Jeannie inside."

Karen's friend, Alice, greeted them at the door. Jeannie was shown to a birthing suite and settled into bed while the three men were taken on a tour. The facility was complete with warm hardwood floors. There were two spa-like birthing suites with queen-sized beds featuring luxury linens, oversized water birth tubs, ensuite showers complete with extra-soft towels and spa robes. The other rooms included a practitioner room, reception and lounging area, full kitchen, lab, and laundry facility, acupuncture/massage suite, and a private suite for the midwife. When they stepped out onto the back porch, they took in the raised garden beds, fruit trees, vines on a trellis, and many flower beds. There was an additional porch where family members could relax in comfort. The men were advised that they would be pampered with hot, freshly-prepared foods.

Frank looked at Tim and said, “Thank God, no burnt cups of coffee from some vending machine.”

Tim was shown to his wife’s room to participate in the birthing process as his in-laws settled in. What he discovered had Tim’s mouth hanging open in surprise. Jeannie was lounging in a tub full of warm water.

“What is going on?” Tim demanded.

Jeannie tried to laugh through her pain at the look on her husband’s face and admonished him to calm down. “This is a birthing pool, Tim. Our baby is going to have a water birth. Alice says it won’t be long now. So, get a grip and shut up.”

Tim did as he was told. There was no way he would argue with a woman in labor.

Tim emerged from the birthing suite two hours later to find both of his in-laws snoring away as they relaxed in recliners in the lounge. After jostling them awake, he said, “Well, looks like you two made yourselves at home. In case you were worried, Jeannie's doing just fine, and she's given me a son."

Frank and Frank, Jr. jumped up and started slapping Tim on the back and offering their congratulations.

Frank said, "Well, what's the baby's name?"

Before Tim could answer, Sophie and Jason entered the building. So, Tim had to repeat what he'd already told his father and brother-in-law.

"Jeannie said we're naming the baby Timothy Lee Jones, Jr. She wouldn't take no for an answer when I tried to talk her out of naming the baby after me."

Sophie said, "That name is an excellent choice, but what about when the two of you are together. I can't tell you how many times the wrong person answered me when I yelled for Frank."

Tim looked dumbfounded, then said, "Well, then we'll just call the baby, Lee. That should solve the problem."

Everyone thought that was perfect.

Two days later, Tim flew his small family home to the ranch in Montana to a joyous greeting. The ranch family was waiting to meet their newest member, Timothy Lee Jones, Jr.

CHAPTER 41

MAK'S life had become exceedingly frustrating, but she was doing her very best not to show how unhappy she was. Everyone on the *Circle R* went out of their way to be sympathetic, and she didn't want to seem ungrateful. Her body was now completely healed, except for her eyesight. She had to be thankful that she'd survived Brian's kidnapping attempt and that she wasn't totally blind. At least she could see shadowy shapes, but the loss of her sight meant she couldn't work. So, she spent her time learning how to take care of herself by feeling her way around the small cabin she shared with Sean. She didn't want to become a burden to anyone, especially him. She loved him so much, but she couldn't help feeling that Sean was getting the short end of the stick. He hadn't signed up for being stuck with a blind woman. Just because they'd gone to bed together and she'd gotten pregnant didn't mean he was responsible for her.

Elli tried to keep Mak busy by including her when the children worked on their studies. Mak also sat on the floor with the twins and helped keep them occupied by building towers with blocks or playing make-believe with cars and trucks.

Elli showed Mak how to diaper the babies and change their clothing. Mak accomplished the tasks with proficiency despite her impediment. She especially enjoyed rocking the little girls and singing lullabies to put them while putting them to sleep.

She couldn't read books to the children, so Mak made up stories about a young brother and sister who lived on a ranch. Mak had a fertile imagination, so the boy and girl shared many grand adventures.

Sean escorted Mak to the bunkhouse at mealtimes, where she would spend time with John, Tom, Jo, and Jake. John was kind enough to place Mak's food on her plate in a clockwise rotation, with her meat at twelve o'clock, the vegetable at four o'clock, and the potato at eight o'clock. Mak thanked him for his consideration, but she didn't eat much. Sensing Sean's frustration, Mak wasn't surprised when he got angry at one point. She was shoving her food from one side of the plate to the other. The fingers of her left hand served as a bumper to prevent anything from spilling out onto the table.

"Mak, I expect you to eat everything on that plate. You're pregnant. I don't want anything to happen to you or the baby. Now, eat your food," Sean demanded.

Trying desperately not to cry, Mak worked her way around the plate, finishing each portion entirely before proceeding to the next. She wouldn't be surprised if she could hear a pin drop during that meal. The tension in the room was so thick she could probably have cut it with her butter knife.

When she was finished, Mak asked Jake if he would be kind enough to walk her to Jo's cabin. Jo had gone to California to see her family. Jo's brother, Bill, and his wife, Lori, had just celebrated the birth of their first child. They had asked Jo to be the baby's godmother. So, while Jo was away, her cabin sat empty. Jake looked at Sean worriedly, then helped Mak from the room.

"Well, I fucked that up, didn't I?" Sean fumed. "I know she's unhappy because she thinks she's a burden. I'm trying to be patient and give her time. But Mak won't even discuss wedding plans, and the baby's due in less than three months. I don't know what to say or do. I feel so damn helpless."

John clapped his hand on Sean's shoulder. "You need to give her time, Sean. She's been through more than one person should have to endure in such a short amount of time. Plus, Mak's hormonal. I'm betting she's worried sick about how she's going to take care of that baby when it's born, too. Has either of you discussed how Mak is feeling with the psychologist she was seeing?"

"No, Mak stopped seeing the woman, but it may be a good idea if we make another appointment. This can't go on. Mak's not eating, and she's not sleeping well, either. This should be the happiest time in her life," Sean admitted.

Jake didn't look happy when he came back into the bunkhouse. He looked at Sean sadly and said, "Don't shoot the messenger, okay. Mak asked me to tell you that she will be spending the night in Jo's cabin. She said she needs some time to think."

"Well, fuck me!" was Sean's response.

Later that night, Sean slipped into Jo's cabin. When he entered the room, Sean found Mak asleep on the bed. He could see the tracks of her tears on the soft skin of her cheeks.

Sean sat on the side of the bed and reached out a hand to gently brush a stray strand of hair behind Mak's ear. Then leaning in, he whispered, "I love you so much, darlin'. I'm sorry for upsetting you."

Mak opened her eyes and started to cry. Then she admitted, "I'm sorry, Sean. I feel so lost and helpless. I don't mean to make you angry."

"Oh, darlin'. Why would you think I'm angry with you? I'm just worried about you. I need you to be honest with me. Do you still want to marry me, Mak? I love you and want you to be my wife. But we can talk about that later. I know that you need time, so I'll try to be more patient."

Mak placed her palms to either side of Sean's face and pulled him in for an intimate kiss. "I love you, too, Sean. Please make love to me."

"Ah, darlin', are you certain? You've been through so much. I can wait until you're ready," Sean responded.

"No. I need you, now. Even though we've been sleeping in the same bed every night, you've been treating me like a piece of fine china that you're afraid you're going to break," Mak admonished.

Removing his clothing, Sean slipped into bed beside Mak and kissed the side of her neck. Mak was wearing a pair of maternity sleep shorts and a loose-fitting top. Gingerly sliding his hand under her top, he inched the material up to expose her beautiful breasts. Sean could see the changes caused by her impending motherhood. The breasts seemed larger, and the nipples had darkened. The large butterfly inked on Mak's right breast appeared to have perched on the very edge of that beautifully soft bud. Sean traced Mak's tattoo with his tongue along her ribcage, up and over her left breast to the tiniest butterfly. After kissing the skin over her heart, he took her right nipple into his mouth and began to suckle. When the tip was peaked, he turned his attention to the left breast. It deserved the same loving consideration. As he laved her nipple with his tongue, Mak smiled tentatively. So, Sean captured her lips in a searing kiss.

As their tongues dueled, Sean positioned himself between Mak's thighs and entered her slowly. When he was fully seated, he let out a contented sigh.

"God, you feel good, darlin'. I could stay right here inside your sweet pussy forever and never get tired of making love to you. I've waited a long time to find you, Mak. Please don't ever make me let you go. I don't think I can live without you," Sean admitted.

"I love you, Sean. Now, could you please move? I've been horny as hell."

"Well, we'll just have to fix that, won't we?" Sean said with a grin.

After Sean had brought Mak to orgasm twice, he couldn't hold back any longer. Shifting his weight, he lifted Mak's legs up over his shoulders and drove into her. When he was close, he took Mak's hand and placed her fingers over her clit.

"Pleasure yourself, darlin'. I'm close, and I want you to come for me one more time."

As Mak rubbed circles over her swollen nub, she could feel her orgasm building until her muscles contracted. Then, as she moaned Sean's name, he found his own release. Finally, when he could catch his breath, Sean flopped down beside Mak, pulled the covers over them, kissed her gently, and fell asleep.

CHAPTER 42

TWO days before Jo was due back from her visit to her relatives in California, Mike received an unexpected and unwelcome telephone call from her. Jo thanked Mike for the opportunity, but she wouldn't be returning. She had reconnected with a man who owned a fifty-thousand-acre cattle spread in the northern part of the state. He and Jo had gotten married.

Mike thanked Jo for the time she had spent working for the *Circle R*. He also reminded Jo that she should be the one to tell Mak. Jo assured him that she would call Mak as soon as she was settled into her new life. Mike congratulated Jo and wished her luck.

After hanging up the phone, Mike sat there scrubbing his face with his hands. Well, that was fast. Jo had only been in California for eight days, managed to meet a man, and was already married. To Mike, that sounded like a disaster in the making, but Jo did seem a little flighty to him. So, maybe not such unexpected behavior. What bothered him the most was that even though she professed to love Mak like a sister, Jo didn't seem overly concerned about how her friend would take the news. Then, there was John. Mike didn't know how John would feel about Jo's defection, either, because he showed all the signs of being in love. What a colossal mess.

Sending Emi a text, he asked her to reach out to the other family members and arrange a meeting. He'd get everyone's input and then decide how he would tell the ranch hands that they were now one short.

This blew Elli's plans concerning the new programs Jo was supposed to spearhead all to hell. Giving it careful consideration, Mike wondered how difficult it would be for Mak to handle those chores if she had some assistance. She could still teach, even though she couldn't see well. Maybe that would help pull her out of her depression. It was worth a try. He'd bring it up at the family meeting and get everyone's thoughts on the subject.

That evening while Jess and Sophie babysat, Mike, Emi, Elli, Tyler, Tim, Jeannie, Alex, and Anna gathered in the living room at the main house. Tyler brought out a tray of snacks, two pitchers of drinks he'd prepared, and another pitcher filled with ice water. Artfully arranged around several ramekins, the food included blue cheese potato chips, crispy kale chips, beer pretzels, roasted cumin cashews, ground beef mini quiches, and an assortment of meat and cheese chunks.

Everyone admired the tray before digging in while Tyler took their drink orders. One pitcher contained a rum ginger concoction combining dark rum, bitters, lime wedges, and ginger ale. The other was filled with a lime squash drink made of limes, honey, and carbonated water for those who wanted something nonalcoholic.

"What are the different dips?" Mike asked.

"Well, clockwise, the ramekins contain your classic hummus, ranch Greek yogurt dip, zucchini Pico de Gallo salsa, a layered Mediterranean dip, hot spinach dip, and honey mustard dip. The last one at ten o'clock is a creamy red pepper veggie dip," Tyler pointed out. "They're from recipes I created while I was hiding out at my cabin in Vermont after I got Elli pregnant with Billy." As Tyler paused, he cleared his throat and turned away. Thoughts about that time of his life made him very emotional.

Mike studied Tyler, then questioned, "What's wrong, son?"

"Making the dips brought back the anguish of almost losing Elli. That's something I have trouble dealing with. I look at her and know that I can't live without her. She and the kids are everything to me. I'll spend the rest of my life proving my love to her, so she never regrets becoming my wife." Tyler mumbled the last part. "Sorry for that. It wasn't something you needed to hear."

Mike squeezed his son-in-law's shoulder sympathetically and responded, "You know that you can come to me any time you feel the need to talk, don't you? Where are your feelings of insecurity coming from, Tyler? Has Elli given you any indication that she's unhappy because, from my perspective, you make my daughter very happy? Don't forget, I visited her and the kids at the farm in Stillwater while you were off creating those dips. She didn't come right out and say so at the time, but I knew she was in love with you. I wanted to pack up her and the children and move them back to the ranch. But I didn't because I knew you needed the chance to realize what you were missing. I had a dream about you and Rick the night before Elli returned to Stillwater for the funeral of Rick's wife. You were always meant to be Elli's husband. She's loved you since she was a young girl, and if I'm not mistaken, you've loved her just as long. You just needed time to realize that. I'd say that she's forgiven you for running off because she entrusted her first four children into your care. Plus, she's given you six more. If that's not love, I don't know what is. Just don't ever do that again, or I might need to beat your ass. Now, I think we're wasting your talents. These are really delicious. Maybe we should consider starting a catering service," to which Tyler grinned and shook his head. Pleased that he'd eased some of Tyler's distress, Mike told him, "Go sit next to your wife and give her a kiss. I'll get this meeting started."

Standing in front of the fireplace, Mike cleared his throat to get everyone's attention. "Okay, I have some disturbing news that I'd like to share. Then we'll discuss how we want to handle it," Mike began. As he glanced around, the members of his family were worriedly staring at him, waiting for him to continue.

"I received a call this morning from Jo Johnston. She resigned her position here on the *Circle R.* She's gotten married, so she's not coming back," Mike informed the others.

The room erupted with everyone talking over each other until Mike held up his hands and asked for silence. “We need to discuss how this affects our bottom line. I have to say that I’m really chafed. Emi, Elli, and Jeannie, with Mak’s assistance, put in many hours creating the advertising for those new services. Thankfully, we haven’t published anything yet, since Jo is no longer available to run the programs. But I hopefully have a suggestion.”

Elli held up her hand to interrupt her father, “Does Mak know yet? This is going to be devastating news. I can tell you that Mak hasn’t been in a good place emotionally. I think she feels worthless right now, so I’m concerned about her. In fact, I would use this meeting to suggest that we talk to Sean about how we can help. I don’t understand how Jo could do this.”

“Talking to Sean is a good idea, Elli. But, then, run into the office and grab a pen and paper, will you? I think we need to take notes. That way, we won’t forget any good ideas that we come up with,” Mike requested.

When Elli had returned to her seat on the sofa next to her husband, she leaned in, gave Tyler a kiss, then told her father, "Okay. I'm ready."

Mike continued, "After I spoke to Jo this morning, I had a thought. Mak can only see shadows, but I don't think that makes her totally handicapped concerning performing equine massage therapy. I would think she could still do that. Isn't that mostly hands-on? She should even be capable of giving classes for young beginner clients in natural horsemanship and roping and reining, especially if we provide her with an assistant. I know that Jessica expressed an interest in equine massage therapy. What do you think? I was thinking that being able to work might help bring Mak out of her depression."

Tim interrupted, "We could get Sophie involved, too. She seemed to have a case of hero-worship where Mak was concerned before Mak was kidnapped. Sophie did a fair amount of crying and praying for Mak while Mak was unconscious."

Tyler interjected, "I agree with that. Jess and Sophie would make excellent assistants for Mak. We could pay the girls a salary that would go into their college funds. They could work with Mak after school and on weekends. The rest of us could take turns during the day. Elli can make up one of her special spreadsheets with a schedule. Let's talk to Sean and get his thoughts on the subject. I think he's worried that Mak doesn't want to marry him anymore."

Jeannie piped up, "Anna and I tried to talk to Mak about wedding preparations the other day. Anna wants to make Mak's dress for the ceremony, and Emi suggested a party for the women to create decorations. Mak told us that she wasn't ready for that yet. Although I can't blame her. Sean hasn't given her an engagement ring. Maybe they've both changed their minds?"

"Well, then, I guess we need to talk to Sean first. So, it's late. Let's table this meeting for now. Tyler, would you arrange a meeting with Sean for tomorrow evening, and we'll all gather again for that?" Mike requested.

"I'll set it up in the morning. Do you want to include John or wait to see if Jo is honorable enough to tell him that she's not coming back herself?" Tyler asked.

Everyone agreed that John should be included in the next meeting.

Tyler said, "Okay, I'll tell John to be here as well. I'll make a sweet and salty tray for tomorrow night's discussion. Maybe bourbon or whiskey for the guys and lemonade for the women to go with that."

Mike thanked Tyler for keeping them all well-fed. After collecting the children, Mike and Emi left by the front door and headed for their home. Tim, Jeannie, and Sophie left by the back door where Tim had parked the jeep. Alex and Anna stayed to help settle all of Tyler's and Elli's children into bed, then retired to their suite at the other end of the house.

CHAPTER 43

"DARLIN', I have to go. Tyler asked John and me to attend a meeting this evening. Will you be okay? I promise I'll rub your feet for you when I get back. I've noticed they've been swelling up a little bit lately. I can rub lotion other places, too," Sean said hopefully and with a suggestive lift of his brows. Then, shaking his head, he admonished himself because Mak couldn't see his stupid facial expressions.

Mak giggled and reached out to run her hand over the bulge in Sean's jeans. She could just make out his shape and had to feel her way to her objective. "I'll just bet you would love to inject some of your lotions in certain places, you horny man, you. So, hurry back, and just maybe you'll be the recipient of one of my blowjobs."

"Holy hell. I gotta go. The sooner I get out of here, the sooner I can get back," Sean stuttered. "Now you've got me all hot and bothered. Give me a kiss, quick."

Sean tried to kiss and run, but Mak latched onto his bottom lip with her teeth, and the kiss turned into a clash of tongues. Finally, when they drew apart, Sean said, "Oh, hell!"

Just then, Mak's cell started to play the theme song to "*Sisters*," which meant she was receiving a call from Jo. Sean grabbed the phone off the dresser, pushed accept and speaker, kissed Mak's brow gently, then darted out the door. Thankfully, the interruption helped to ease the ache in his groin. He didn't want to show up to a meeting with a hard-on.

Mak could hear Jo saying, "Mak, are you there?" Since the phone was on speaker, Mak didn't need to hold it while she talked because being visually impaired meant she had a bad habit of disconnecting her calls.

"Hi, Jo. I'm right here. Are you having a good time with your family? Tell all of them how much I miss them. I can't wait for you to come home. I've missed you a bunch, ya know."

"Oh, honey. I've missed you too," Jo told her.

Mak could hear that Jo's voice sounded a little wobbly. Finally, worried, she asked her, "Are you alright, Jo? Did something bad happen? You sound like you're trying not to cry."

"No, sister-mine. Nothing bad has happened, but I have some news for you, and I know that you're going to be hurt," Jo admitted.

A knot fisted in Mak's stomach. She knew Jo because they'd been together forever. "You're not coming back, are you Jo?" she haltingly asked her.

"No, sweetie, I'm not. Please let me explain. I know you're going to think I'm crazy, but I'm thrilled, Mak. So, please try to understand, okay?" Jo begged.

"I'm listening, Jo. Go ahead. Tell me what's going on."

Mak could hear Jo take a deep breath. She also thought she heard the sound of a familiar male voice in the background and little girls giggling and squealing.

"Okay, I guess I'll just bite the bullet and come right out with it, and then give the particulars. I got married, Mak. I'm now Mrs. Jack Hamilton."

Mak gasped. "Oh, no. Jo, are you insane? Did you forget what that man did to you? Did you forget what his best friend did to me?" she demanded.

As Mak curled into a ball on her cot, she muffled her sobs with her pillow. Then, she listened as Jo laid waste to their friendship with her explanation.

"I ran into Jack in the park the day after the christening for Bill's daughter. I was babysitting for my sister and took my niece and nephew there to play on the equipment. Jack had just come from an attorney's office across the street. He's, now, father to two young girls, Mak. He was godfather to the children, but their parents perished in an avalanche while on a skiing vacation in Colorado. The parents owned a fifty-thousand-acre cattle ranch in northern California. Jack has inherited the property and is responsible for parenting the little girls. They're two-year-old twins, Mak, and so cute. I'm now a mother, and I'm so excited!"

Jo took a breath and asked, "Are you still there, Mak? I'm so sorry, honey. Please be happy for me. Jack never married the donkey-faced debutante. He still loves me, Mak, and I've never gotten over him. He's everything I've ever wanted. Please tell me that you don't hate me, Mak. I don't want to lose your friendship."

Mak wiped her eyes with her fists and her nose with the sleeve of her cotton shirt. Then, with an anguished reply, she said, "I love you, sister from another Ma and Pa. Please be happy, Jo, but promise me you'll be careful. I'm concerned for you." Then Mak pressed against the bottom of the screen on the cell phone where she knew the disconnect button was located.

Throwing the phone back on the mattress, she curled in on herself and cried herself to sleep.

While Mak was having her heart broken by her best friend, Sean and John were seated in the living room at the main house. All of the adults on the ranch, except for Mak, were present at the meeting.

Tyler had put together another one of his snack trays. This one contained a pineapple boat full of a mixture of pineapple chunks, blueberries, raspberries, and strawberries as a centralized theme, surrounded by crunchy crackers, veggies, cheese slices, cured meats, nuts, and olives. Two ramekins, nestled in amongst the other food, contained basic hummus and a mint lemon hummus as dips.

Tyler had used the other half of the pineapple to make pineapple coconut champagne cocktails. A second pitcher offered non-alcoholic strawberry pomegranate mojitos. The final pitcher contained iced water.

After her first cocktail, Anna hiccupped, giggled out an apology, and asked if they could have a meeting every evening. She blushed and hid her face against Alex's shoulder when everyone started to laugh. Alex kissed his wife's forehead tenderly and said, "God, you're such a lightweight. No more booze for you, sweetheart."

Mike filled a plate, then took his position in front of the fireplace as head of the meeting. At the same time, everyone dug in and demolished the charcuterie platter.

"Sean? John? We have some news to impart, then we want to talk about Mak," Mike told them.

Both men paused with food halfway to their open mouths with stupefied looks on their faces. Silently they waited for Mike to continue.

"Everyone else in the room already knows that Jo Johnston called me yesterday with her resignation." That got both men's attention. Mike looked at John to gauge his reaction as he told them, "Jo got married. She isn't coming back to take up her duties here on the *Circle R*."

Everyone watched silently as John winced, closed his eyes, and lowered his head. Then he got to his feet and told them, "If you'll excuse me for a few minutes, I just need to get some air. I promise I'll be back." Then he left the house through the front door. Elli wanted to go to John, but Tyler placed his hand on her arm to forestall her.

"Give the man some space, Elli. He'll be embarrassed if you catch him crying," Tyler told her.

Elli nodded her understanding and sat back down beside her husband. Then, having a kind and compassionate heart, she hid her face against Tyler's chest to hide her sobs. Tyler picked his wife up, excused himself, and carried Elli into the kitchen where he could comfort her in private.

Sean sat on one of the armchairs, stunned into silence. A million things raced through his head, all involving what this news was going to do to Mak. She was already in a depression. How would she handle her best friend's defection?

Finally, finding his voice, he asked, "Did Jo say anything at all about Mak? Oh, fuck! Jo called Mak right as I was leaving the cabin. I've gotta go."

Mike grabbed Sean's arm as Sean tried to ease past him. "Hold up, Sean. We have a possible solution to help Mak. We're hoping what we've come up with will help Mak feel useful again. So, stay and finish before you go rushing out of here, please."

Sean, realizing it was probably already too late to prevent the pain that Jo would cause Mak, nodded and sat back down.

"Let's give John, Tyler, and Elli a few minutes, and then we can continue. I know you want to go comfort, Mak. I promise we won't take long so you can get out of here. While we're waiting, can you tell me where you and Mak stand? I've noticed some distancing, and Jeannie mentioned last night that Mak refused any discussion regarding wedding preparations. She also mentioned that you haven't given Mak an engagement ring yet."

"Oh, fuck me. With everything that's happened, I totally forgot. I told Mak that she could pick out the one she wanted. That was the night that bastard got his hands on her. So now she won't be able to see to make a choice. I've really messed up. She probably doesn't believe me when I tell her how much I love her. I haven't given her any proof." Sean hung his head. "What a cluster!"

Emi spoke up, "Sean, why don't you let Tyler, Mike, Alex, and Tim go with you tomorrow to a jeweler's in Billings. All four men have excellent taste. I believe I can speak for all of the women that we're happy with the rings we've received."

Mike said, "That's a perfect idea, sweetheart. So, what do you say, Sean? Want some help shopping for the perfect ring?"

Before Sean could answer, John returned and eased onto the piano bench. His eyes were red-rimmed. Tyler and Elli came in from the direction of the kitchen. Elli's eyes were swollen from crying. She made her way to John, who stood to receive Elli's embrace. After Elli whispered something in John's ear, he nodded his head. Placing a gentle kiss on Elli's forehead, he thanked her for her concern and hugged her back. Then she took her place on the sofa next to her husband and snuggled into his embrace.

Mike spoke up, "The men are going jewelry shopping tomorrow morning after the chores are done. We're going to help Sean pick out an engagement ring for Mak." Tyler motioned that he was in agreement, but John asked that he be excluded. Sean imperceptibly nodded his head in understanding.

"Okay, so Sean, this is what we were thinking might help pull Mak out of her depression. She needs to feel useful. She's had plenty of time to heal from her injuries. Her only problem is her sight, but at least she isn't totally blind. Mak can see shadows. We think she should still handle the programs Jo was hired to do if Mak's given some assistance. We're in agreement that Jess and Sophie would be perfect for that."

"Wait. You're telling me you think Mak can still perform equine massage therapy? Plus, give classes for young beginner clients in natural horsemanship as well as roping and reining?" Sean asked.

"Yes, Sean. I'm betting Mak can do those things with her eyes closed. So, being able to see shapes is a plus, in my opinion. We can work with her to perfect those duties before bringing any strangers into the mix. As soon as we know that she'll be able to handle things, we can start to advertise."

"You do realize that she's seven months pregnant, right?" Sean questioned.

Emi interjected, "That's not going to prevent Mak from working, and working will be a much healthier alternative to lying around fighting depression, don't you think? I'll keep a very close eye on Mak. We won't let her do more than she can handle. Let's talk to her and see how she feels about it and go from there."

Anna sighed, "Oh boy. Can we do it tomorrow night in another meeting? I want to see what kind of drink Tyler concocts to go with the tray of food. We could make it a celebration. If Sean finds the perfect ring, he could get down on one knee and propose."

As everyone laughed, Alex looked at Anna quizzically and asked, "Do I need to start worrying about you, dear?"

Anna hiccupped, then squeaked out, "Nope, I'm good, honey." The rest of the group laughed harder.

Everyone, including Sean, agreed that Anna had an excellent idea. So, Mike told them, "Okay, the meeting is adjourned until tomorrow night. The men will meet in the ranch office as soon as the chores are done in the morning."

Sean wished everyone a good night, then beat a hasty retreat. He was worried sick about how Mak had taken Jo's news. When Sean reached the cabin, he stripped and slipped into bed beside Mak. Sean pulled her in close, wrapped his arm around her waist, and kissed her softly on the temple. He'd found Mak curled into a fetal position facing the wall. The tracks of dried tears stained her cheeks, her nose was red, and her eyelids were puffy.

Mak turned towards Sean and pressed her face into the curve of Sean's neck where it met his shoulder.

"I'm sorry, darlin'. I know you're hurting, but I'm here for you, Mak. I love you so much, and I'm here for you. I'll always be here for you."

When Mak started to sob, Sean pulled her in tight and let her cry. It was the best medicine. Get it all out, and then move on. He'd be there for her and never let her fall. Mak had been through enough and didn't deserve any of it.

When Mak's sobs started to ease, Sean tipped her chin up, stared into her eyes, and said, "Does this mean that I don't get my blowjob?"

Mak choked out a final sob and then started to laugh. "God, I love you so much, Mr. Sean Fitzpatrick Hannity. I'd say take me to bed, but I think we're already here." After giving him a swift, hard kiss on the mouth, she left a trail of kisses along his torso, making her way south until she reached her objective. Sean tried to stop her, but she pushed his hands away and took him into her mouth. When Sean let out a groan, she smiled, then took him as deep as she could and started to pleasure him.

Sean stiffened, trying to hold back his release. Finally knowing he couldn't last much longer, he pulled Mak off him and eased her onto her side. Lifting her leg, Sean found her opening and eased inside until he was fully seated. Finding her tiny bundle of nerves at the apex of her sex, he pleasured her until he could feel that Mak was close, then he began to move with hard thrusts. When they both came together, Sean saw an exploding starburst behind his eyelids. It was the most intense orgasm he'd ever experienced, and he was fully sated.

After he'd caught his breath, Sean went into the tiny bathroom to get a warm washcloth. He used it to gently clean between Mak's thighs. Then, climbing back into bed, Sean pulled the covers over them, wrapped Mak in a tight embrace, and whispered, "Go to sleep, darlin'. Tomorrow is the beginning of the rest of your life. I'm going to work every day to make it a good one for you, Mak." With that promise hanging in the air, they both fell asleep.

CHAPTER 44

BREAKFAST completed, Mak told Sean that she'd like to help John with the dishes. John gave Sean a look as if to say that he'd take good care of Mak. So, Sean gave Mak a hug and told her that he'd see her later.

After Sean left the bunkhouse, Mak felt along the tabletop for the dishes and handed them to John as he washed. When the table was cleared, John handed Mak a dish towel and placed her in front of the drying rack. Mak knew that there was plenty of counter space to the right of the dish rack. Running her fingertips over the area, Mak judged it to be open. Carefully taking each item from the dish rack, she dried then placed it on the countertop. John had washed the dishes and stacked them so that Mak would feel the larger plates first and be able to assist with the chore so that she'd feel useful.

When they were finished, John made a cup of tea for Mak. Then he sat down at the table across from her. Reaching out, he took Mak's hands in his callused ones. Her hands were so slender that John's large ones covered hers completely.

Mak swallowed hard, unsure what to say because she didn't know if she was correct in her assumption that John was in love with Jo. It wasn't something she could actually see. It was just a feeling Mak had gotten over the weeks since waking up in the hospital. Maybe she'd be overstepping by saying anything.

Well, there was only one way to find out. So finally, she squeezed John's hands and started to tell the story about the first time she'd met Jo. Mak didn't leave anything out or try to paint Jo in a better light. She was Mak's sister from another Ma and Pa, an excellent friend, and Mak's savior. But Jo had been through many men, and Mak wasn't confident that Jo knew what she was actually looking for in a life partner. Then Mak told John about Jack Hamilton and what he had put Jo through when Jo lived with the man in Philadelphia.

"I don't think Jo ever got over him," Mak told John. "Anyway, she called me last night. Jo ran into Jack at the playground in a park where Jo had taken her niece and nephew to play. They married three days ago, so apparently, she loved him enough to forgive him. She's not coming back."

"I'm sorry that she hurt you, John. You're such a good man, and you don't deserve that. I'm just really, really sorry." Then, Mak started to cry. She was so sick of all the tears she'd been forced to shed of late and angrily brushed them away with the sides of her hands.

John had been quiet while Mak told her story. Not being able to see John's face, she had no idea that silent tears were streaming down the sides of his cheeks. The tears were more for what Mak had been through than for himself.

Finally, Mak heard John sigh. Then he kissed the palms of her hands and told her, "You're a good person, Mak, and I'm happy to have you as a friend. Thank you for telling me. Sounds like I might have dodged a bullet. I know there's someone out there for me. I just haven't found her yet. Hopefully, it will be soon. But I'm not giving up, so you don't need to worry about me. Now, let's walk you over to the main house. Elli's probably wondering what's keeping you. Then I can get on about my chores."

After helping Mak to her feet, John gave Mak a soft hug, took her hand, and led her from the room. He would spend his day remembering what Mak had told him and praying that his words about finding the right woman for him were true. He was tired of being alone. Especially when he was surrounded by couples who were deeply committed.

Sean was coming from the stable when John exited the kitchen door of the main house and went to meet him. "Are you okay, John?"

"Yeah, I think I am. Mak and I had a good talk. Do you know how lucky you are, Sean? Mak is an extraordinary woman. If I didn't know how much she loves you, I'd give you a run for your money," John said with a grin, trying to rile his friend up.

Sean took off his cowboy hat and gave John a swat. "Hands off my woman, John. Don't make me beat your ass. That filly's mine, and she's carrying my baby. Now, I just need to hogtie her into a lifetime commitment. I know she's it for me. Are you coming to the meeting tonight? Mak could sure use your support. But I'll understand if you don't want to watch me make a fool out of myself when I get down on one knee."

John laughed. "Sean, I wouldn't miss that for the world. I'll be there. Now, don't you have an appointment with a jewelry store?"

"Yeah, come with us. It won't feel right without you there. You're one of my best friends. Plus, it will give you a head start on finding just the right ring for when it's your turn."

John could see that it would mean a lot to Sean to have his support. "Okay, I'll come. Jewelry shopping isn't exactly one of my strong suits, but I can put in my two cents. So, let's go before I have the chance to change my mind."

Sean and John headed for the ranch office, where they met up with Tyler, Tim, and Mike.

Mike said, "Let's do this. I was in that jewelry store for hours before I found the right ring. Almost lost Emi that day, too. I'd pissed her off and then didn't show up for supper. She didn't talk to me for weeks and was ready to leave. I've gotta tell you, don't ever piss off the woman you love."

The men just nodded their heads in understanding. Even John had been in their shoes. He'd thought he was in love with a girl in high school. Then she'd dumped him for a football jock the summer before junior year.

Sean's mouth dropped open when the five men entered the jewelers in Billings. The store was called "*Love Comes in Small Packages*." But Sean figured they should have included the word "expensive" between the words "small" and "packages" in the title when he got a glimpse of some price tags.

The woman behind the counter noticed that Sean looked like a deer caught in the headlights and rightly assumed that he was the one who was hoping to get engaged. When she asked him if she could be of assistance, Sean and the other four men crowded forward.

Mike said, "Our friend here is looking for an engagement ring."

"Well, let's start with some basics. What does your special lady do for a living? It's usually best to purchase a ring that fits her lifestyle," the saleswoman suggested.

"Mak works on a ranch with horses, but she has slender fingers. Her hands are kind of delicate. So maybe something that won't get caught on anything but is sturdy enough to hold up to hard work?" Sean suggested.

Mike, Tyler, Tim, and John all nodded in agreement. This was the first time five grown men had shown up together to pick a ring for one lucky woman. The saleswoman was finding the situation rather enjoyable.

"So, let's see," she began. "You want something that will hold up under tough conditions. Well, platinum settings offer the most protection. Platinum is four times more durable than gold, but those bands are also expensive at about twice the price. A more cost-effective alternative to that would be palladium. Palladium is not as strong as platinum, but it's known for being resistant to tarnish caused by constant wear that comes with hard work. For women that work with their hands, palladium is a great option. Just be aware that palladium isn't a good choice for any type of setting with many small details like filigree. It also doesn't lend itself to lots of small gemstones or tall settings. Luckily, none of those things are good for an active lifestyle anyway! Let me show you some engagement rings in both platinum and palladium. If set with round diamonds, they don't have any hard corners that might catch on anything."

Several trays of rings were set on the counter before the five men. Tyler was the first to choose a ring with an infinity twisted band. The other four shook their heads. "That doesn't remind me of Mak," John told him. Tyler said that he had to agree and slipped the ring back in its place in the tray.

"Mak's a beautiful woman, but I think she'd like something simple. Nothing ostentatious. Don't you think?" Sean asked the others.

Tim picked a half bezel solitaire out of another tray. The matching wedding band had five matching bezel set diamonds.

"I don't know. That set seems kind of tacky to me," Sean told him. "But that's closer than the other one."

"Well, how about this one?" Mike asked. "I think it looks more feminine and kind of romantic." Then, when the men all stared at Mike like he'd lost his man card, he chuckled, "Well, I did spend nearly half of a day looking at rings for Emi."

"I like that one, too," John said.

The woman took the matching wedding ring and slipped it over the ring finger on a mannequin's hand. Then she took the engagement ring from Mike's fingers and placed it behind the wedding band.

"This is what is known as a cross split-shank band. It has a solitaire diamond held firmly in a rounded setting. So, it won't catch on anything. The matching band has small diamonds embedded in the surface to protect them. This set is platinum, so it will be a little pricier."

"Do you have a band for the groom that would go with those rings?" Sean wanted to know. "It would be kind of nice for our bands to match, I think, but I don't need anything with diamonds. I'm not really a diamond kind of cowboy."

Tyler agreed, "I thought the same thing when I picked out Elli's rings. I wanted our rings to match. I'd been in love with her for years. I wanted every man to know Elli belonged to me and they'd better not touch. Of course, it helped that she was already carrying my child. So, you have that part nailed down too, Sean." That made everyone laugh.

The saleswoman produced a cross-shank men's wedding ring with an engraved design to make it look like the women's band minus the diamonds.

Sean produced a ring that Mak sometimes wore on her ring finger when she felt like dressing up. It fit her perfectly, so the jeweler could use that to get the right size. After the woman measured his finger, Sean said, "Wrap them up. I'll take them."

When the woman rang up his purchases, Sean swallowed and jokingly said, "Does anyone know where I can sell a kidney?" Then, grabbing his receipt and the jeweler's bag, he followed Mike, Tyler, Tim, and John from the store to the sounds of raucous laughter.

Tyler said, "Let's go home. I still have to make the food tray for tonight's meeting, and Anna is expecting something special to drink to celebrate. Who knew the woman who was my best friend's housekeeper when we were kids couldn't hold her liquor?" All five of them laughed at that comment.

CHAPTER 45

AT 8:00 p.m. all of the adults on the *Circle R Cattle Company Ranch* gathered around the dining room table to hold their meeting. Tyler had produced three trays this time. One which included vegetables, meats, and cheeses with various dips. The second contained fresh fruits. The last one showcased a lemon ricotta Bundt cake surrounded by strawberry brownie kabobs, chocolate-dipped strawberries, and cream cheese-filled strawberries. He paired the food with a cocktail made with fresh strawberries, tequila, and rhubarb bitters. The women who weren't drinking were provided with a nonalcoholic grape sparkler made from just-pressed grape juice and dry sparkling water.

Mike said, "Okay, that does it. Maybe we should open our own barroom and make Tyler the bartender. This is really good."

Alex removed Anna's glass after she inhaled her drink and switched her over to ice water. Anna gave him a dirty look and said, "Party-pooper."

Mike stood at the head of the table and said, "Okay, everybody. Now that Anna's drunk, we can bring this meeting to order. Mak, everyone in this room has come to admire and respect you. We all want you to stay here with us on the *Circle R* and make this your home."

When Mak went to object, Sean placed his fingers against her lips to halt her flow of words. "Just hear us out, Mak." So, Mak shut her mouth.

Mike continued, "Jo has left us in a bit of a quandary, as I'm certain you are well aware. You worked with Emi, Elli, and Jeannie to advertise the new programs we want to offer paying customers. So, you know how much time went into that. We've all agreed that we think you should be offered the position Jo vacated. We want you to spearhead those classes."

When Mak tried to remind him that she couldn't see, Emi interrupted her. "You'll do just fine, Mak. I bet you've done those things so often over the years that you could do them in your sleep. Besides, Jessica and Sophie would like the opportunity to work with you after school and on weekends. The rest of us would also like to learn. So, the adults could work on a rotating shift. Then there would always be someone to assist you. We just ask that you give it a try. If you cannot handle those chores, we won't be worse off than we are right now. Jo's kind of left us in the lurch, so to speak. We're all hoping that you can save us from what would otherwise be a wasted endeavor."

Mak opened and closed her mouth several times, but she couldn't decide what to say. She was pretty confident these people were just trying to help. Mak loved all of them for giving her a chance. She just didn't know how much longer she could go on feeling totally worthless, so she guessed it wouldn't hurt to give their suggestion a try. When Sean took her hand in his and gave it a gentle squeeze of reassurance, she finally found her voice.

"I don't know what to say. This is the first time I've felt like part of a family in a really long time. I love all of you so much and don't want to ever let you down. So, I guess my answer is yes. I'll try really hard to make this work. Thank you."

Everyone cheered and applauded. Unbeknownst to Mak, Jessica, and Sophie, Tom and Jake had brought all the children into the room. They all moved to stand by the side. Once they were in position, Sean got down on one knee alongside Mak's chair and took both of her hands in his.

Leaning in, Sean whispered against Mak's ear, "Darlin'?"

Mak turned her head towards the sound. She could make out the shape of Sean's face so close to hers, so she reached out to run her fingers along the curve of his jaw.

"Mak, I count the day you dropped your drink in the grocery store parking lot in Butler as the best day of my life. When I touched your sweet face, it felt like I was jolted with a lightning rod's worth of love. You were all I could think about after that, and you became my reason to breathe every minute of every day since. So, Mak, will you marry me and make me the happiest cowboy in Montana?"

Mak was so overcome with emotion that this sweet, gentle, incredibly handsome cowboy could possibly want to saddle himself with a woman with a disability that she couldn't say no. She was too selfish anyway because she loved him so much. So, the only answer she could give him was, "Yes!"

As Sean slipped Mak's engagement ring on her finger, he leaned in for a kiss and said, "Thank you, darlin'. I intend to give you lots of babies."

The room erupted in hooting and hollering, making Patti and Annie cry. Elli and Tyler rushed over to soothe their daughters, and everyone took turns congratulating the newly engaged couple.

Anna said, "Finally! Women's meeting tomorrow. We have a wedding to plan, and Mak needs to choose a pattern so I can get started on sewing her wedding dress. Then we need to have meetings to make the decorations. This is going to be so much fun! I vote that Tyler makes the food and beverages." That got a laugh out of everyone.

CHAPTER 46

ON the last Friday of May, all of the adults from the *Circle R Ranch*, plus Jessica and Sophie, took seats on the bleachers at the high school football stadium. They were there to witness Tom's and Jake's graduation ceremony. Jake held the honor of class valedictorian. As he gave his speech, Tyler turned his attention to the look on his oldest daughter's face. Tyler was confident he had looked just like that when Elli had given her speech on the day they had graduated sixteen years before. It was a look that was full of love and pride. Tyler also knew that Jake had feelings for Jess, so he had been keeping an eye on the young man. Tyler trusted Jake and Jess, but he knew all about the hormones that drove a young man crazy. Tyler didn't want anything to sidetrack Jake's or Jess's plans to become veterinarians. They had years of schooling ahead of them. Unfortunately, something like an unplanned pregnancy could sideline those plans in a hurry. That had happened to Elli because of one night spent with Tyler's best friend, Rick. If not for Bill and Peggy Roberts' loving care, Elli might never have realized her dream of becoming an elementary school teacher.

All of the proud parents, relatives, and loved ones cheered and whistled as the graduates, now turned adults, walked across the stage, collected their diplomas, switched their tassels from right to left, and threw their caps in the air. Now, it was time to celebrate. Graduating was a significant accomplishment, so Tom and Jake deserved the party of their dreams. Tyler thought that the party should incorporate all of their favorite dishes.

All graduating class members were invited to attend the party the following day. A large tent was erected in the backyard behind the main house. When Tom and Jake were consulted, they both decided that they'd like the party to be a day-long affair. Their classmates could take trail rides, spend time swimming in the spring-fed pond, have a picnic for lunch and a sit-down dinner, and dance with a live band in the evening. Tyler managed to have a carnival set up in the south pasture to make the day even more memorable. It came complete with a Ferris wheel, musical chair swing, a super slide, tubs of fun, and a roller coaster. There was also a dunk tank and game booths. It was an ambitious undertaking, but Tyler pulled it off with the help of all of the family and ranch members. Even the children pitched in to make the day special. To keep the littlest children occupied and make them feel included, Mak and Elli helped them make decorations.

As Tyler worked to make the final preparations for his planned picnic lunch menu, Elli paused in the kitchen. She was on her way to the backyard and wanted to see if her husband needed anything. Tyler laid down the knife he was using to cut fruit, washed and dried his hands, and pulled Elli into his arms. Nuzzling the side of her neck, he said, "Hi, sweet girl. Who is watching the little ones?"

"Mak, Momma, and Anna are on kid duty. I was going out to check on Jessica and Sophie and the decorations. But I thought I'd check on my wonderful husband first. Is there anything that you need, Tyler? You had such a serious look on your face when I came into the kitchen. Is anything the matter?"

Tyler kissed Elli's wrinkled brow to ease her concern. "The boys' graduation last evening and planning their party has just made me a little introspective. It made me think about when we graduated from high school. I was so very proud of you when you gave the valedictorian speech. I bet I whistled the loudest when you were finished speaking. The kids on either side of me gave me a look because I'd hurt their ears. Then I was thinking about what happened at the graduation party we attended. You were so beautiful when you stepped out onto the deck by the pool. Do you remember when I stopped to talk to you?"

Elli stared at Tyler's face, wondering where he was going with this. "I remember, Tyler. Why are you bringing this up? What's wrong, sweetheart?"

"I was so stupid, Elli. I stood there tongue-tied. I wanted so badly to tell you that I was in love with you. I wanted you to be mine, and the only thing that came out of my mouth was good luck in college. I felt like such a loser. Can you forgive me, Elli?"

Elli cupped Tyler's handsome face in the palms of her hands and responded, "What brought this up? There's nothing to forgive, Tyler. We've been over this before. I loved you too, but I was too shy to tell you how I felt. But it doesn't matter. We're together now, and we have a beautiful family. You make me so happy. I can't imagine my life without you in it. I love you so much!"

The kiss Tyler gave Elli was full of remorse for the times he had failed her. Elli was his heart and soul. His now and forever. She would always be his reason to breathe every minute of every day until there wasn't any breath left in his body.

When they broke apart, Tyler took Elli's face in his hands and said, "I love you so damn much, sweet girl!"

"Well, you know what? I think that you and I need to take a vacation. Just the two of us. Maybe after Sean's and Mak's wedding, we can go to the cabin in Vermont, where I'm certain I can think of a few ways that I can show you just how much your love means to me." Then Elli rubbed her hand over the bulge in Tyler's jeans, giggled when he tried to grab her and ran out the kitchen door. She needed to help with the final preparations for the graduation extravaganza.

Tyler watched the love of his life leave the house and thought, "You're going to pay later for leaving me hanging with a hard-on. I have big plans for you tonight, my sweet girl!" Then he chuckled and got back to work. The guests would be arriving soon, and being teenagers, they were sure to be hungry.

Jess and Sophie had been up since dawn, blowing up blue and gold balloons (the school's colors) from a helium tank, attaching strings, and tying them in bunches about the tent. Streamers and twinkle lights dangled from the tent's ceiling supports. Blue and gold tablecloths covered the tables.

Tyler set the food out buffet-style with blue and gold plates stacked and waiting to be heaped with food. Large baskets of rolls were ready to be topped with slow-cooked barbeque beef, pulled pork, chicken salad, seasoned turkey, sloppy joe, and sun-dried tomato burgers. In addition, there were trays of sticky honey chicken wings, oven-fried chicken drumsticks, and barbequed turkey legs. The sides included bowls of corn-on-the-cob, baked beans, barbeque pork Cobb salad, loaded potato salad, broccoli salad supreme, macaroni salad, fruit salad, and scalloped taters to round out the main course. The drinks table offered the usual coffee, sodas, and waters with pitchers of honey-citrus iced tea and iced raspberry tea. The dessert table boasted a giant super soft vanilla graduation cake covered in gold buttercream roses topped with a graduation cap-shaped cake coated in blue fondant icing and a diploma decorated in white fondant with a red buttercream ribbon. Arranged around the cake were chilling trays of homemade ice cream sandwiches.

After everyone had their fill, the kids all ran off to enjoy the rides for the rest of the day. While the women packed up what little was left of the food, Mike, Tyler, Sean, John, and Tim made quick work of clearing the tables. Then they straightened up the chairs in preparation for the formal dinner later that evening. Tyler had arranged to have that meal prepared and served by a catering service from Billings. After that, the band would arrive and set up on a stand that the men had built. Then, dancing would be on the lawn in front of the podium.

While everyone else was occupied, Jake grabbed Jessica by the hand and led her to the stable.

"What's up, Jake?" Jessica questioned. "I need to help my mom with the babies."

As Jake clasped Jess's hands, he studied the delicate lines of her face. He'd fallen in love with her when she was just twelve years old. Leaning down, Jake grazed Jess' petal-soft lips with his. Then, getting down on one knee, he asked her the most serious question any young man could ever ask his best girl, “Jess, I know we aren’t finished with school yet. We have years ahead of us while we study to become veterinarians. But I’m worried sick that you’ll find someone else, and I couldn’t live with that. So, Jess, will you wear my promise ring until we’re both old enough? Then I’ll replace it with an engagement ring? Will you promise to marry me, Jess?”

Jess couldn’t believe what she was hearing. Even though most people would say she was still just a kid, she knew her own mind and what her heart wanted. Like her mother, who loved her father and stepfather when Elli was just a girl, Jess loved Jake with the same intensity.

“I love you, Jake. My answer is a thousand times, yes.”

Jake had a ring ready. With shaking hands, he placed the ring on Jessica’s finger. It was a sparkling white topaz with a brilliant garnet set in a sterling silver band with twenty-four-carat gold accents. The names “Jessica & Jacob” were engraved inside the band. When the ring was seated on Jessica’s finger, Jake kissed it to seal their commitment to each other. Then he took her sweet face in the palms of his hands and kissed Jess with as much passion as an eighteen-year-old could muster. And that was quite a lot! Then he grabbed her by the hand again, and they ran off to enjoy the day, stopping first to get Elli's permission.

Elli noticed the flush in her daughter's cheeks and the ring on her finger but chose to ignore things for the time being. She had known for a long time how Jessica felt about Jake.

"Go have some fun. You've worked really hard to help with setting up for the party. I think your grandma and I can handle taking care of the babies."

Jess grabbed her mom in a swift hug then ran off to enjoy the carnival rides and games with Jake.

As Elli watched, Tyler stepped up behind her and pulled her back against his chest. "What's up, Elli? You look a little sad."

Elli swiped a tear from her cheek. "Just a little bit, Tyler. Our daughter's becoming a beautiful young woman. It seemed like only yesterday that she was just a little girl. Before you know it, she'll be off to college and then creating a life and a family of her own."

Tyler squeezed his wife in sympathy. He knew just how she felt. Jessica may not be his daughter by blood, but he loved her just as much. "Come on, wife. Let's go check on the rest of the Whrite-Thompson brood and give them lots of hugs and kisses. We can't keep them from growing up, but we can love them as much as possible while they are."

The rest of the day went off without a hitch. The formal dinner included roast beef or chicken served with mashed or twice-baked potatoes, salad, three types of vegetables, and rolls. Various drinks were offered that were non-alcoholic equivalents of those served to adults. It was all very elegant.

When the meal was concluded, the kids all ran out to enjoy the music while they danced and sang along.

It was very late when the last guest offered their thanks for being invited and made their departure.

Tom and Jake would be working on the ranch for the summer. So, after hugging all the women and shaking the hands of the men, they went to the bunkhouse. Morning chores would still need to be done, so they needed to get some sleep. And the next few weeks would be full of preparations for the Whrite-Thompson's trip to Stillwater, New Jersey, and Sean's and Mak's wedding ceremony.

CHAPTER 47

MAK ran her hands over her abdomen, hoping to relieve the cramping. It was kind of like applying a hands-on deep tissue technique to reduce a muscle spasm on one of the horses. It certainly seemed to reduce some of the tension she had been experiencing ever since Brian's father had shown up unexpectedly two days earlier. Mak had never expected to see the man again. Not that she could honestly see him, that is.

Every adult male of the *Circle R Cattle Company Ranch* was present at a meeting to finalize plans for Sean's bachelor party when the limousine parked in front of the ranch office. Sean was at the main house discussing wedding plans with Elli, Emi, Jeannie, and Anna.

Mike answered the door when the driver knocked. And he was displeased when the driver informed him that Brian Alexander Hillhouse II wished to speak to Makailyn Elsbeth Jamieson.

While Tyler, Tim, John, Tom, and Jake surrounded the silver-haired gentleman, who had climbed out of the back seat, Mike went to the stable to get Mak. She was working with Jessica and Sophie on one of the horses that Mike had just purchased. Mike told the girls to put the horse away and led Mak out into the yard where she could make out the shadowy figures of Tyler, Tim, John, Tom, and Jake. Mak's diminished eyesight had heightened her other senses. Mak had gotten good at telling people by their scent, so that's how she knew who was standing there. It was the scent that reminded her so much of Brian that scared her. Plus, there was a crucial scent missing. When two hands pressed lightly down onto her shoulders, and she was pulled back against Sean's chest, his scent enveloped her in its embrace. Finally, Mak could relax because she knew that she was safe.

As the shadow with Brian's scent stepped forward, the man spoke, "Makailyn Elsbeth Jamieson, do you remember me?"

Mak nodded, "I believe so, sir. But, first, I want to offer my condolences. The pain of losing your only child must be acute. So, I'm sorry for your loss. May I ask why you've come here to see me, sir?"

Sean stepped around Mak and placed himself in front of her. Mak took his arm and gave it a gentle squeeze to let him know that she appreciated his support.

"Mak, I just came to offer an apology for what my son has put you through. I'm very sorry for what you had to endure, my dear. I had hoped that you would be my daughter-in-law and give me the grandson I so desperately wanted. You had such a calming effect on Brian, and you were so perfect for him. But unfortunately, that was not to be. So, I've just come to see if you're getting along alright. I wanted to find out if there is anything at all that I can do to make it up to you."

Sean tried to step forward. He wanted to get right up in the older man's face to tell the pompous ass what he could do with his good intentions, but Mak held on tight and gave Sean's arm another squeeze.

"Mr. Hillhouse, there isn't anything that I need from you. I am very blessed because I am surrounded by people who love me. They've gone out of their way to make me a part of their family. I also have a good man who loves me and intends to marry me in a couple of days. But, as you can see, he's also given me a wonderful gift. I'm carrying this man's son."

That got a gasp out of all the men of the *Circle R*. Mak hadn't revealed the baby's sex. Until that point, she had kept it a closely guarded secret.

Sean leaned in and cupped Mak's face with his work-roughened hands. "Oh, darlin', you've made me the happiest man alive."

Then Sean turned towards Brian Hillhouse II and said, "If you'll excuse us, sir, I need to take my fiancée to our cabin so I can kiss the ever-lovin' daylights out of her in private." Not waiting for a response, he wrapped his arm around Mak's waist and led her away.

After Sean and Mak left, Hillhouse turned towards Mike and told him that he had opened an account for Mak at the local bank in Butler. "My son Brian bequeathed twenty-million dollars of his estate to Mak. So, I've had those funds moved to that account. As a result, Mak is now a very wealthy woman."

Mike scoffed and said, "I don't think Mak is going to want that money, Mr. Hillhouse. Your son not only caused the loss of Mak's sight, but he also caused her the loss of a child and a lot of other pain and suffering."

"Well, Mr. Willis, the money is Makailyn's to do with as she pleases. Hopefully, she can use it for medical treatments to help restore her eyesight. One can only hope that may be a possibility. Would you please tell Makailyn that I wish her all the best? She'll be receiving documents from the estate attorney confirming what I've just told you."

Then the chauffeur helped Brian Hillhouse II back into his limousine. Finally, the vehicle disappeared down the driveway of the *Circle R Cattle Company Ranch*.

Mike would find out a few weeks later that the man had taken his own life, distraught over the loss of his only son and heir. Brian Hillhouse II was buried next to his son in the family plot on the grounds of the Hillhouse family mansion. Brian Hillhouse III was the last of a long line of Hillhouses. There would never be any more.

Hillhouse's wife discovered that she'd only inherited the family mansion and the surrounding acreage at the reading of the will. The balance of the estate would be used to create a foundation in the name of her late son, Brian Hillhouse III. The funds from that foundation would generate grants toward research to provide preventions, treatments, and cures for people affected by retinitis pigmentosa, macular degeneration, Usher syndrome, and the entire spectrum of retinal degenerative diseases. The foundation would also provide financial aid to blind and visually impaired individuals to improve their quality of life. In addition, the construction of an assisted living facility on the hospital grounds of *OSU* was in the planning stages. Upon completion, the facility would aptly be named the *MAK House for the Blind and Visually Impaired*.

Mak received an invitation to attend the ribbon-cutting ceremony for the grand opening. However, there was plenty of time to think about that because construction would take at least two years. Mak responded that she would do her best, depending on what life presented in the interim.

Mak was pleased that something good had resulted from the pain she'd suffered. In the meantime, she'd go about her business developing the skills she needed to live in a world of shadows.

EPILOGUE

ON the 30th of June, exactly nine months to the day that Sean had first kissed Mak, he stood in front of the fireplace in the living room of the main house on the *Circle R Cattle Company Ranch.*

John and Tyler stood beside him as his groomsmen. It was good that there were two of them because they might need to hold him up. He was so nervous, he felt like he was going to faint.

Tyler, Elli, their ten children, and Alex and Anna had cut this year's trip to Stillwater, New Jersey, short so that they could assist in the preparations for the wedding.

Everyone else who was a part of the ranch sat expectantly, waiting for the ceremony to begin. It would be a simple service since neither the bride nor the groom had any living relatives. The people of *Circle R* were their only family. Sean felt blessed in that regard.

Mak would soon be giving birth, and they'd add one more member to the people they'd come to love.

Also included as guests were Maimee Ritter, Herald Cleary from the *Rent-A-Wreck* company in Billings, and Martha and Charlie Gormley. They were Mak's adopted grandparents, so they were also considered family.

Because it was now summer, the women had chosen light fabrics so that everyone would stay comfortable but remain stylish. Sean was wearing a western-style linen suit in a light tan with a bolo tie the same color as the groomsmen's attire. A shiny new pair of cowboy boots covered his feet. He'd just had his hair cut and had even gone to a nail salon. It was Sean's first-ever manicure, plus the manicurist worked to rid his hands of some of his calluses. He intended to use those smooth hands to give his bride a massage later. Then, maybe if he was fortunate, she might gift him with one of her unbelievable blowjobs. He was horny as hell. That son of his couldn't be born soon enough as far as he was concerned. He was looking forward to making another.

Tyler and John were dressed in a light shade of blue to match the bridesmaids' dresses. Their bolo ties were the same shade as Sean's suit.

Since the bride and groom didn't have any relatives, the women had decided that they'd change things up a little. So, all of the females were sitting on the groom's side. All of the males were seated on the bride's side of the aisle. Tom and Jake were given the option of inviting a guest, but the girl Jake wanted was already at the wedding and wearing his promise ring. So, he said thanks but no thanks. Tom had his eye on Sophie, so he opted out, too.

Anna had done an excellent job creating the bridal gown and bridesmaid dresses. Sean's gift to his new bride would be a surprise. She would be the proud new owner of a seeing-eye dog. Mak would receive her gift when the dog would act as a flower girl for their wedding ceremony. Anna had made a ruffled collar with a matching bow for the dog. The Whrite-Thompson's male golden retriever, Toby, would act as ring bearer. He would be wearing a vest and bolo tie to match the groomsmen. The rings would be attached to the dog's bolo tie. Jessica would walk between the animals, tossing daisies from a basket.

Elli and Emi entered first. They wore tea-length sweetheart style dresses that flowed into A-line skirts with a midi hem and side slit that almost reached their hips. The gowns featured V-necklines with adjustable spaghetti straps. With fitted waists, the dresses beautifully accentuated the women's figures. Tyler got a good look at his wife and almost swallowed his tongue. He was in big trouble. He'd forgotten to pick up some condoms when he'd stopped at the drugstore early that morning.

The golden retrievers entered with Jessica, padding softly on each side of her. Jess was wearing a frilly ruffled sundress and her first pair of high heels. When she reached the end of the row of chairs, she led Toby to her father so that Tyler could undo the rings attached to Toby's bolo tie. He handed those to John for safekeeping.

Then Jess handed the female golden retriever's leash to Sean, and the animal sat down beside its master. Sean thanked Jess kindly and kissed her on the cheek. Jess blushed prettily and went to sit beside her female siblings.

As the pianist struck up the chords of the bridal procession, Mak entered on Mike Willis's arm. Mike was wearing a linen suit to match the groomsmen. Anna had designed a lovely silk, ivory-colored maternity dress for Mak. It was made of one hundred percent silk with a fully-lined skirt draped lavishly over her very pregnant curves then down to a dramatic floor-sweeping finish. The lace bodice kept her shoulders delicately covered while stylish eyelash edging and keyhole detailing at the back completed the look. A subtle stretch panel, also at the back, ensured a flexible fit and covered the zipper that would allow an easy escape from the garment. A stunning jeweled belt provided the perfect finishing touch, defining Mak's empire waist and drawing the eye towards her slimmest point. Mak was wearing a pair of satin ballerina flats so that she could walk comfortably.

When Mike placed Mak's hand into Sean's, he gave her a gentle kiss on her cheek. Then he whispered in Mak's ear, "Sean's a good man, Mak, and a damned lucky son of a bitch because he found you."

Mak gave Mike a brilliant smile in return.

After they'd recited their vows, the minister said, "You may kiss your bride."

Sean took Mak's face in the palms of his newly buffed hands and kissed her as if it were the first time. Then he took her hands and placed them against the gift that would aid his bride through all the coming good days and bad.

Mak ran her hands lovingly over the silky fur of her new companion. "What's his name, Sean?" she asked.

"It's a girl, Mak," Sean responded. "She's a golden retriever just like Toby. She's a seeing-eye dog, so she's trained to help you get around. No more feeling dependent or worthless. I love you, darlin', and I want you to be as independent as possible."

"Does she have a name, or can I pick one of my own?" Mak questioned.

"You can name her anything you want, darlin'. So, what's it gonna be?"

"I think I'll name her Ava."

Sean brought Mak's hand to his lips and kissed her over her wedding ring. I think that suits her to a tee. Now let's go get something to eat. My stomach was too tied up in knots to eat any breakfast. I was afraid you'd change your mind."

Mak laughed, "Never even gave it a thought, husband-mine."

Tyler had set up the wedding feast on the covered patio at the back of the house. The bride and groom had opted for a barbeque, so John and Jake were busy tending the meat they'd placed on the grill. Elli and Jeannie assisted Tyler in an assembly line style as the meat came off. First, he turned out chicken skewers that he put on a platter with ramekins containing a cool avocado sauce. Pineapple chicken sliders were created next. They included a mixture of ground chicken, unsweetened crushed pineapple, shredded carrot, grated onion, soy sauce, and garlic powder formed into burgers. Placing the burgers on whole wheat split dinner rolls, Tyler covered them with a mixture containing low-fat sour cream, mayonnaise, and ground ginger. That was topped with lettuce. Then Tyler paired buttermilk biscuits with boneless chicken breasts sprinkled with salt, thyme, and pepper. These were topped with cranberry chutney, lettuce leaves, sliced tomato, and red onion. Finally, the table was covered with bowls of various salads, both fruit and vegetable, slaws, and a massive bowl of barbequed meatballs made with a combination of ground beef, bread crumbs, chopped onion, egg, minced parsley, milk, salt, and pepper covered with a sauce made of grape jelly and Worcestershire sauce.

Other platters included deviled eggs, toasted ravioli puffs with warm marinara sauce, garlic herb mini-quiches, and cucumber stuffed cherry tomatoes. Last but not least was mini mac & cheese bites to tempt the kids.

Tyler had outdone himself with the wedding cake, too. A work of art, it included three tiers dripping in white buttercream icing flowers with the primary focus on tiny thistle icing greenery and purplish pink icing florets. Small icing butterflies of varying sizes floated above the flowers. A large butterfly perched near the top.

The cake was so closely decorated to resemble his new bride's tattoo that Sean narrowed his eyes suspiciously. Then, taking Tyler aside, he asked him accusingly, "Have you seen my wife naked?"

Tyler stared at Sean, then laughed. "Hell, no, Sean. Mak showed her tattoo to Elli. Elli drew me a picture."

"Shit, Tyler. I'm sorry. You've worked so hard preparing everything so that Mak and I could have the perfect wedding day, and then I went and ruined everything by getting jealous. I don't know what to say. Can you forgive me?"

Tyler clapped Sean on the back and said, "If someone showed me a rendition of Elli's butterfly, they'd be picking pieces of their teeth out of their poop after I'd knocked their teeth down their throat. Thankfully you didn't punch first, then ask me how I knew what Mak's tattoo looked like after. So, therefore, I think we're good."

"Thanks, Tyler. Again, I'm sorry. I should have known better. A blind man could see how much you love your wife. You're the last man I should have suspected of cheating. It won't happen again. I promise. Now, I think I'll go kiss my bride before she eats one of the sliders with the red onion on it."

Tyler laughed as Sean walked away. Then stared speculatively at his wife. Going over to his in-laws, he asked them if they could keep an eye on the kids for a few minutes. He needed to discuss something with Elli.

Grabbing his wife by the hand, Tyler quietly walked her to the back door. Entering, he pulled her down the hall to the bedroom, where he quickly divested his wife of her panties.

"This is going to be quick, he told her. Damn, you look good in that dress, sweet girl." Yanking down his pants and briefs, Tyler pulled his wife's dress up around her waist, lifted her so that she could wrap her legs around him, and entered Elli with one quick stroke. While he took her mouth in a fierce kiss, he pounded into her. When she moaned out his name and tightened around his hard length, Tyler was right there, ready to go over with her. When their breathing had slowed, he went into the bathroom and cleaned himself up. Then he went back into the bedroom to take care of the mother of his children. After righting their clothing and Elli's hair and makeup, Tyler said, "Can we do that again after the kids are all in bed? I promise to take it slower."

Elli just grinned at him. "I think you forgot something again, Mr. Thompson."

Tyler grinned back. "I know. I forgot to pick some up when I went to the pharmacy for the baby Tylenol this morning. Are you angry with me?"

"Not in a million years," was Elli's reply. "Let's get back to the party before everyone figures out what we've been up to." Taking

Tyler by the hand, she kissed him gently, then led him down the hall and out onto the patio.

Mike had to poke fun at his son-in-law, of course, by whispering in his ear, “Did you remember to use protection this time?”

Tyler blushed and shook his head.

As the happy couple cut the wedding cake, Mak let out a groan and grabbed her belly.

Everything was a blur after that as everyone worked together. Sean rushed Mak to the car they’d planned to use for their trip to the honeymoon suite in a fancy hotel in Billings that was reserved in the names of Mr. and Mrs. Sean Hannity. But amazingly, it looked like they’d be spending their honeymoon in a private suite at the hospital instead.

John ran to the cabin to get Mak’s suitcase. He placed that in the trunk of the car. When Sean was safely in the back seat with his bride, who was now in active labor, John jumped in the driver’s seat and started the car. Before he could pull away, Mike tapped on the hood to get his attention. Rolling down the windows, Sean and Mak could see all of the residents of the Circle R standing near the entrance of the house, hoping to wish them luck. Mike poked his head in the window and said, “As a show of solidarity, a few of us will be along as soon as we clean up from the wedding feast. While you’re waiting for your son to be born, we’ll fill up the waiting room, drink the bad coffee from the vending machines, and walk a path in the tile. Now get the heck out of here before Emi has to deliver that baby.”

Mak was probably the first bride to be carried through a hospital entrance by her new groom while still wearing their wedding attire.

Several of the nurses and family members of patients took pictures and video clips with their cell phones. Those ended up on a lot of *Facebook* and *YouTube* accounts online.

When Mak’s water broke, she was moved to a birthing room. Sean was by her side, helping and offering encouragement.

“Just breathe, darlin’,” he said. “You’ve got this, Mak.”

Mak just rolled her eyes and told him, “Next time, you’re the one giving birth.”

That made Sean laugh. “No, I like my part much better.”

At 9:57 p.m. on June 30th, Lyle Duncan Hannity made his appearance in Mak’s and Sean’s lives. The baby’s name honored

Mak's father because he was a special man who had fathered an extraordinary daughter. Baby Lyle weighed six pounds, nine ounces, had soft hair the same color as his mother's, and eyes the same color as his father's. They say that babies can't smile, but his tiny bow lips pursed into the most beautiful smile as his mother kissed him gently on his forehead for the first time. Then Sean helped bring him to his mother's breast for his first meal. Sean thought his son was one lucky kid getting to suckle on those tits. Maybe later, when everything was quiet, and the baby was sleeping, Sean would have to get a taste. After that, his son would just have to learn to share.

As soon as Mak and his son were settled, Sean went out to the waiting room. Mike, Tyler, Tim, and John jumped up when he entered the room and started pounding him on the back in congratulations.

"Mak and the baby are doing well," he told them. "I may have helped deliver a bunch of calves over the years, but I've got to tell you, I thought I was gonna faint at one point during the delivery. I don't know how women go through that. I'm surprised they let men anywhere near them again after experiencing the pain of giving birth."

As the guys laughed at Sean's pronouncement, Tyler said, "Wait until your wife has twins. Elli squeezed my hand so hard when she had the girls last year, I couldn't feel it for days after."

John was very quiet while Mike, Tyler, and Tim swapped childbirth stories. Since he'd never been married, he couldn't relate. Heck, the last time he'd had a steady girlfriend was in eleventh grade. Her name was Cheryl Langbien. They'd been an item for two years. Then she'd blossomed into a beauty over summer vacation and become all long legs and high pert breasts. That fall, Cheryl had caught the eye of the captain of the football team. John couldn't blame the guy for seizing the opportunity. The last thing he'd heard, Cheryl and the jock had moved to Utah and had six kids. Good for them!

But he hadn't really known what love was until he'd spent one glorious day with another girl. After high school graduation, Bill and Peggy Roberts had thrown a party for John on the *Circle R*. Everybody from his graduating class had been invited, just like the one held for Tom and Jake.

What happened at the party was the reason for John's introspection. That's when he'd fallen for Lilibeth MacEwan.

John called Beth "*Little Bit*" every time he thought about her. But she'd probably hit him if she knew. Beth was petite next to John, even before he came into his mature height. She'd definitely be tiny next to him now. At the end of high school, she was a 5'3" tall, green-eyed pixie with fair skin and a short-cropped hairstyle. It was the first time Beth had shown up at a dance or a party in all the years John had gone to school with her.

John was standing with Bill and Peggy when Beth made her way over to them to thank the Roberts for the invitation. John's eyes almost fell out of his head at the sight of her in that sundress. She may have been tiny, but she had curves in all the right places.

So, John asked her if she could ride, to which she'd shaken her head negatively. Excusing himself to the Roberts, John grabbed her hand and led Beth to the stable.

Once he'd saddled the horse, John put Beth up in front of him, and together, they had ridden out along the trail to the line cabin. When they got to the pond, John slid his hand over the length of her silky-smooth leg before lifting Beth down from the saddle. Leaving the horse to graze, he and Beth sat down in the grass to talk. Beth was shy at first, so John questioned why she'd never attended any other functions during high school. Beth explained that she had a younger sister, Betty, who suffered from Batten Disease. John asked Beth what that was because he'd never heard of the illness before. He thought Beth was just making it up.

John would never forget the glimmer of tears in Beth's eyes or the sad look on her face as she explained the symptoms of Batten disease. She told him the illness usually started between the ages of five and ten years and included vision loss or seizures. Betty's illness had manifested when she was eight, and blindness had followed swiftly. Beth continued to tell John that there would also be a loss of muscle control and some wasting of brain tissue, causing dementia over time. With no treatment available to cure or slow the progression of Batten disease, it was always fatal, with death usually in the late teens or early twenties. Since Betty was now twelve years old, clearly, her days were numbered.

Beth had become so distraught, John had gathered her into his arms and held her head tight against his chest. What happened next just seemed like a natural progression of what he was feeling. John claimed Beth's lips in a searing kiss, and there was no turning back.

They both seemed to be driven by an undeniable hunger. Because Beth tasted so sweet, he needed more. After pulling Beth's sundress over her head, he kissed a path from her mouth down the side of her neck. Leaning back, John noticed the look of desire in Beth's eyes. He was positive it matched the look in his own. After ripping off his own shirt, shorts, and briefs, he helped Beth remove her bra and panties.

John wanted to cringe at how inexperienced they had both been. Without any foreplay, John was between Beth's legs and inside her before he could even think about what they were doing. John was filled with remorse whenever he thought about how he'd hurt Beth when he'd taken her virginity. She'd stiffened in his arms, and a single tear had slid down her cheek, but she never uttered a word of recrimination. When he'd asked her if she was okay, she'd just nodded her head. That first time didn't last long, but thankfully Beth had stayed wrapped up in his arms, and they'd talked some more. After going for a quick swim in the pond, John had led Beth to the line cabin where they'd made love two more times. Each time had been better than the one before.

John grimaced at what a young fool he had been. He should have told Beth that he'd joined the service right then and there. Three days later, John had gone to Beth's house to tell her that he was leaving for boot camp the following morning. He wanted to ask Beth if she would be his girl and wait for him. Beth's father refused to allow John to see his daughter. The man glowered at him when John tried to explain why he was there. Then Mr. MacEwan told John to get lost and not come back. Beth had responsibilities that didn't allow for boyfriends.

John left for boot camp, and he never saw Little Bit again. After four years of military life, he came home to discover that Beth's parents had been killed in a car accident. She'd taken her little sister and moved away. That was that. John hasn't experienced a long-term relationship since. He still judged every woman he met by that girl. His story was similar to Mike's, but at least he hadn't left the girl with a baby in her belly. Hook-ups at the local barroom were just that. Not meant to lead to anything permanent. Well, unless you counted Sean and Mak. They'd hooked up at that same bar, and look where that had led. Sean was a lucky bastard as far as John was concerned. Maybe he should hit the saloon again. A guy could only hope. Right?

Two days later, the Hannity family came home to a vast Welcome Home surprise party on the *Circle R Cattle Company Ranch*.

The ranch family was growing, and Lyle Duncan Hannity became its newest member. Elli and the children had created a memorial plaque to commemorate the baby's birth with the names of all the people who would form a village of love to help raise him properly. The adults included Alastair Caelan Thompson, Annabelle Thompson, Roger Michael Willis, Emilia Addison Willis, Timothy Lee Jones, Jeannie Jones, Tyler Logan Thompson, Eloise Lianne Whrite-Thompson, Sean Fitzpatrick Hannity, and Makailyn Elsbeth Hannity. The children included ten Whrite-Thompsons: Jessica Blair, Richard Blair, Peggy Lynne, Tyler Logan, William Timothy, Lianne Susanna, Alastair Lachlan, Caelan Angus, Patricia Emilia, and Anna Bella. Roger Michael Willis, Jr. and Addison Mackenzie Willis, Sophie Hannah Brown, Timothy Lee Jones, Jr., and Lyle Duncan Hannity brought the number to fifteen.

John Andrew Marshall, Jacob Campbell MacGowan, and Thomas Graham McKinney were included as honorary family members.

"Who will be the next person to become a permanent member of the *Circle R Cattle Company* family? Only time will tell," Mike told everyone as he passed the plague around.

John winced at that. He was hiding a secret out at the line cabin, and he'd need to tell everyone soon. That secret wouldn't stay hidden for long, and John would need the *Circle R* family's help.

THE END

About the Author

B. E. Stalter grew up in Butler, a small town in Morris County, New Jersey. An obsessive bookworm, her formative years were spent with her nose in a book or walking to or from the Butler Public Library, where she exchanged those books for others. It didn't matter the genre. She read anything she could get her hands on, including the back of the cereal box at breakfast if no other reading materials were handy. In the rare moments when she wasn't reading, she was busy studying or doing housework for her mother. She was also drawn to the great outdoors, where she did yard chores for her father and participated in sports. Her younger brother was a constant companion for games, dunks in the pool, or long walks or bike rides to enjoy picnics in the woods. Now, when she can get her nose out of a book, she splits her time between caring for her husband and son, two cats, a herd of American Aberdeen Angus beef cattle, and a flock of chickens. ***HIS REASON TO BREATHE – Caught Up In A Deception*** is the 3rd novel in the ***WITH ALL the HEART and SOUL*** *Series*.

Also by B. E. Stalter

Book 1 in the

A WITH ALL the HEART and SOUL Series

HEART OF GLASS

WHAT HER HEART WANTS

When Jessica asked for all the "dirt" about her parents' childhoods for her ancestry project, she thought their stories would be happy until she heard the truth.

Elli Roberts' childhood was filled with a sense of longing—the longing to be loved. Dominated by an abusive father and emotionally unavailable mother, a love of books, volunteering, and a longing for two boys would become her life.

Rick Whrite lost just about everything a young boy could possess. Then he met two girls. An angel named Elli would hold Rick's heart. The other, a she-devil named Carly, would control his life.

Tyler Thompson's parents were tired of him getting into trouble. So, they moved him to the country. Tyler and his new best friend, Rick, would share a love of sports, practical jokes, and passion for the same girl. Unbeknownst to them, she had given each of them a gift. One held her heart, and the other held her soul. Would either of them realize the value of the gift and claim it?

Book 2 in the

A WITH ALL the HEART and SOUL Series

SECOND CHANCES

WHAT HIS HEART WANTS

Sixteen-year-old Emi Mackenzie has given her heart and soul to Michael, but after his family moves, Emi discovers that Mike has replaced them with an unexpected gift. Nine short months later, Emilia's mother gives the gift away before Emi even has the chance to see it.

Seventeen-year-old Mike Willis has given his heart and soul to Emi. Before Mike's parents move the family halfway across the country, he and Emi make vows to each other. Ones he will be unable to keep.

Thirty-two years later, will Emi and Mike be given second chances at love when they are brought together again in an unexpected way?

In this sequel to *HEART OF GLASS – What Her Heart Wants*, Elli Roberts discovers that she has been lied to by the people who were supposed to love her. Will Elli be able to forgive the lies, mend her broken heart, and accept what her heart has always wanted—a family that truly loves her?

(Each Book in the Series is a standalone Novel)

www.ingramcontent.com/pod-product-compliance
Lightning Source LLC
LaVergne TN
LVHW050914080826
845145LV00001B/79

* 9 7 8 1 7 3 7 1 3 4 0 3 9 *